DEFENDER

A WITCHES OF CLEOPATRA HILL NOVEL

CHRISTINE POPE

DARK VALENTINE PRESS

DEFENDER

ISBN: 978-1-946435-03-3

Copyright © 2017 by Christine Pope

Published by Dark Valentine Press

Cover design by Lou Harper

Formatting by Indie Author Services

1

———

Kate Campbell sat in her Volkswagen Jetta, hoping that the darkness would help conceal the way she'd been lingering there, parked on the street, for the last twenty minutes. People came and went from the condo complex across the small residential road, pulling in and out of the entrance to the complex, or sometimes merely heading out for an early-evening stroll, taking advantage of the mild April temperatures while they still could. Within a month, Scottsdale would be blasting into the upper nineties, the day's heat lingering long after the sun had set.

An innocuous-looking manila envelope lay on the passenger seat of Kate's car. Now it was dark enough that she'd have to turn on the overhead light in the car or get out her iPhone to shine its beam on the papers the envelope contained, but she'd read over them enough times that the words had already imprinted themselves on her brain.

Petition for Dissolution of Non-Covenant Marriage Without Children.

How exactly she'd gotten here, Kate couldn't even say. Although she would never admit such a thing to Jeff, her estranged husband—his ego was already bruised enough—she knew the first rumblings of discontent had started a long time ago. It had taken seeing the happiness of her brother Colin with his wife Jenny, though, for Kate to realize that she wanted something more. *Deserved* something more.

Because Jeff had insisted, she'd tried counseling, even though she knew the marriage was a lost cause. Those joint therapy sessions had only served to solidify the realization that she had nothing in common with him anymore…if she ever had.

Best to get this over with, even as her jumpy stomach and slightly shaky hands told her she still wasn't completely prepared to face her estranged husband. She'd handled all the paperwork herself, not wanting to waste the money on a lawyer when she and Jeff really didn't have any assets. They were renting the condo they lived in when she walked out. No debt except her student loans and the car payment for Jeff's truck, which he'd agreed to take over. Kate's car had been purchased by her parents when she was a junior in college, and she knew she'd keep driving it until the wheels fell off.

As it turned out, the rules for this sort of thing were pretty simple. Serve the papers to your spouse at home if no lawyers were involved, or take them to the attorney's office if your estranged significant other had decided to lawyer up. She'd called ahead, made arrangements with Jeff so she wouldn't have to waste a trip over here. Of course, he didn't live all that far from her, since he'd moved to Scottsdale after they separated, claiming the relocation made his commute easier. That was an outright lie, but Kate hadn't called him on it. She knew he was having a hard time with their split, and being closer to her while everything shook out was his way of coping. If he'd started stalking her at work or loitering around the apartment complex where she now lived, she would have complained…gotten a restraining order or something.

Or sicced Jenny's family on him.

That thought did make Kate smile slightly, despite the anxiety humming along every nerve. Who would have ever thought she'd be related by marriage to a family of witches?

Good witches, from what she'd been able to tell, but still….

The truth was, Jeff was really too lazy to be a stalker. He'd gained even more weight since she'd moved out, probably because he was living on takeout and pizza rather than the somewhat more nutritious meals she'd tried to keep on the table during their marriage.

And now she knew she was just procrastinating, because the moment had come, and even though she wanted to be free more than anything else she could think of, handing over those divorce papers still felt like an admission of failure. She'd made a bad call, marrying Jeff while they were both still in college just because it felt like the best thing to do at the time. It wasn't that he'd been abusive or anything, only… neglectful. Like she was a piece of the furniture, rather than his partner in life. She wanted more than that. She wanted…no, she *needed* someone to love her the way Colin loved Jenny, unreservedly, with his whole heart.

Her phone pinged, and she started, then pulled it out of her purse.

Colin. He wasn't psychic, but sometimes he sure acted like it. Or rather, he knew her so well that he might as well be reading her mind.

Let me guess…you're sitting in your car and stalling.

What gave it away? she typed back.

The complete radio silence. You said you'd text me after you'd done the deed.

I know. I'm just about to go up.

Courage, little sister.

I know.

A small pause, and then the text came back. *You sure you don't want to come up for the weekend? It might help to get away.*

Colin had invited her to come to Jerome after she'd given Jeff the divorce papers. As enticing as the prospect had sounded—she'd come to love that crazy little mountain town—Kate had declined. It felt like running away. She needed to hand over the papers and go home, and try to pretend this was just another normal night.

A night of sitting alone. Her friends had tried to get her to go out and start dating again, telling her that if she and Jeff were formally separated, it wasn't a big deal if she began seeing other people, but she just couldn't bring herself to do that. Once she'd delivered the papers and really started the ball rolling…maybe. Even so, she didn't know who the hell she was supposed to date. She hadn't met anyone so far who'd piqued her interest. A few guys at work had sent out some signals, but she'd shut them down. Life was complicated enough without getting involved with a coworker. When she finally decided it was time to meet someone, she'd do it the old-fashioned way… online, or at a bar. Just because her marriage to Jeff had ended in failure didn't mean that the right guy wasn't out there somewhere. She just had to work up the nerve and get herself out there. Being legally separated seemed like a step in that direction.

And if the bars and the online dating apps and the introductions from friends didn't work, then maybe she would take a page from Colin's book and crash a wedding. That had worked out pretty well for him.

No, I'm good, she texted back. *And I'm going up to Jeff's now. I swear.*

Okay. But text me when it's over with & you're home. I want to know you're all right.

I will. Thanks, Colin. She put a little heart emoji at the end of the text, so he'd know how much she appreciated his support. Then she dropped the phone back into her purse, removed her keys from the ignition, and picked up the manila envelope with the life-changing papers inside.

As she got out of the car, she tried to tell her rapidly beating heart that it was being ridiculous. This should be simple enough. After all, she and Jeff had been in contact, had spoken on the phone, had even met in person for lunch one time so she could sign the paperwork to let his employer know that she now had health coverage through her new job as a planning assistant with the City of Scottsdale, and therefore she could be dropped from the policy Jeff had through his own work at the logistics company.

All right, she had met with Jeff since they'd separated. But this would be the first time she'd brought him divorce papers.

She clicked her remote to lock the car doors, then resolutely made her way across the quiet street and down the path that wound through the condo complex. From someone's open window, she could hear a television blaring away. Some kind of game, she thought, wondering what it might be at this time of year. Basketball? Maybe. She had to admit she'd tuned most of that sort of thing out. Jeff loved sports, and she'd dutifully gone to Diamondbacks and Cardinals games with him in an effort to share his interests. But when he had that stuff on in the house, she'd always tried to ignore it. There was something fun about the excitement of watching a game in person, but she could never get into televised sports.

His condo was at the back of the complex. The evening air was mild and pleasant against her skin, and she breathed it in, glad that it hadn't been too hot today. She hadn't changed out of her work clothes, still wore the slim skirt, silk blouse, and ankle-strap sandals she'd put on that morning. The outfit wasn't all that different from something she would have worn to court, although she told herself she wasn't on trial here. This wasn't that kind of divorce. So much easier when you didn't have any property to split up, no child custody to squabble over. She'd told Jeff they'd talk about kids after she was done with her master's degree, and now she could only be deeply grateful that they hadn't dragged an innocent child into their mess of a relationship.

Up the stairs to his condo on the second floor. The people across from him had a little cactus garden in pots on their section of the landing, but Jeff's side was completely bare, not even a doormat. Short-sighted, she thought, if he wanted to get his cleaning deposit back. He must be tracking in all sorts of dirt.

That wasn't her problem, though. She'd have to stop worrying about Jeff's choices, because in the very near future, they wouldn't be connected at all. Just two people going their own way in life, two people who'd known each other once but now had nothing to tie them together.

Kate pressed the doorbell and waited. And waited. Half a minute went by, and she frowned. At least one light was on inside the condo; she could see its glow up against the mini-blinds.

Maybe the doorbell wasn't working. Instead of pressing it again, she knocked, three smart raps.

Still nothing.

Mystified, she stood there, trying to figure out what was going on. Had he gone on an errand, even though he knew she had said she would be over at seven-thirty? Yes, she'd spent some time sitting in the car, but that was because she'd gotten here early, knowing she'd need some time to gather herself before she confronted him.

He couldn't have forgotten. Jeff was a lot of things, some of them not particularly appealing, but he'd always been good about being on time, about being where he'd said he would be, when he said he would be. This wasn't like him.

She knocked again, then called out, "Jeff? It's Kate."

Still silence. Nothing from the people next door, either; their unit was dark, all the blinds closed. Either they were working late or were out for the evening. So she couldn't knock on their door and ask if they'd seen Jeff.

Almost without thinking, she placed her hand on the door latch. To her surprise, it moved, and the door opened a fraction of an inch.

Her frown deepened. Jeff was not the type to leave his front door unlocked; he had an expensive TV and stereo system, and a newish laptop. Not to mention all those boxes of baseball cards. She'd never asked how much they were all worth, not even when they were going over their meager assets together, because they were something he'd collected on his own and which she didn't think she had any claim to.

An icy tingle moved down her back, and she shivered.

Don't creep yourself out, she thought. *For all you know, he's just down at the laundry room or something, and didn't bother to lock the door because he knew he'd be right back.*

That sounded plausible, but....

Gingerly, she pushed the door open an inch more, and called inside, "Jeff? Are you in there?"

Silence.

Well, since she'd gone so far as to open the door a little, she figured she might as well go all the way. Yes, Jeff might be annoyed that she'd barged into his condo while he wasn't there, but she could simply explain that she'd been worried and hadn't meant to intrude. Frankly, there were about a thousand other places she would rather have been right then.

She opened the door wide enough so she could enter, and paused immediately inside. The light she'd seen must have been coming from over in the dining nook, because the living room itself was nearly dark. She couldn't make out much of anything.

"Jeff?"

Her fingers found the light switch next to the door, flipped it on.

And then the manila envelope she held slipped from her fingers as she raised her hands to her face and screamed, and screamed.

2

NIGHT SHIFTS. JACK SANDOVAL SQUINTED AT THE clock on the opposite wall and hoped this one would pass without incident. Or at least, an incident where his services wouldn't be required. A full moon always meant car accidents and domestic disputes and your usual assortment of crazies in addition to the regular run of burglaries and assaults, but he wouldn't be called to handle any of those sorts of crimes unless the other detectives on duty were occupied elsewhere.

Problem was, the number of murders also tended to rise when the moon was full. Got in people's blood, he guessed; even witches and warlocks couldn't exactly explain it, although any witch worth her salt would tell you that most spells were more powerful when the moon was full. His relatives in the de la Paz clan probably weren't casting many spells tonight, though. No reason to, when their world had been safe and calm and placid for more than a year now.

The phone on his desk rang, and he couldn't keep himself from grimacing before he picked it up. He knew all too well what the call probably meant, especially since the readout on the phone indicated the person on the other end of the line was Larry Jansen, lead detective for the Scottsdale P.D.'s homicide department.

Still, this was his job, and Jack knew he would be first on the hook to pick up any new homicide cases, since he'd just closed the books on a double murder that had been the result of a drug deal gone bad.

"Sandoval," he said.

"Jack, we need you on-scene for a possible homicide at 2344-A Cactus Circle." A pause. "It's…bad."

It would have to be, for Larry to have offered even that brief disclaimer. Usually he was neutral to a fault, wanting his officers to make their own determinations when it came to individual crime scenes. "Any witnesses?"

"Not to the actual crime, as far as we can tell. The first responders report that the next-door neighbors were out for the evening, and the people living under the victim said they were watching TV and didn't see or hear anything."

"Who reported it?"

"The victim's wife. Soon-to-be ex-wife, actually. She'd gone to his place to deliver divorce papers."

"Has she been questioned?"

"They got some basic details, but they're waiting on you."

"I'm on my way."

"I figured you were."

Larry ended the call, and Jack got up from his desk, then slipped into his sport jacket, which he'd left hanging on the back of his chair. The night was probably mild enough that he really didn't need it, but he'd found that the public liked to see plainclothes officers in jackets. Made them seem more professional, or something.

Two calls to make before he left, to Grace Pedersen, one of the city's CSI techs, and Ian Tolliver, another homicide detective. Together, they made up the remainder of his team. Neither of them sounded thrilled to be called in after they were technically off shift, but of course there were no arguments, only a quick "I'll be right over" from both Grace and Ian. Jack hadn't expected anything less. Actually, the two of them would probably make it there before him, since they lived closer to the crime scene.

The condo complex in question was off Scottsdale Road, about ten minutes from the police department headquarters. As Jack emerged from the building, he shot a jaundiced glance upward at the large yellow-tinged moon hanging overhead. "Thanks a lot, you bastard," he muttered.

His department-issued Ford Taurus waited for

him in one of the spots designated for official use. He got in and headed north on Scottsdale Road, mentally preparing himself for whatever might lie ahead. If Larry said it was bad, then it was.

At times like this, Jack almost wished he had a partner, someone to chew things over with while on the way to a crime scene. Back when he'd been a beat cop, he'd resented having someone in his lap all the time, just because the job was hard enough without having to hide that he wasn't exactly your standard-issue police officer, was actually a member of Arizona's largest witch clan. Luckily, he'd been able to avoid exposing the truth of his nature, but he had to admit things became much easier when he was promoted to detective and rode a desk every day instead of a squad car.

He turned onto Cactus Circle. About halfway down the block, he saw a swirl of police lights, flashing a raucous blue and red. Three patrol cars, a fire truck, an ambulance, and a van from the medical examiner's office. About what he'd expected, but still, he couldn't help being impressed by the turnout. All those personnel, just for one body.

A body of a man who'd been murdered, Jack reminded himself.

He pulled up behind one of the squad cars and got out. Immediately, a uniformed officer came over to him. "I'm Officer Lopez. Detective Sandoval?"

"That's right," Jack replied, moving the lapel of his

jacket slightly so the officer could see the badge clipped to his shirt pocket. "What do we have?"

"Deceased male Caucasian, twenty-nine years old."

Jack could feel his jaw tighten. Damn. Somehow it always felt worse to him when the victim was under thirty. All that potential…gone. "Go on."

"No sign of forced entry. Nothing taken, as far as we can tell." Lopez didn't look like much more than a kid himself, twenty-five, if even that. His dark eyes were strained, but he sounded composed enough as he continued, "I'm no expert, but this killing…it looks like something ritual to me."

God, Jack hoped not. His clan had had enough of that sort of thing to deal with—and sweep under the rug—when Matías Escobar and his thug cousins kidnapped those young witches from up north and tortured them, killing one of the girls. Yes, Escobar had been dealt with, but the last thing Jack wanted on his plate right now was another crime with evidence that pointed toward witch-kind. "Witnesses?"

"Not really. The immediate neighbors either weren't home or didn't see or hear anything. We're talking to people in some of the other buildings, just in case they might have noticed any suspicious activity earlier in the evening. The wife came on the scene afterward…or so she claims."

Jack frowned. "What makes you think she was involved?"

"Oh, nothing in particular." Lopez stood up a little straighter and lifted his chin. "It just seems to me that the timing is a little suspicious."

Sounded like someone wanted a promotion. Jack wouldn't exactly brush off the other man's words, but, on the other hand, he also intended to take them with a very large grain of salt. He'd wait for input from his team, who should already be up in the condo, gathering evidence. "Where's the wife?"

"Over there, with my partner." Lopez pointed toward a low wall of stacked stone that bordered the pathway next to the building. A woman sat there, but because she was partially obscured by the uniformed officer standing in front of her, Jack couldn't really see what she looked like.

Well, he supposed he'd get a good look at her soon enough, take her measure. "Thanks," he told Lopez.

Jack walked over toward the wall Lopez had pointed out. As he approached, the patrol officer who'd been blocking her turned and gave him a brisk nod. "Detective Sandoval?"

"Yes."

"I'm Officer Manning. This is Ms. Campbell, the victim's wife."

The woman stood as the patrolman said her name. Seeing her clearly for the first time, Jack almost started, then told himself the last thing he should be doing right then was paying any attention to her appearance.

But…she was beautiful. Late twenties, with long sandy brown hair streaked with gold. He couldn't be sure of her eye color because the lighting out here wasn't very good, but he could tell that she had the kind of graceful bone structure that didn't require much makeup, even though right then she was stricken and wan, her eyes shadowed and reddened from shock and grief.

Somehow Jack managed to gather himself. "Ms. Campbell, I'm Jack Sandoval. I'll be the lead detective on this case. Do you mind if I ask you a few questions?"

She shook her head. "No," she replied. Her voice was somewhat low-pitched and husky, but he couldn't know for sure if she always sounded like that, or whether the word had come out that way because she'd been crying. "I'm not sure how much I can tell you, though. I didn't see anything."

"That's fine," he said. He gave the patrol officer a slight nod, indicating that he wanted to continue the interview alone. Luckily, Officer Manning didn't seem inclined to argue, because he nodded in return and headed off toward the spot where the team from the medical examiner's office was beginning to set up its own field operations. Jack returned his attention to the woman in front of him. "Just tell me what happened."

She pressed her lips together, then let out a breath.

"I—I was coming over to bring Jeff our divorce papers so he could sign them."

How completely ridiculous was it that Jack experienced a slight sensation of relief at hearing she really had been separated from the victim? As if it mattered. "What time was that?"

"A-around seven-thirty, I think. I got here a little earlier than that, though. I parked on the street and went over the papers a few more times, and—" A small chuckle, and she sent a nervous look up at Jack. "Really, I was just sitting there and trying to work up the nerve to go see him."

Voice neutral, Jack inquired, "Were you worried he would react badly?"

"Oh, no," she said at once, her tone so emphatic that he knew she must be telling the truth. "I mean, he'd pretty much reconciled himself to the divorce happening. He wasn't happy about it, but he wasn't going to fight it, either."

Her reply relieved him somewhat. It probably meant that, whatever had happened, it hadn't resulted from a struggle between the two. Besides, this Ms. Campbell didn't look as if she'd been involved in any kind of an altercation. Her face was strained and pale, but the clothes she wore—a silk blouse with elbow-length sleeves and a dark pencil skirt—appeared relatively unmussed, except for a few wrinkles she'd probably picked up while sitting in her car. "Did anyone see you when you were in the car?"

"I don't know. I think a few people went past—walking their dogs or whatever—but I couldn't really tell if they were paying any attention to me."

Well, that wasn't so good. He'd have to wait for the exact time of death from the medical examiner, but it did sound as if there was an unspecified period where Ms. Campbell had been by herself, with no one to back up her claim that she'd been sitting alone in her car. "Ms. Campbell—" he began, and she shook her head.

"Kate...please. And actually, legally it's still Kate Nichols. I've just been using my maiden name lately, trying to get used to it again."

"All right, Kate." Jack paused, trying to think of the best way to phrase the question without sounding too accusatory. "Do you have any way of proving your whereabouts in the time immediately before seven-thirty?"

"I—" She broke off there, worry entering her eyes, as if she'd just realized for the first time that the police might regard her as a possible suspect. Then she hitched in a little breath and said, sounding relieved, "I was texting with my brother right before I went up to Jeff's place. You know, for encouragement."

"May I see those texts?"

"Of course." She began rummaging through a large brown leather purse that sat on the wall behind her. No doubt the patrol officers had already inspected its contents, including the phone, although they probably wouldn't have asked her to unlock it. She pulled out a rose gold iPhone and entered the code, then went to the messaging app. "Here."

Jack took the phone from her and looked down at the exchange displayed on the screen. Sure enough, there was a convo between her and someone named Colin, with time stamps between seven-nineteen and seven twenty-three. That still didn't cover the entire time she'd supposedly sat in her car, but it did prove she really had been texting. "Colin is your brother?"

"Yes," she said. "Colin Campbell. He lives up in Jerome."

That particular revelation made Jack look at Kate more sharply. All right, just as many civilians lived in Jerome as did McAllister witches, but....

And then it clicked. Colin Campbell had married a McAllister witch—Jenny, whose sister Roslyn had died at Matías Escobar's hands. Jack hadn't recognized Colin's name right away because, after all, the McAllisters weren't his clan, although his niece Zoe had married one of them a little more than a year ago. The de la Pazes and the McAllisters had always gotten along well enough, and under normal circumstances, Jack would have been happy to meet someone who was connected to the Jerome witches, if only peripherally.

Now, though.....

The night air was pleasant enough, but he couldn't prevent a thrill of cold from moving down his spine.

This had to be a horrible coincidence. This woman's brother might have married into the McAllisters, but clearly she was living a normal civilian life down here in Scottsdale. It shouldn't make any difference that Colin Campbell's wife had a sister who was murdered by a dark warlock.

But Lopez had said it looked like a ritual killing….

"Thank you, Kate," Jack said as he handed the phone back to her. "I'll need you to wait with Officers Manning and Lopez while I go take a look at the crime scene."

"All—all right." Something about her expression seemed even more stricken as he made the request, but he wouldn't flatter himself that it was because he was about to leave her with someone else.

She was quiet as he guided her over to the officers' patrol car. Lopez still appeared to be giving her the side-eye, but Manning was much friendlier, telling her to sit down on the back seat, asking her if she'd like some bottled water. Kate murmured a "yes, please" in response to the offer and then took a seat as directed, sitting sideways so her feet touched the ground outside the open car door.

Jack did his best not to look at her long legs, or at the pretty feet in the high-heeled sandals. It was really insane for him to be paying any attention to those sorts of distractions, considering the circumstances. He'd be the first to admit that he was a devotee of the female form, but there was a time and a place for everything, and a crime scene where a woman's estranged husband had just been murdered was definitely not it.

After excusing himself, he headed back to the building where the victim's condo was located. As he paused at the bottom of the steps, taking in the layout of the place, a young woman in a deputy's uniform approached. Lisa Peters—that was her name. Her face was pale, but her tone precise and level as she said, "We've done our preliminary inspection of the scene. It's all yours."

"Thanks," Jack replied. He wouldn't ask any questions of her now; he always liked to go into a crime scene with his mind fresh, no preconceived notions to possibly fog his perception of the site. Later they'd go over every single piece of evidence in excruciating detail, but that was for later, in the days and possibly weeks ahead. "I'm going up."

Peters nodded and headed off toward one of the squad cars parked on the street. Jack didn't even bother to take in a breath, but headed up the stairs to what had once been Jeff Nichols' condo.

The door stood open, the entrance barred with yellow crime scene tape, even as light glared from the unit. Jack ducked under the tape and paused just inside the door. His heart gave a heavy, disapproving thud. Yes, he'd seen his fair share of homicide investigations, had witnessed more ugliness than he ever wanted to consciously recall, but none of that had prepared him for the scene that confronted him now.

The blood spatter wasn't exactly spatter. Its coppery stink assailed his nose, but he realized right away that the bloody markings on the walls and the floor weren't there by random chance, that there were distinct patterns to those markings. Nothing as crude as an upside-down pentacle or the horned symbols used by today's Satan worshippers, true, but Jack thought he recognized some of them, sigils old as civilization, signs used to invoke the dark powers, to summon the forces of the underworld to the spell-caster's aid. Some were sharp and spiky in shape, others intricate circles with arcane lettering surrounding them, but all of them were evil.

Again that icy trickle of dread traced its way down his spine. He knew he would have to tread carefully here, because of course none of his coworkers had any idea that he was in fact a warlock, and therefore in possession of knowledge no ordinary homicide detective should have.

Grace Pedersen came up to him as he made himself take a step forward. Her blue eyes, usually cheerful as a summer sky, were shadowed, and the lines around them seemed far more pronounced than they normally were. Even so, she tried to summon a watery smile. "Hey, Jack. Just another night in Scottsdale, huh?"

"Something like that," he responded. His gaze

tracked to the huddled form on the floor, now mercifully covered by a rubber sheet. Even with the sheet concealing the worst of the damage, however, he could tell there was something wrong about the shape of the body under that sheet. "Time of death?"

"A little after seven, near as we can determine without an autopsy," she said.

Steeling himself, he knelt and pulled a pair of latex gloves from his jacket pocket and slipped them on, then reached out with a thumb and forefinger to pull back one corner of the rubber sheet.

Holy Mary, Mother of God.

It took all his effort not to murmur a spell of protection under his breath right then, a barrier of white light against the darkness. Surely he was in need of such a thing, as were Grace, who looked on worriedly, and Ian, who methodically moved along the bloodstained walls and took picture after picture of the various symbols painted there.

Even half-obscured by the sheet, Jeff Nichols' face was a mask of terror, eyes staring white-ringed, mouth open in a silent scream. A fine mist of red coated his features, residue from arterial spray. Fighting back a sick feeling, Jack looked down and realized the victim's hands had been severed and now lay neatly on either side of his head. The fingertips were coated with blood, almost as if….

His gaze moved to the sigils on the walls. They were precise enough, and yet the streakiness of the outlines made him realize that they hadn't been painted on with any kind of brush. No, it seemed that....

He let go of the rubber sheet and stood. "The perpetrator used the victim's fingertips to paint those signs on the walls?"

Grace nodded, then swallowed. She'd always seemed the soul of competence to him, tough and almost impossible to rattle after twenty-five years investigating crime scenes, but right then she looked as if she was doing everything in her power to prevent herself from throwing up. "That's what Ian and I think. Of course, it'll take further analysis to be absolutely sure." A pause, and then she asked, her voice nearly a whisper, "Jack, who the hell would do something like this?"

"No one sane," he replied. Normally he didn't make those sorts of armchair diagnoses—after all, he was no psychiatrist—but he didn't see how anyone in their right mind could do this sort of thing. "So we need to find them, and fast."

"Understood." She hesitated before saying, "Unfortunately, so far we haven't found anything here except the victim's blood."

"No tracks?" Jack inquired. With the amount of blood spilled, you'd think the killer would have stepped in some of it.

"None that we can find." Her gaze moved down to the plastic covers she wore on her shoes. Jack hadn't bothered with them, since the bloodstained carpet had already been protected by more plastic, but Grace had taken the precaution since she was one of the first people on the scene. "Maybe the killer had made sure he was protected, and wore gloves and plastic covers on his shoes. The cuts that removed the hands from the victim's body were done with surgical precision, as far as I've been able to tell. Whoever killed Jeff Nichols, he—or she—was very careful about it."

"And no one saw anything."

Her shoulders lifted, even as Ian paused in snapping pictures and walked over to them, then said, "No one on this side of the building. The patrol officers also questioned the people in the four units on the north side, but one of those condos is empty—apparently it's used as a vacation rental—and of the remaining three, only one person was actually home. Lily Perez, fifty-two. She said she was watching Netflix and didn't hear anything."

Of course. Right then, Jack wished the public was a little more the way it tended to be portrayed in books and movies, hyper-vigilant and noticing everything. Unfortunately, his experience told him that most people tended to ignore anything that wasn't directly under their noses.

"What about the surrounding buildings?"

"One of the other uniforms on-scene is going door to door, but I doubt he's going to turn up anything. Whoever did this was in and out without anyone noticing."

Jack nodded. Sometimes you got your clues handed to you, and sometimes you had to pry them out of the minutest traces of evidence. So far, it sounded like the killer had taken care not to leave anything behind to identify him—somehow, Jack doubted the murderer was a her—but it was far too early to declare defeat.

Besides, he had all those symbols painted on the walls. Dark magic, the blackest possible…which meant there were few warlocks in the world who would have risked their very souls to perform that kind of conjuring. Certainly no one in the de la Paz clan, and none of the McAllisters, either. A few years ago, he might have suspected Damon Wilcox, but Damon had been dead for nearly four years now, and none of the other Wilcoxes appeared inclined to take over his more dubious experiments.

Which left Jack with…what? The Santiagos? Certainly they had several bad eggs among their clan, but with Matías Escobar and his two cousins stripped of their powers and sentenced to life in three separate civilian prisons, that didn't leave many other suspects.

Also, there were the Castillos, the witch clan in New Mexico. They kept to themselves, although they'd long been friendly with the Wilcoxes, which made them somewhat suspect in Jack's eyes. Still, he'd never heard of any Castillos coming anywhere near de la Paz territory. Surely Luz Trujillo, his clan's *prima*, should have been able to sense any interlopers trespassing on their land.

He'd have to talk to her, just in case. Actually, there were several people he needed to talk to, once he had copies of all the photos Ian had just taken. There were several in the clan who had knowledge of the old, dark ways, even if they didn't practice those forbidden arts themselves.

"Okay," he said, after a long pause during which both his assistants studied him with worried expressions, as if they guessed he had the beginnings of certain suspicions going through his mind, suspicions he didn't yet wish to share. "I'm going to check out the rest of the condo."

"You won't find anything," Ian said. "Nichols was killed here in the living room. Nothing in any of the other rooms was disturbed."

"Maybe," Jack replied. "But I still want to check it out."

Ian shrugged and returned to his photographs, while Grace went to retrieve her fingerprint kit and head into the kitchen, which appeared relatively untouched. The whine of the camera seemed to penetrate Jack's eardrums as he moved down the short hallway to the bedroom.

As Ian had pointed out, there wasn't all that much to see. Jack didn't know how long Jeff Nichols had lived here, but it was obvious enough that he hadn't bothered much with trying to make the place his own. The bed was rumpled and half-covered with a dark blue comforter, as if that was all the effort he'd put into making it that morning before he left for work. The walls and the dresser and nightstand were completely bare, except for a clock radio and an unplugged cell phone charger on the nightstand.

Well, there was one thing....

The dresser had a framed wedding photo of Jeff Nichols and Kate Campbell. *Kate Nichols,* Jack reminded himself, even if it sounded as though she had already started using her maiden name again. In the photograph, Kate's smile was luminous, although Jack thought he detected something almost strained about it, as if she'd just realized that maybe this wasn't the happiest day of her life after all. The Jeff in the photo was in much better shape than the man whose body now lay under a rubber sheet, but even back when the picture had been taken, he gave the appearance of someone who was carrying too much weight...a certain puffiness around the eyes and chin.

Trying to dismiss that uncharitable thought— *what kind of asshole goes around criticizing the appearance of someone who's just been brutally murdered?* he admonished himself—Jack turned away from the photo and stuck his head in the bathroom to take a quick look around. Someone had already turned on the lights above the vanity, so he didn't have to worry about getting out his gloves so he could touch the switch.

Again, nothing much to see here. Flecks of dark bristles, remnants of that morning's shave, were dusted over part of the cultured marble vanity top and in the sink itself, and the mirror needed to be wiped down, but what else would you expect from someone newly returned to the bachelor life? Jack had to admit that his own bathroom probably would be in similar shape if it weren't for Teresa, the woman who came in to clean his place every Tuesday. It would be waiting for him in freshly scrubbed splendor whenever he got home tonight, a notion he found reassuring. He wanted things to be clean after having to see this kind of filth.

As Grace had already pointed out, all evidence suggested that the killer hadn't ventured farther into the apartment than the living room. Jack headed back out there, where Ian was already packing up his photographic equipment and Grace was entering some notes on her iPad.

"Was the TV on?" Jack inquired. He'd noticed it earlier, an enormous curved 60-incher sitting on a low entertainment console.

"What?" Grace replied, looking up from the iPad.

"The TV. Was it on?"

Her fair eyebrows pulled together. "No. That did seem kind of strange, because we found a half-eaten sandwich on a plate on the coffee table, as if the victim had been sitting there, eating and watching TV, right before the crime occurred. You think it's significant?"

"Not sure." Actually, he did have a theory, but it wasn't one he could share with Grace. In most cases, you'd think it would make more sense for the killer to have left the television on, simply because the sound would have helped drown out any of the noise of the murder itself. But that same sound, whether it was from a basketball game or watching the evening news, would also disrupt the casting of those dark spells. Sound was energy…as was magic. "Just trying to figure out what the hell happened."

She nodded. "Not much to go on yet, I'm afraid. I just have to hope that once I can get back to the lab and process some of this evidence, I'll find something."

If there was anything to find. The person responsible for the murder clearly was methodical and cool, an organized killer, not someone who would be careless enough to leave anything significant for the authorities to detect. But he'd just have to hope. Sometimes the flimsiest of clues provided a pathway to a conviction.

"I'm going to go down and talk to Ms. Campbell again," he said.

"You think she had anything to do with it?"

Not a chance, he thought, but he only replied, "No. I just want to follow up on a few things, and then I'll have Lopez and Manning take her home. She's had a hell of a shock."

Grace offered a sympathetic nod. While it was their job to be wary, anyone with eyes to see could tell that Kate Campbell was innocent.

Besides, she was a civilian, a non-magical person, and so she couldn't have cast those dark spells even if she wanted to.

Saying that he'd see everyone back at the station, Jack left the condo and headed over to where Kate still sat in the back seat of Lopez and Manning's squad car. She had a plastic bottle of Costco-brand water in one hand and was staring off into the distance, clearly trying to avoid focusing on the immediate scene around her.

When she saw him approaching, however, she got out of the car and tucked the bottle of water into her oversized purse. Questions filled her eyes, but she waited for him to speak.

"I'm going to have these officers take you home," he told her with a slight tilt of his head in the direction of the two men, who were standing in front of the car and having a muffled convo.

A sort of wary relief entered Kate's expression. "You don't want to question me?"

"I interviewed you already, Ms. Campbell. For the moment, you're not a suspect." He hesitated, then said, "Is there someone you can have come and stay with you? It's probably better if you're not alone."

"I'm fine," she began, but he cut through her protests.

"Maybe, but I still think it would be better if you had someone with you. Or someplace you can go stay. Do you have family in the area?" Sooner or later they'd need to discuss her brother Colin and his connection to the witching world, but that could wait.

"My parents are down in Tempe. But I'd rather not go there. It would feel strange to try to sleep somewhere that wasn't my own place." A slight pause, and she went on, "I'll call my friend Samantha. She lives here in Scottsdale, too."

"Good."

Kate's face looked so pale, so stricken. Jack wished he knew her better, that he was a friend instead of the detective called in to handle this case, because right then he wanted to reach out and give her a hug, let her know that she'd survive this.

Instead, he offered her what he thought of as his "official" smile—not too wide, meant to be reassuring more than anything else. "I'll contact you tomorrow, Ms. Campbell. In the meantime, try to get some rest. And probably take the day off from work."

Her lips compressed. "I think I'd rather go to work. Maybe if I'm surrounded by other people, I'll be in better shape."

While he understood the sentiment, Jack knew generally that wasn't the case. People needed time to process these sorts of tragedies. Still, he didn't want to prod her. This was her life, her choice. "Well, don't make a decision now. See how you feel in the morning."

She offered a dubious nod. Then she said, her voice tight and desperate, "Who would do such a thing? Why would they do...*that?*" Her gaze tracked up to the condo where her estranged husband's body lay, then back down to Jack, pleading, fear and worry and horror all blending in her eyes. Now he saw they were hazel, a warm mixture of green and gold.

Right then, he really didn't have any answers for her. "I don't know, Kate," he said gently, using her first name on purpose, hoping the more casual form of address might help to put her at ease. "But we're going to find out."

3

A NIGHTMARE. THIS WHOLE THING HAD TO BE A nightmare. Any minute she'd sit up in bed and blink into the darkness, and realize everything was fine, Jeff was fine, that she'd had a horrible dream born of her anxiety about taking him the divorce papers.

Problem was, she knew this wasn't a nightmare. This was reality, her sitting in the back seat of a patrol car while she was being taken home, the nice cop—Manning—behind the wheel, while his decidedly not-so-friendly partner followed them in her Jetta. Not to relieve her of the stress of driving, though. No, Lopez was going to take her car to the police station so they could check it for evidence. She'd wanted to protest, but realized they were only doing their job. If she really decided to go to work after all, she'd call an Uber or something.

Officer Manning hadn't said much of anything to

her, except to ask if she wanted the heater on. Silly question, wasn't it, when the night outside was so mild? But she realized then that she'd begun to shiver, that goosebumps pimpled the exposed skin of her forearms. Shock, of course. What else did she expect?

She managed to murmur a reply, saying that would be fine, and then lapsed into silence as she watched the familiar streets of her adopted town pass by. How happy she'd been to move here eight months ago, how thrilled to land her dream job with the city's planning department. Getting the job when so many other applicants were vying for the position seemed to be a sign that her decision to leave Jeff had been the right one, that the universe was trying to lay an easy path before her.

Dear God, how wrong she'd been about that.

Her tears were a hard, burning lump lodged somewhere in her throat. Kate knew if she actually talked to her best friend Sam, then she really would start to cry hysterically, and she wasn't going to do that. Not while sitting in the back of a cop car, anyway. No doubt Officer Manning had seen his share of women sobbing in the back of his patrol car, but Kate refused to be one of them. Once she was safely home, then she could fall apart.

Anyway, she texted Sam to let her know something terrible had happened, and would she mind coming over and staying the night? Bless her, Sam hadn't asked any questions, had said she'd be over in twenty minutes, even though she probably had about fifty other things to do with her evening downtime, including heading out for a drink to unwind.

Or not. Samantha had broken up with her boyfriend two months earlier and wasn't quite ready to get back out there. She and Kate liked going out together because that way they weren't being hermits, but they also could feel safe in knowing that they had each other's backs in case any over-eager guys didn't get the hint that the two women weren't looking for anything except a chance to relax and have a few drinks together.

Officer Manning pulled up in front of Kate's apartment complex, while Officer Lopez parked her Jetta immediately behind the squad car and got out. He still looked unfriendly as ever, although this time she wondered whether that was because he'd drawn the short straw when it came to babysitting her car.

"We'll walk you to your door," Officer Manning said.

She nodded. Right then, she was all too glad to have the escort, although she shuddered to contemplate what her neighbors might think if they saw her go to her apartment, flanked by a couple of uniformed cops. Well, the news about Jeff's death would get around eventually, and people would realize the policemen had been there to protect her, not the other way around.

Officer Manning got out and came around to the

rear door, which he opened so she could climb out. Officer Lopez was already waiting for them on the sidewalk, dark eyes grim and unsmiling. He didn't say anything as she got out of the squad car.

They walked her down one of the paths that wound through the complex, the moon overhead so bright that the landscape lights set out to illuminate the area were hardly needed. Her building was toward the front of the complex, so they didn't have too far to go.

When they got to the landing, Samantha was already waiting there, a flowered SportSac weekender bag sitting on the landing next to her. The light from the fixture beside the door gleamed in her red hair. Her eyes widened at the sight of the two police officers, and her mouth opened, probably to ask what the heck was going on.

Kate forestalled her by saying, "Thanks so much for getting here so fast, Sam. Officer Manning, Officer Lopez, this is my best friend, Samantha Davis. Detective Sandoval thought it would be better if I wasn't alone tonight."

"Good advice," Officer Manning said, and gave Sam a brisk, no-nonsense smile. He shifted his attention to Kate and added, "Go on inside. Lock the door. Don't open it for anyone without a badge."

She assumed he was just trying to be helpful—and make sure nothing happened to her on his watch—but Kate couldn't repress the chill that went over her. Had Jeff opened his door to a stranger, or had the murderer simply broken in? Detective Sandoval hadn't let slip anything of what he'd found in the condo, but she supposed that was to be expected.

"I won't," she promised, and dug her keys out of her purse. It wasn't until she tried to insert the key in the lock that she realized how badly her hands were shaking—so badly, in fact, that Sam came to her and took over, turning the key and opening the door. Then she went back to where she'd been waiting and retrieved her weekender bag.

"Let's get inside," Sam said. "Thanks for bringing her home, officers."

Both Manning and Lopez nodded. Kate went inside, glad that she'd left the torchiere lamp in one corner of the living room switched on. She'd turned it on before she left for Jeff's place because she hated coming home to a dark house.

Then Sam closed the door behind them and turned the deadbolt. She set down her bag and said, "Kate, just what the hell is going on?"

"Jeff's dead," Kate said. That was all she could manage, because immediately afterward the tears finally came, flowing down her cheeks, and she sobbed, in awful spasms that wracked her entire body.

At once Sam came to her and took her by both hands, guided her over to the sofa so she could sit down. "God, I'm so sorry, Kate," she murmured as she stroked her friend's arm. "What—what happened? Was there a car accident?"

"N-no," Kate replied. She didn't want to say anything more than that, but she knew the murder would be all over the news soon enough. It wasn't the sort of thing that could exactly be covered up. "He—he was murdered."

Sam went stiff with shock. "*Murdered?*"

"Yes. And—and oh, God, Sam, you should have seen the blood. It was all over the walls, like…like graffiti made with blood rather than paint."

A shocked sound, and Sam dropped an arm around Kate's shoulders, hugging her fiercely. "Jesus Christ. So…is that what happened when you went over to take him the papers? You found him?"

"Y-yes." Kate gulped back her tears as best she could and sucked in a deep breath, telling herself that she needed to try to get a little control back, if for no other reason than she wouldn't be able to tell her friend what had really happened if she kept having hysterics. "It was like something out of a horror movie. Worse, because it was real. I don't—I'll never forget it. Ever."

Another hug, and then Sam pulled away slightly. "I'm getting you a drink. What'll you have?"

"There's some Cuervo on the top shelf of the pantry."

"Okay."

Sam got up from the couch and headed into the

kitchen. Kate could hear her rummaging around for a minute or two, and then she returned to the living room, a bottle of Cuervo Gold in one hand and a pair of shot glasses in the other. She set everything down on the glass-topped coffee table and poured tequila into each shot glass, filling both of them nearly to the top.

"For what ails you," she said, and handed Kate one of the shot glasses.

Kate took it, and bolted the contents of the glass, letting it hit the back of her throat and drop straight into her stomach with a thud she could almost feel. The heat of it spread into her shocked and chilled limbs, and she nodded.

"Better?"

"A little," she said. "I'd better have another, though."

Without comment, Sam refilled the glass, and once again Kate tossed back the liquor, glad of the way it had already begun to blur the edges of reality, was making her feel for the first time in the last few horrible hours that she might somehow be able to get through this.

Sam picked up her own shot glass and drank about half its contents before setting the glass back down on the table. "Well, now I know why those cops were walking you to your door. They don't think…?" She trailed off there and sent Kate a questioning look.

"No," she replied at once. "I mean, I'm not sure

Officer Lopez is entirely convinced of my innocence, but the lead officer on the investigation, Detective Sandoval, basically told me I wasn't a suspect. I'm not saying that might not change, but for now it's not something I need to worry about."

"No, all you have to worry about is some crazed killer roaming around out there," Sam blurted, and then almost immediately put her hand to her mouth. "Oh, shit. I am so sorry. That's not what I—"

"It's okay," Kate said. "It's not like I haven't thought the same thing. Although right now I'm trying to figure out...why Jeff? Why in the world would anyone want to kill him?"

Sam pressed her pink-glossed lips together and shook her head. "I don't have a clue." She paused there for a few seconds, then lifted her shot glass and drank the tequila that remained. "Although...didn't you say that he'd been doing some kind of online sports gambling?"

"That was two years ago," Kate pointed out. It made her feel a little calmer to be looking at the whole hideous situation with something resembling logic. That way, she could get her racing brain to slow down and attempt to work its way through the problem. "He told me he stopped."

"He told you," Sam said, her tone very gentle. "But do you know for sure?"

"I—" Kate began, and hesitated. Truth was, she really *didn't* know. Not for sure. Yes, they'd had a joint checking account for the household expenses, and she'd never seen anything strange there, but they each also had a separate personal account for their own little expenditures. Nothing major; Kate had never had more than a couple hundred dollars in her personal account. But who knew what might have been going on in Jeff's? It wasn't like she'd ever been able to see the balance. Gathering her breath, she went on, "You're not suggesting that someone murdered Jeff because of online gambling debts?"

Sam poured herself another shot of Cuervo. "I don't know. It's just the only thing I can think of that makes any sense."

And Sam was all about making sense. She'd been getting her master's in microbiology at the same time Kate was working on her master's in urban planning, and now split her time between working at a lab in North Scottsdale and teaching a few classes as an adjunct at the local community college. Sam wanted facts, numbers, data. She certainly wasn't the type for wild hypotheses or conspiracy theories. And because her world was focused on order, not chaos, she probably didn't want to entertain the notion that there might be a madman running around Scottsdale who got his rocks off by murdering people and then finger-painting—literally—with their blood.

That last thought made Kate's stomach heave, and she grabbed the bottle of Cuervo and poured herself some more. All right, logically she knew that throwing back shot after shot of tequila when her stomach was already upset probably wasn't the best idea, but she supposed she hoped, somewhere in the back of her mind, that if she drank enough of the stuff, she might finally be able to blot out the hideous scene which now seemed imprinted on her mind, on the insides of her damn eyelids, so all she could see with her eyes open or shut was Jeff's body sprawled on the floor of his condo, arcane symbols she couldn't recognize painted all over the bare white walls.

"Hey," Sam said, her no-nonsense, problem-solving tone of a minute earlier gone, replaced by something much more gentle. "It's horrible. I know. But getting drunk won't help. Especially a tequila drunk. You're going to have the mother of all hangovers tomorrow if you keep this up. Let me get you some water, order some takeout."

Kate's stomach roiled again. "I couldn't eat anything. I'd throw up."

"You say that, but you know you need food. When was the last time you ate?"

"I had some yogurt at lunch."

A shake of Sam's fiery head. "That's not going to cut it. What sounds better? Chinese? Pizza?"

"We can't order anything in. Remember what Officer Manning said."

Her friend looked so crestfallen at that remark, Kate almost chuckled, despite everything. "Don't despair. I kind of loaded up at Trader Joe's the last time I went. There's got to be something in the freezer, if you're determined to feed me."

"That I can work with."

Sam got up from the couch—taking the bottle of Cuervo with her—and went into the kitchen. Kate stared at the half-inch of tequila left in her shot glass and wondered if she should drink it now or wait. *Better now,* she thought. *Nothing I have on hand pairs all that well with tequila.*

What a stupid thing to be thinking, when her husband lay dead a few miles away. Were the investigators still working on the crime scene, or had they finally wrapped things up? She tried not to imagine Jeff's body being carried out on a gurney, taken to the medical examiner's van so they could cut him up even further.

Her stomach lurched, and she gulped down the last bit of tequila. It really didn't help all that much, but at least now it was gone.

She sat there, listening as Sam bustled around in the kitchen, and stared at her living room, at the vertical blinds that concealed the sliding glass doors leading to the balcony, at the ficus in the corner by the front window, the cherished painting of the Superstition Mountains that Jeff complained she'd paid way too much for, but which she loved. Because of her guilt at leaving, she'd let him keep way more household stuff than she took, but that painting had come with her.

It hurt, but as she tried very hard not to look at any one thing in particular, to not *think* of any one thing in particular, she realized part of the reason it hurt was because it didn't hurt *enough*. Which she knew was a crazy thing to be thinking, but there it was. She and Jeff had been separated for months. She'd acknowledged to herself a long time ago—even as she tried not to say the words aloud to him, because they sounded so cruel—that she didn't love him anymore, hadn't loved him for some time. Even with all that, though, she had loved him once, and she thought she should be feeling more than she was right now. What had happened to Jeff was beyond horrible, and she could be shocked and grieving over such a brutal death...but it wasn't grief over someone she loved. And that sounded absolutely dreadful.

Sam came into the living room, a full glass of water in each hand. She set one of the glasses down, but extended the other toward Kate. "Here. You probably need this more than anything else."

Kate took the glass, sipped obediently. Then she placed it on a coaster.

"What is it?" Sam asked. "You look—well, even worse than you did a few minutes ago, frankly."

"Thanks, I appreciate that," Kate returned, a wan smile touching her lips.

"Sorry. But...."

"No, it's okay. I'm just wondering if I'm a horrible

person because I'm not feeling much of anything right now."

Sam frowned slightly. "It's perfectly natural for you to be in shock. I'd be surprised if you weren't."

"It's more than that. It's…." Kate paused there, wondering how much she should say. Yes, she and Sam had been friends for almost four years now, and they'd been through a lot together, but what would Sam think if Kate openly confessed that she didn't feel as deeply shocked and grieved as she should be?

Her friend was looking at her with such worry that Kate knew she had to say something. If such revelations made Sam think less of her, well, there wasn't much she could do about that. But she hated secrets. It had been hard enough to keep the truth about her sister-in-law's family from everyone Kate knew, even her own parents.

But Colin had begged her, had explained that the witch clans had only survived this long by keeping their true natures hidden from the rest of the world, and how on earth was she supposed to say no to that? Anyway, she had a feeling their parents wouldn't have believed a word of it without a proper demonstration of some sort of magical ability, and no way was Colin going to ask his wife or any of her relatives to perform tricks on command. Kate was close to her parents, and keeping secrets from them was not something she was at all comfortable with. However, difficult as it was for her to remain silent, she could see how important it was to Colin, and so she hadn't argued, had tucked the knowledge away as best she could.

At any rate, as soon as Kate had come to terms with the shift in her feelings toward Jeff, she'd been up front with him, hadn't tried to pretend the situation was anything but what it was. Because they were estranged, it had been easy enough not to say anything about the McAllisters—or the other witch clans that apparently existed in Arizona—but she'd almost slipped a few times in front of Sam.

And here she was thinking about witches, simply because it was a lot easier than trying to focus on the problem at hand. Still, she'd rather Sam knew the ugly truth about her. At least that way she wouldn't have to hide what she was feeling.

"It's just that I'm upset about what happened to Jeff, and horrified, but I'm not...grieving, if you know what I mean. We were still married, but he wasn't my husband anymore. I know that sounds terrible."

In response, Sam leaned over and hugged Kate, the embrace strong and fierce. "No, it sounds normal. You didn't love Jeff anymore. Why should you feel the same way as someone who lost a husband, a boyfriend, a lover? Your relationship was totally different. You can't judge yourself now because of the way you once felt about him. What happened is horrible, and I pray to God they catch whoever did this and lock them up forever, but you can't beat yourself up for not rending your garments and rubbing ashes in your hair. Or whatever it was that people used to do when they were in mourning."

That comment made Kate smile weakly. She disentangled herself from her friend's embrace and said, "I don't remember. Anyway, I don't have so many garments that I can afford to 'rend' any of them." That was only the truth. Yes, her job with the city planner's department paid well, but the apartment wasn't cheap, and the payments for her student loans were truly horrifying. She figured if she kept to a strict budget and didn't encounter any insane expenses along the way, she might be rid of those loans by the time she was forty. Maybe.

"Well, then." Sam paused for a moment before adding, "Everyone handles shock and grief differently. You're going through enough without guilting your-self into thinking you should behave a certain way."

Very sensible advice. Maybe it was even true. Kate knotted her hands in her lap and stared down at the now-bare ring finger of her left hand. She'd taken off her engagement ring and wedding band some months earlier, and now wore on her right hand the white gold and diamond cigar-band ring that had once belonged to her grandmother. Why Grandma Delores had left it to her, rather than her mother, Kate didn't know. But she was glad of it, proud of how it looked on her finger. People tended to notice it, rather than the absence of any wedding rings on her left hand. At least she'd started her job after she and Jeff had separated, so no one at work really knew her as anyone except "Kate Campbell." It made life so much easier.

Not that it was going to be all that easy to go into work and try to explain to everyone that her estranged husband had been brutally murdered. She wouldn't be able to cover it up, though. Detective Sandoval's advice came back to her, that maybe she should take the day off. Her six-month anniversary at the job had come and gone, so at least she could take a day if she needed to. But what was she supposed to do with a day off? Sit around the apartment and brood? When things had gotten bad with Jeff, she used to get in her car and just drive, heading out into the desert so she could be alone with her thoughts. That option was denied her now, until the Scottsdale P.D. returned her car to her. She couldn't really afford a rental. Besides, wouldn't that look suspicious, to rent a car and drive out into the Sonoran Desert just so she could get her head screwed on straight?

The toaster oven made the *bing* noise that signaled it had gotten to the end of a cycle, and Sam excused herself to go into the kitchen. Kate remained where she was, although part of her was thinking that she should really get up and help her friend. But no, Sam would just tell her to sit down and let herself be waited on, so Kate didn't move, only sat there and twisted the ring on the middle finger of her right hand while Sam got things ready.

A few minutes later, she emerged with a plate full

of various appetizers—mini quiches, and cut-up pieces of phyllo pastry with mushroom, and macaroni and cheese balls. Kate looked at the plate and raised an eyebrow. "You expect me to eat all that?"

"Not all of it," Sam replied imperturbably. "Just half. I'll take care of the rest." She set the plate down on the coffee table, handed a paper towel to Kate, and then settled herself back on the couch and spread another makeshift napkin across her lap.

To Kate's surprise, everything looked good. It smelled good, too. She picked up a mini quiche, blew on it, and popped it into her mouth. Yes, that tasted good as well. Total comfort food, which was what she needed right then.

They ate in silence for a few minutes. Then Sam asked, "Do you know when you're going to get your car back?"

Kate set down a half-eaten piece of phyllo pastry. "Officer Manning made it sound as if it might be sometime tomorrow, but I don't know for sure. It's annoying, because Detective Sandoval basically told me that I wasn't a suspect. But I guess they just want to be thorough. Anyway, they're supposed to call me when they're done...whenever that ends up being. Just another reason to stay home tomorrow, I suppose."

"It's better if you do," Sam said. "I know you probably want to act like everything is normal, but it's not, and you need to take care of yourself. I'd drive you, but I've got an eight o'clock class tomorrow, and it's on the opposite side of town from city hall."

"It's fine," Kate replied. "I think I will take the day off." Her apartment needed to be cleaned anyway. A few hours of mindless scrubbing might be just what the doctor ordered.

"Good." Then Sam shifted on the couch, the leather creaking slightly. "Do you need me to call your parents?"

Oh, God. Of course they would have to be called—and Colin, too. For all she knew, he'd been texting her for the last half hour, trying to find out what had happened after she dropped off the divorce papers. Well, she'd let the food soak up most of the tequila before she dived into any of those obligations. It wasn't even that late yet—not even nine o'clock. They probably wouldn't think there was anything strange about getting a call at that hour.

"No," Kate said. "It's all right. I'll call in a little bit. And—and I guess I'd better call Nancy."

Nancy Nichols was Jeff's mother. She lived up in Anthem, and hadn't said two words to Kate since the separation.

"Don't you dare call her," Sam said, her pretty features hardening with dislike. "The woman called you a bitch, remember?"

Oh, Kate remembered that incident all too well. At least Nancy had done it over the phone instead of name-calling her to her face, but still, it hadn't been a pleasant experience.

"Besides," Sam went on, "the police would have contacted her, since she's the next of kin. You don't need to get involved, at least not right now."

Possibly she should have protested further, but Kate didn't have the energy right then. She and Nancy had never gotten along very well, since her mother-in-law had made it clear that she didn't think Kate was good enough for her precious boy. Mostly Kate had done what she could to stay out of the way, which was easy enough while going to school full-time and working as a T.A. to earn some income on the side. Inwardly, though, she couldn't help blaming Nancy for some of Jeff's more obvious character flaws. A single mother, she'd dealt with her situation by over-compensating, by giving Jeff basically every damn thing he wanted and waiting on him hand and foot. He'd expected pretty much the same treatment from his wife, taking it for granted that she'd handle the cooking and cleaning and shopping, even though she was putting in sixty-hour weeks at school.

Oh, well. He still hadn't been able to comprehend the true reason for Kate's walking out, that she'd gotten fed up with being treated more as a servant than a wife. And there was no way in hell she could ever tell the truth to Nancy, because Nancy would have viewed any such statements as an attack on her parenting skills. Kate had been as diplomatic as she could in explaining why she'd left, saying only that she and Jeff had gotten married too young and that they were two different people now, but Nancy still didn't want to hear any of it. That was when the "bitch" remark had been trotted out, accompanied by the oh-so-friendly adjective of "selfish."

So Kate was all too happy to let the police handle Nancy. At some point there would be funeral arrangements and all the messiness of clearing out Jeff's condo, but for now, Kate would keep her distance. One slightly cheering thought was that both Colin and their mother hated Nancy like poison—Liam Campbell, Kate's father, hadn't interacted with Nancy as much, and therefore was more neutral on the subject—and would be only too happy to go to bat to protect Kate.

"Okay," she allowed. "You're right. That's one conversation I'd rather not have."

"Good." Sam helped herself to a macaroni and cheese ball, and chewed thoughtfully for a moment. "I know this is going to be hard, but you need to turn your brain off for a while. Let's see what's on Netflix and just tune out for the rest of the evening."

"I'll still have to call my parents, and Colin."

"True, but eat first and watch one show. If nothing else, it'll help to get the tequila out of your system before you call them."

That sounded like a plan. Kate couldn't guarantee that she wouldn't still break down while talking to her mother or her brother, but it would give her some time to collect herself. She really couldn't ask for much more right now.

"All right," she said. The world might still blow up in her face the next day, but she'd take this moment while she could. *Sufficient to the day,* as her grandmother used to say.

Yes, this day had definitely had its own share of evil. About all she could do was hope that the worst was over.

4

JACK SANDOVAL STARED DOWN AT THE photographs spread across his desk and rubbed the bridge of his nose. By that point, it was past midnight, and he should have been off shift, but he really didn't feel like going back to his apartment. Not with something this disturbing staring him in the face.

The symbols were much clearer in the photos than they'd appeared on the walls of Jeff Nichols' apartment. Ian had done some retouching in Photoshop, it looked like, before he printed out the images for Jack to inspect. Although he didn't know the individual meanings of all those sigils, Jack could tell now more than ever that they were evil. Tomorrow he'd have to start talking to people in his clan, but for now he was just trying to piece together what had happened, based on the scanty evidence they had so far.

The M.E. had logged the time of death as somewhere between 6:50 and 7:05 p.m. Kate Campbell had said she waited in the car for a while before going upstairs to see her estranged husband. Best guess, she'd first parked on the street outside the Nichols' complex roughly fifteen to twenty minutes after the crime had been committed.

But as to when the killer had actually gone inside the condo—that was more difficult to nail down. The medical examiner's report indicated that Nichols had been alive while his hands were removed, then used to paint the walls of the living room. Best guess was that he would have bled out in ten to fifteen minutes, with brain death occurring before that, which meant the killer could have broken in as early as 6:45, or as late as 7:05 p.m. Probably earlier than seven, though; Jack couldn't imagine even the most skilled warlock being able to paint all those symbols in just a few scant minutes.

Larry hadn't been all that thrilled with him for letting Kate Campbell go home, even with having her car impounded so a forensics team could go over it for any evidence. "She's the most likely suspect," he said, not bothering to hide the irritation in his voice.

"She didn't do it," Jack replied. And Larry probably knew that as well as he did. No way could Kate have looked so pristine if she'd just brutally murdered her husband. Even if she'd covered up her clothes with a jumpsuit or something, arterial spray still probably would have gotten on her hair or face. She wouldn't have had time to get cleaned up in that small space between the probable time of death and when she'd called 9-1-1.

"You're that sure? What, did you suddenly develop mind-reading skills or something?"

Unlike some of the members of his clan, Jack didn't possess that particular gift. However, he knew that no civilian had painted those symbols on the walls of Jeff Nichols' condo, and he also knew the reason why there was no sign of forced entry was that witches and warlocks didn't need keys to get through locked doors. It was one of the simplest talents they possessed, although one they took care not to abuse.

Unfortunately, he couldn't mention either of those data points to Larry, since they involved witches and warlocks, and Jack had to keep his mouth shut when it came to that particular subject. "No," he said calmly. "I know because, for one thing, she doesn't possess the physical strength to overcome someone like Jeff Nichols. He outweighed her by more than a hundred pounds. And there was no trace of any drugs in his system, so it's not as if he was knocked out before the killer got busy cutting off his hands."

"Bone saw?"

"Or something like it. The cuts were too clean for a knife, or even an axe. Also, I spoke with Kate Campbell at the scene, and she didn't look like someone who'd just spent the previous half hour cutting off body parts and painting the walls with blood. She looked like she'd just come from work—skirt, silk blouse, open shoes. Not a hair out of place."

"Pretty girl, huh?"

"I don't see what that has to do with any of it," Jack replied, an edge entering his tone.

"Just making an observation, Jack. Well, don't stay too late. I have a feeling this investigation isn't going anywhere soon."

Larry had hung up then, and, presumably, had gone home to enjoy the rest of his evening. His comment continued to rankle Jack, though, even as he made notes of the symbols painted on Jeff Nichols' condo walls. He'd take the photos, too, when he spoke with his clan members the next day. Every little bit helped.

What difference did it make if Kate Campbell was pretty? Her appearance didn't have any bearing on the case. Sure, if he'd met her at a bar or a club, he probably would have tried to talk to her, buy her a drink... if she'd let him. On the surface, she seemed approachable enough, with her wide, friendly mouth and beautiful girl-next-door looks, but he'd also sensed a certain steeliness about her, as if she'd show her backbone when you least expected it. Good. Because she was probably going to need that strength during the days and weeks ahead. Homicide investigations were never fun, even if you did happen to be cleared of any suspicion early on in the proceedings.

Anyway, she was part of the investigation, and nothing else. He'd let himself admire her, because he wasn't one to ignore a woman's looks, but that would be the end of it. Anything else would be downright unprofessional, if not dangerous.

As he scratched out his notes, he made a few mental ones as well, the sort of thing he really didn't want to commit to writing, in case anyone else might want to see his research. First thing, he'd have to talk to Luz Trujillo, see if she'd gotten any sense of an outside witch or warlock infringing on her territory. Jack wasn't entirely sanguine about the outcome of that conversation, because he knew that Luz, while a strong witch, wasn't quite as powerful as her mother Maya, the former *prima* of the de la Paz clan. In her prime, Maya could sense an interloper from a hundred miles away. He had to start somewhere, though.

After that, he'd seek out Consuelo de la Paz, a distant cousin, a woman who'd spent her long life exploring the darker corners of the witching world. As far as he knew, Consuelo had never practiced those dark arts herself, but she had done extensive research. She should know what all these symbols meant, and might have some insight as to who had drawn them, and why. That mission would take up a chunk of his day, since Consuelo lived down in Tucson and rarely ventured into the Phoenix area—as far as Jack knew, she didn't even drive—but she was the best resource he had.

He had to hope she'd have something to offer. Because if Consuelo couldn't help him, he'd be back to square one, just fumbling in the dark. That a warlock had committed the crime, Jack was one-hundred-percent positive. That was why he had to be the one to catch the perpetrator; the non-magical cops who staffed his department wouldn't have a chance when going up against someone like that. No, this was for the witching community to handle, and quietly. Maybe Luz could convince Angela and Connor Wilcox to do the same thing they'd done to Matías Escobar, using their combined powers to completely destroy any trace of magical ability he possessed. That way the perpetrator of this particular crime, whoever he turned out to be, could be safely locked up in a civilian prison. Everyone wins.

Except, of course, Jeff Nichols. Jack had already performed the unwelcome duty of calling his mother to inform her of what had happened. Just the barest details, of course, along with the usual condolences such occasions demanded. She had burst into noisy sobs, claiming it was impossible, that he had to be mistaken, that the dead man had to be someone else. Jack let her weep for a few minutes, then did his best to extricate himself from the call, telling her he'd be back in touch when the medical examiner was ready to release the body.

That remark had set off another round of sobbing, but at last he was able to hang up. Next-of-kin notification was one of the worst parts of the job, but a task he had to handle, since he was lead investigator on the case.

Jack glanced up at the clock that hung on the wall above the file cabinet. A quarter past twelve. He really needed to get home. Technically, his shift didn't start until noon the next day, but schedules didn't mean a whole hell of a lot when you were working on an active investigation such as this one. He knew he'd be on the phone with Luz before ten, and then, with any luck, on his way down to Tucson soon afterward. However, he wouldn't tell Larry he was actually going to Tucson, only that he would be out and about, following some leads. Because of his track record, Jack's boss tended to give him more leeway than was usual, and thank God, since otherwise engaging in this particular extracurricular activity would be difficult to explain.

And what the day would bring after that, he had no idea.

Kate rolled over and stared at the clock next to her bedside. 4:44 a.m. Ugh. In the bed beside her, Sam breathed deeply, not loudly enough to really be classified as snoring, but enough that Kate knew her friend was down for the count, as long as she didn't do anything to disturb her.

You need to sleep, she told herself, but she knew that wouldn't do much good. Usually, she didn't have any problem sleeping, was so tired at the end of the day that she could easily sleep eight hours through without waking up once or even having any dreams that she could remember. Now, though, it felt as if she'd gotten up almost every hour on the hour, trying to find a position that felt comfortable, but not moving around so much that she'd wake up Sam. Kate had her personal tragedies to deal with, but Sam still had to get up and put in pretty much a twelve-hour day, starting with the classes she taught from eight until noon, and then working the second shift at the lab in North Scottsdale. She couldn't afford to lose sleep just because her friend was suffering a bout of trauma-induced insomnia.

Problem was, every time Kate closed her eyes, she kept seeing that blood-spattered condo, Jeff's disfigured body lying on the bloodstained carpet. Maybe with time the details would begin to fade, but right now she could still see everything—the way a plate with a half-eaten sandwich sat on the coffee table, how he'd been in his sock feet because he'd probably kicked off his shoes the minute he got home from work.

Think about something else. Anything.

Her mother had been horrified when Kate called,

but she soon lapsed into questions, wanting to know where Kate was, why she had gone to her apartment instead of calling her parents to come get her and take her home. Kate didn't want to point out that the house her parents now occupied wasn't "home," was someplace they'd purchased after she'd started college and wasn't any true refuge for her. Instead, she said she'd called Sam because she lived closer, and that way she could stay over tonight. And when her father got on the phone, she'd had to repeat the whole story. He didn't sound thrilled, but he also didn't press her the way her mother had. Being insistent just wasn't Liam Campbell's way.

"Maybe tomorrow," Kate promised her parents, and hung up afterward.

Colin had been easier to manage, just because he was all the way up in Jerome, and Jenny was now eight months pregnant and not in any shape to go tearing down to Scottsdale in the middle of the night. While her brother made the offer to come stay at Kate's, he'd backed off soon enough when she told him she already had Sam watching out for her, and that she'd be fine. And she had to appreciate that he didn't ask a lot of questions, even though the reporter side of his mind was probably screaming to get all the details.

Well, she supposed he could get some of that information from the evening news. They got the Phoenix stations up in Jerome, didn't they? She was kind of hazy on that particular detail, simply because the times she'd gone to visit Colin, he and Jenny had kept her busy enough that she didn't need to waste time watching TV.

However, Kate herself hadn't seen any of the evening news, because Sam had made sure they stayed on Netflix and didn't flip over to any of the local channels. Just as well. Kate really didn't want to know how the local news might spin such a lurid crime, even though she got the feeling Detective Sandoval wouldn't give out anything more than the barest details. He had the sort of self-assured air that made her think he probably ate local reporters for breakfast. Too bad, in a way, since with his looks he would be a natural in front of the cameras.

Whoa. Kate had to stop herself there, because what in the hell was she doing, thinking about Jack Sandoval's looks? Talk about inappropriate. What he looked like didn't matter. What mattered was that he would be tracking down the madman who'd killed Jeff.

Too distracted, too tired and scared and worried. That was why her brain kept going off at these weird tangents. She thought of how Officer Manning had told her not to open the door for anyone who wasn't a cop—or, presumably, one of her immediate family—but why? Just because they weren't sure whether Jeff's murder was an isolated incident, that the killer might have targeted her as well, for whatever reason?

A chill went over her, even as she tried to tell herself that line of reasoning didn't make any sense at all. As far as she knew, Kate didn't have any enemies… well, unless you counted her mother-in-law, who'd clearly taken Kate's betrayal of her precious only son to heart, and then some. Even so, while no doubt Nancy Nichols would have been all too thrilled to hear that her erstwhile daughter-in-law had contracted some kind of hideous venereal disease after going back out on the dating market, she really wasn't capable of murder. Trash talk, sure. But words couldn't draw blood.

If she'd been by herself, Kate might have slipped out of bed and gone to the kitchen, gotten herself a glass of water and some ibuprofen for the dull ache she could feel lurking behind her temples. For some reason, the analgesic worked better to help her sleep than anything else. But she didn't want to wake up Samantha, and she didn't know how light a sleeper her friend really was. No, she'd just have to stay here and tough things out. Eventually, she should be able to fall asleep.

The building creaked, and she had to keep herself from startling. Her apartment did that all the time; it wasn't like some crazed axe murderer was trying to creep up the sheer stucco walls outside. Luckily, the day had been mild enough that she could keep all the windows closed and locked. Was it enough, though? She couldn't afford an alarm system, even if the management company would have allowed her to install one.

It all seemed to hit her then—that Jeff was gone, and in one of the most gruesome ways possible. That some kind of psychotic killer was roaming free on the streets of Scottsdale, and that she didn't know if she'd ever be safe again.

Sobs rose in her throat, but she reached up and clamped her hand over her mouth, hoping to muffle the sound that way. She didn't want to wake up Sam. Yes, her friend had come here to offer support and comfort, but right then, Kate needed to know that she could go it alone if she had to. After all, Sam wouldn't always be here for her.

Tears leaked down from the corners of her eyes, wetting the hair at her temples, but she made no sound. She wouldn't. She knew she had to be brave.

No matter what happened.

Jack didn't give Luz a lot of details over the phone, only told her that he needed to talk to her as soon as possible. Sounding somewhat mystified, she said that she had a lunch date downtown with her husband David, but she could see him late that morning.

He'd been to the house before, of course, the gracious hacienda-style home that had belonged to the former *prima* and had come to Luz when she assumed the title and responsibility of guiding their clan. Even though Luz and David had now lived here for several years, it still felt somewhat jarring to Jack to know that Maya wouldn't be there to greet him when he arrived. She had been such a fixture in his life—and the lives of all their clan members—for longer than he could remember, that sometimes he still forgot that she was now gone from this world, her vital life snuffed out by that evil little bastard, Matías Escobar.

Luz herself looked very cool and gracious, wearing a turquoise-blue linen dress and sling-back sandals. Only Luz, he thought, could wear linen and not turn into a rumpled mess.

"This shouldn't take long," he said as she welcomed him inside. Today promised to be warmer than the day before, and ceiling fans already whirled quietly overhead.

"It's no problem," she replied. "I don't need to leave for another forty-five minutes or so."

She led him into the living room, where a blue-rimmed pitcher of Mexican glass and a pair of matching tumblers sat on the coffee table. As Jack settled himself on the couch, she poured him some iced tea and sent him a quizzical glance.

No point in beating around the bush, he supposed. "I got called in on a homicide last night. Nasty one, too."

No reply except a slight lift of her eyebrows, as if

to indicate that she knew it was his job to work homicide cases, so why was this one any different?

He reached for one of the tumblers of iced tea and took a sip, then set the glass back down. "I'm positive the killer is a warlock."

Shock flashed in her dark eyes. "How do you know that?"

"Because these are what he left behind." Jack picked up the manila envelope containing copies of the crime-scene photos and extracted several of the 8x10s. He handed them to her.

Her gaze moved to the photos she held. She didn't respond immediately, although he saw the muscles in her slender throat work as she swallowed, as if trying to choke back a gag reflex. After a long moment, she said, "Is that…?"

"Yes," he replied grimly. "The killer used the victim's blood to paint those sigils on the wall."

"*Madre de díos.*" Luz suddenly looked very pale, her expertly applied blush standing out against her normally warm-toned skin. She drew in a breath, then said, "I am not trying to dispute you, Jack, but isn't it possible that a civilian could have drawn these symbols? These things have been recorded, after all, and exist in some obscure texts, even though they are quite difficult to find."

The thought had occurred to him—it would have made life so much easier if this were simply your garden-variety whacko—but he'd had to put it aside.

"I don't think so. For one thing, there was absolutely no sign of forced entry. A warlock wouldn't need to force his way in. And also, although I don't yet know how his identity relates to the bigger picture, the victim is loosely connected to the McAllisters. His estranged wife's brother is married to Jenny McAllister."

That revelation made her draw in a breath. "I see," she said slowly. "Yes, that does put a slightly different complexion on things. I doubt such a connection is mere coincidence."

Jack doubted it as well, as much as he would have liked to chalk it up to the capriciousness of the universe. "Which is why I have to ask—have you sensed any witches or warlocks in the area who aren't members of our clan? Because I really can't believe that a de la Paz did this, and I doubt it was a McAllister or a Wilcox, either."

"No," she said immediately, the frown returning to her face. "Things have been very calm lately. Robert and Danica Rowe visited Caitlin and Alex in Tucson last week, but they were expected, and were the only outsiders who passed through our territory."

While Jack had been expecting to hear something along those lines, he couldn't quite prevent the sinking sensation that passed over him at her reply. If a powerful outsider had come onto de la Paz lands, Luz should have been able to sense the interloper, and would have contacted him immediately, since he was the clan's best practitioner of defensive magic.

Which meant…what? That the murderer really was one of the de la Pazes? Or that the culprit was a stranger and had somehow managed to mask his presence, thereby making himself invisible to the clan's leader?

Matías Escobar had done something similar when he came to Arizona several years earlier, but he was no longer a threat. Still, he had come from Santiago territory. Perhaps he had learned his evil tricks from someone who remained back in California, but who had now decided to come to Arizona and stir up trouble, for whatever reason.

"You are worried," Luz said. Her voice was calm, but a certain tightness around the edges belied her outwardly tranquil expression. "You think it might be the Santiagos again?"

Jack didn't know why he should be surprised at Luz's perceptiveness. True, she wasn't as powerful a witch as her mother had been, but that didn't mean she didn't see clearly. "I don't know. It's where my mind wants to go first, for obvious reasons. Do you know anything about what's been going on with them?"

"Very little," the *prima* replied. "Simón Santiago was not happy with the way we handled Matías Escobar and his cousins. He thought we should have sent all three men back to California to be dealt with

there, and said that Angela and Connor Wilcox over-
stepped their bounds."

"They had every right, considering Escobar's
crimes were perpetrated against members of their
clans."

"Precisely. I do not think either Angela or Connor
stays awake at night, worrying that they might have
done the wrong thing in that instance. But Simón is a
proud man, and no doubt already finds his situation
rather precarious."

That was one way of putting it. Technically, the
Santiago clan was ruled by a *prima,* just as all witch
families except the Wilcoxes were. But Simón's wife
had suffered a terrible accident years earlier, and had
been confined to a wheelchair ever since, and so
Simón had taken over the day-to-day running of the
clan. What if his grip had begun to slip, though?
What was the line of succession? Jack asked as much
of Luz, who shook her head slightly, her features still
taut with worry.

"Her name is Marisol Valdez," Luz said. "She is
Beatriz Santiago's niece, the daughter of Beatriz's
younger sister. Because Simón's and Beatriz's daughter
Lucinda was not a strong enough witch to be considered for the position of *prima*—a fact which pains
him greatly, I have no doubt—Marisol was named the
prima-in-waiting. I know very little of her, except that
she is in her middle twenties and is bonded to her
consort, although they have yet to start a family. I

suppose it is something that I have even that much information—much of it was passed to me by Alex's wife Caitlin, who heard it from Lucinda. It seems that things have been very quiet over there lately, which could be good or bad. I simply don't know, since Simón made it very clear after the Escobar incident that he did not want any members of our clan visiting his territory."

Stubborn old bastard. Then again, up until four years ago, the clans here in Arizona had been fairly isolationist as well. The de la Pazes and the McAllisters had better relations than most, but despite the friendship between the two families—and the enmity the McAllisters had held toward the Wilcoxes—Maya had actually allowed Connor Wilcox to attend graduate school here. Clearly, she'd seen something in him that no one else had, a bit of foresight that had more than paid off in the end.

"Well, I'm going to assume it's a Santiago until I'm proved wrong," Jack said. "They have the most motive for wanting to cause havoc over here. For all I know, Matías left some groupies behind in California. Maybe they've just been biding their time until they figured out the best circumstances for them to strike."

"What about innocent until proven guilty?" Luz asked. "I'm not saying your instincts might not be correct, but I hate to suspect the worst when we know so little."

"In this case, we may not be allowed that luxury."

He picked up his glass of iced tea and drank the rest of its contents, then put it down and stood. "Thanks for the tea, Luz, and your advice. I need to get going now."

"Where?"

"To Tucson. I need to talk to Consuelo. I'm hoping she can offer some insights on all this." He gestured toward the photos of the crime scene, still sitting on the coffee table.

Back in the manila envelope they went, as Luz said, "Yes, she's probably your best resource. I hope you find what you're looking for."

"So do I," Jack said grimly. He didn't want to think about Kate Campbell, who'd awakened to a world that would be forever changed. Should he have requested a uniform detail to watch out for her?

Problem was, a couple of civilian cops wouldn't be able to do squat against a warlock or witch. About all he could hope was that she'd decided to go stay with her parents. Safety in numbers. She was much less of a target when surrounded by other people.

He'd check on her when he got back from Tucson, even though that sort of follow-up really wasn't part of his duties. Still, he thought it might help her peace of mind.

As for his own peace of mind...well, a lot of that depended on what Consuelo de la Paz had to tell him.

5

SAM LEFT AT SEVEN-THIRTY, IN A HURRY SO SHE wouldn't be late for the class she taught at Scottsdale Community College. Even as she was walking out the door, though, she said, "You call me if you get the least bit hinky. I mean it. I'll find someone to cover for me, or I'll just cancel. One missed class won't kill anyone."

Kate had only nodded, although she knew she wouldn't do anything to jeopardize her friend's work. The world seemed a lot less scary now that the sun was up, blazing against a hard blue sky. The day promised to be warmer, and she was glad of that. Maybe later she'd sit on the balcony and soak in some sun, and try to tell herself that things would be okay.

Eventually.

In the meantime, she ate some yogurt and a couple of leftover mini quiches, had two big cups of coffee. She also called in to work, saying that she'd woken up with a stomach bug but hoped she'd be back in the next day. Right then she just couldn't bring herself to explain what had really happened, partly because the more she talked about it, the more real Jeff's murder seemed. She just couldn't relive that scene right now. There was a good chance the lie would eventually catch up with her, since word always got out about these sorts of crimes. However, she didn't think her supervisors would give her too much grief over it, considering the circumstances.

And then a long hot shower, as hot as she could stand it. That helped a lot, too, scrubbing away the horrors of the night before. After she was dressed but while her hair was still damp, she took a glass of water with her out to the balcony and sat there in the sun, letting the long strands dry naturally. She'd always preferred that method to blow-drying it, but she only had that luxury on the weekends, when she didn't have to be any place in particular, at any particular time.

This felt good. She sat quietly, trying not to think of anything much at all. It seemed the best way to help her heal from what she'd seen the night before. No doubt there was a team of people at the police station trying to piece together what had happened, but she didn't have to be involved in any of that. They'd do their work, and they'd catch whoever was responsible, and then she'd be free to figure out what the hell she was supposed to do next.

"Kate!"

Her name took her by surprise, because she'd been almost dozing, eyes half-shut against the bright morning sunlight. She started, and looked down to see, of all things, a well-coiffed woman in her early thirties in a bright pink dress standing on the path below the balcony, and just behind the woman, a thickset man a few years older, carrying a TV camera.

What the—?

Kate blinked down at these apparitions. "Excuse me?"

"Kate, can you give us a statement about what happened to your husband last night?"

Estranged husband, she wanted to say, but that sounded petty. Even so, a slow anger began to rise in her, that this reporter had somehow managed to track her down at her apartment, couldn't even be bothered to come knock at her door, but instead had seen an opportunity and pounced.

"No," she said distinctly, and picked up her glass of water. "The police have asked me not to comment on an ongoing investigation." *Take that,* she thought, and went inside and locked the sliding glass door, then turned the vertical blinds so they presented a blank white barrier to the world.

Goddamn it. Yes, she'd known that the bloodhounds would come sniffing around eventually, but she'd also hoped she'd be allowed a bit more peace and quiet to get herself together. As it was, she didn't know exactly what to do. Maybe it was time to call her parents and have them come rescue her, but Kate wasn't all that sanguine about being able to avoid reporters down in Tempe, either. Then again, her father, a no-nonsense engineer, would probably just call the cops on them. That could be amusing.

Knocking at the door. "Ms. Nichols!"

Were they trespassing? She wasn't sure whether the landing to her apartment counted as a public space or not. The reporter probably knew the law better than she did, but Kate figured it couldn't hurt to try.

She went to the door, unlocked the deadbolt, and opened the door a crack. "I'm not going to comment. So I'll ask you to please leave, or I'll call the police and report you for trespassing."

"But Ms. Nichols—"

Kate shut the door and reengaged the deadbolt. For some stupid reason, the thing that irritated her the most was the way the reporter kept referring to her as "Ms. Nichols." All right, it was still legally her name, but she hadn't used it for the last six months and more, and the sound of it was jarring to her ears. And how the hell had they found her? All right, the lease was under her married name, because she couldn't change her driver's license or anything else until the divorce was final, but....

Even though the reporter clearly wasn't ready to

give up, and kept knocking, Kate ignored the commotion on the landing and went to the rear of her apartment, which was, luckily, where the bathroom and bedroom were located. Jaw set, she got out her makeup bag and went to work, putting on mascara and blush and gloss. Eventually, the sound of the reporter banging on the door went away, and she allowed herself to let out a sigh of relief.

A short-lived relief, as she realized that someone else might be along in the near future. She really did need to get out of here. The most appealing prospect was to call Colin and ask if he would come down and get her, but she had a feeling the police might not like it if she picked up and headed someplace that was two hours away. It would have to be her parents' house, down in Tempe but still in the greater Phoenix area. No one could fault her for going to stay with her parents.

She fetched her phone and called her parents' house. Her father would be at work, but her mother should be at home. As she waited for Lynda to pick up, Kate found her thoughts wandering to Detective Sandoval. What was he doing right now? Making progress? She sincerely hoped so. She didn't want any of this to drag out any longer than it absolutely had to.

Tucson. It shimmered in the sun, brighter and harder than Phoenix, probably because there was always less air pollution down here. Jack Sandoval's destination didn't lie in the tall buildings and revitalized shops and restaurants of downtown, though, but out on the periphery, where the suburban sprawl met the original landscape, the sharp, rocky slopes of the foothills with their sentinel saguaros.

Consuelo de la Paz lived at the end of a dirt road, her nearest neighbor probably a quarter-mile away. Jack was glad he'd driven his personal vehicle, a Jeep Wrangler, rather than one of the department's unmarked vehicles. A Taurus might have survived the washboard surface, but he really didn't want to take bets on that.

He got out of the Jeep and approached the house, a squatty, sprawling adobe structure that looked more as if it had grown out of the landscape than had actually been built. Wind chimes sang in the brisk, warm breeze as he followed a gravel path that wound among more species of cactus than he could recognize, many of them now studded with bright blooms in shades of magenta and yellow, scarlet and coral.

The front door was dark wood, hung with a crucifix. The religious symbol didn't bother him, since most of the de la Pazes, in addition to being witches and warlocks, were quite devoutly Catholic. They didn't see anything strange about the combination, didn't find it contradictory in the slightest. Jack himself hadn't set foot in church in years, except to attend weddings and funerals and baptisms, but his family members tended to overlook his lapse, blaming it on working with too many jaded types at the police department. He never bothered to tell any of them that he'd come to his not-quite agnosticism on his own, born mostly of a realization that while God probably did exist, He didn't seem to have much influence on people's day-to-day lives.

A creak of floorboards and a squeak of hinges, and the door opened. Bright black eyes, almost buried in wrinkles and chubby cheeks, glinted up at him. "Come in, Jack."

"Thanks for seeing me, Consuelo."

"Ah, well, I like visitors. Not many venture out here to see me, although my niece Juanita brings me a care package once a week. This way."

She waved him inside with a plump hand, and he followed her inside the house, which smelled of incense and dried herbs. The place was packed with antique furniture, mostly from Mexico, with intricate hand-carving and painted motifs. Every surface likewise covered, with crystals in all shapes and sizes and colors, religious statues, incense burners, vases stuffed with dried flowers, books, and various knick-knacks he couldn't quite identify.

To someone who kept his own apartment nearly as bare as a monk's cell, the clutter was quite appalling. However, he did his best to ignore the chaos as he threaded his way along a narrow open path between the furniture, until Consuelo led him into a small room with built-in bookcases on every side, and more books piled on the table in the middle of the room, a table so large there was barely room to squeeze between it and the bookcases themselves.

At one end were two chairs placed side by side. "Sit," Consuelo said, as she settled her bulk into one of them. It creaked under her weight but appeared to hold. "Let me see what you've brought me."

He handed her the manila envelope with the crime-scene photos. "These were taken last night."

"During the full moon."

"That's significant?"

"Everything is significant. You only need eyes to see." After delivering that pronouncement, she undid the clasp that held the envelope closed and poured the photos out onto the table, into a space she'd cleared immediately in front of the chair where she sat. One by one she picked them up, mouth pursing, deepening the wrinkles that framed her lips. Then she laid them out so she could see all of them at once, although doing so required her to push more books out of the way. At last she said, "Ah."

"'Ah'?" Jack repeated. He knew Consuelo had a reputation for being a bit eccentric, but he'd been hoping for a little more than that. "That's it?"

Her eyes narrowed, and one heavy eyebrow lifted. "Tell me, Jack—how deeply do you want to pursue this? Because what I see here" — she gestured toward the photos arrayed before her — "is something that will take you places you may not wish to go."

"I'll go as far as I have to," he replied, somewhat nettled by the assumption that he wouldn't do everything in his power to bring this killer to justice. "A man is dead, Consuelo. It's my job to find the person who committed this murder and make sure they never do it again."

"Ah, Jack." She settled against the back of her chair, which once again creaked but otherwise held on. "For a warlock, you have such a rational mind. It is all about evidence and facts for you."

"Well, evidence and facts are kind of what you need in a court of law."

She didn't reply immediately, but sat there for a moment in silence, watching him with her shrewd brown eyes. "Perhaps, but that is not what will help you here. This investigation will take you to places you cannot imagine…if you choose to pursue it."

"It's not really a matter of 'choice,'" he protested. "This is my assignment, my case. And thank God for that, because this isn't the sort of crime that a civilian could have adequately investigated. I know that it will have to be handled by the clan, and not by civilian authorities. But don't think I'm going to shy away, even if it takes me down some pretty dark paths."

"Very well." Consuelo contemplated the photos before her, then shuffled them around, as if putting together a jigsaw puzzle. "This is powerful magic, dark magic. We are talking about entities who have no care for human life, except when they can use its energies to feed their hungry spirits."

"What kind of entities?" he asked, not bothering to keep the skepticism from his voice. "Demons?"

Once again she tilted an eyebrow at him. For a moment he got the impression that she was going to scold him for being disrespectful, but then she said, her voice calm enough, "You can call them that, although they are not demons in the sense that most people would think of such things. God created this world, but he did not create *them*. They are other, from the time before."

Despite himself—and despite the warmth of the room, which lacked even a ceiling fan to moderate the temperature—Jack could feel a thin trickle of cold move down his back. He'd been trained in defensive magic, some of which by necessity included dispelling the otherworldly beings commonly referred to as demons, but his training hadn't involved itself with their natures, only the best means of getting rid of them. For some reason, the thought of them as entities outside of time, rather than fallen angels banished to hell, was more unsettling than he wanted to acknowledge.

"What was the purpose of this summoning?" he asked, trying to sound cool and disinterested.

From the knowing glance Consuelo just sent him,

he hadn't sounded too convincing. "To draw power, I think. Someone is doing their best to gather dark energy around them, but as for their final goal?" A lift of her chubby shoulders. The silver crucifix around her neck glinted in the half-hearted sunlight that made it past the brown open-weave curtains hanging at the window. "I can't say for sure. Not without more information. What you see here"—she touched a finger to one of the photographs, then quickly withdrew it, as if she feared she would somehow become tainted by the contact — "these are all spells of summoning, to bring forth those whose true names I will not utter. The lord of chaos, the great changer, the destroyer, the lord of cunning…all of their sigils have been painted here."

"How many?" Jack inquired. His voice was steady, even though the list of epithets unnerved him more than he wanted to admit. It sounded like the murderer—whoever he or she was—had summoned everything except the kitchen sink.

"Twelve in all," she said. "Twelve to mock the natural order of things—the months of the year, the great turning that none of us can ignore."

"Twelve demons is a lot."

"It is," Consuelo agreed. Incongruously, she smiled. "The person who summoned them must have a great deal of confidence, to seek to control so many."

"You mean they're still here?" That was a prospect

he really didn't want to contemplate. Bad enough when his niece Zoe had accidentally summoned a single creature, who then proceeded to wreak havoc all over Scottsdale until his transformation was complete and he morphed into the man she'd been expecting when she first cast the spell. In that case, it was all's well that ends well, although Jack couldn't help feeling a bit sorry for Levi, the erstwhile creature, who was now living in Jerome because it turned out the true match of her spirit wasn't Levi at all, but a McAllister warlock.

Anyway, Levi, even in his previous monstrous form, didn't constitute quite the same threat as twelve demons wreaking havoc across the greater Phoenix metropolitan area.

Again, Consuelo didn't immediately answer him. She closed her eyes, one hand clutched around her crucifix. Jack waited, hoping all this wasn't theatrics on her part. His cousin didn't have any real reason to inflate the seriousness of the situation, but maybe she wanted to feel just a little more important than she was.

When her eyes opened, they fixed on him immediately. "No, they are not here," she said. "I can sense the evil they left behind, like an oil slick on water, but whatever it was that they were summoned for, it appears they have served their purpose. For now, at least."

"What do you mean, 'for now'? The murderer might summon them again?"

"Possibly. Or I should say, probably. The summoner was successful, and so will most likely want to repeat that success by having another need or wish fulfilled by these demons. Once someone gets a taste for power such as that, they generally don't want to give it up."

Of course they wouldn't. "What happens if the summoner isn't successful?"

"The entities summoned would take his life in exchange for being bothered in such a way. Demons— I'll use the term, because it's a convenient shorthand— tend to have quick tempers. I can't say I blame them. After all, how would you feel if you were going about your business and kept getting summoned to a different plane of existence to fulfill some mortal's wishes?"

"Well, I—"

To his surprise, Consuelo chuckled. "It's all right, Jack. I may be teasing you a little. I can't really ascribe human emotions or reactions to demons, because of course they aren't human, are entirely other. But they're also notoriously irritable. Sooner or later, the summoner will run afoul of them."

That would have been reassuring, except that Jack didn't want to depend on "sooner or later." The person behind Jeff Nichols' killing needed to be caught before he had a chance to strike again. A thought occurred to him, and Jack inquired, "You said the full moon was important. Does that mean there won't be another summoning until the next full moon?"

"That would make life easier, wouldn't it?" She shook her head. "Unfortunately, no. Each phase of the moon has its own power. The request does have to be tailored to the spell of summoning, though. The full moon is strongest, of course, but the dark of the moon…." Consuelo trailed off then, her round, dried-apple face grim. "The dark of the moon has a power that is nearly as strong. That, I think, is when you will need to be most on your guard."

"And that's two weeks from now."

"Yes."

Two weeks. He could work with that. Yes, there was the possibility that the killer might decide a waning third-quarter moon was adequate for his needs, but this was strong magic…dark magic. The sort of thing that probably flourished when the moon was hiding its face, and the world was bathed in darkness.

"The man killed was distantly related by marriage to the McAllister clan," Jack went on. "Coincidence, or is there some significance here that I'm missing?"

Consuelo offered him another one of her enigmatic smiles. "There are no coincidences, Jack, only patterns we cannot yet see. I would say that the killer was trying to send a message. If this person is working alone—except for the demonic assistance he has summoned—then even he might think twice about attacking a member of the McAllister clan directly, because they live surrounded by so many of their own kind. Strength in numbers, and especially if their *prima* and *primus* are there with them."

Which was only a fifty-fifty proposition, since Jack knew that Angela and Connor divided their time between Flagstaff and Jerome, depending on the season and whichever particular events might be taking place in a given locale. However, they did tend to stay in Jerome through the end of April, which meant they were probably there now. Even a warlock with a bunch of demons in tow might think twice about going up against the combined power of those two clan leaders.

So maybe Jeff Nichols had simply been an easy target. However, wouldn't Kate Campbell have made just as good a target, especially when her own brother was married to a McAllister witch?

Jack found he really didn't want to think about that. In the eyes of the law, all were supposed to be seen as equal, and yet somehow he couldn't prevent the uncharitable thought from crossing his mind that the world could much more easily spare Jeff Nichols than it could Kate Campbell.

Consuelo watched him, shrewd dark eyes missing very little. Jack had never heard any family stories to indicate that she was psychic, and yet he had the distinct feeling that she could somehow guess at what he was thinking, could tell that his interest in the young widow was something a little more than professional. Crazy, of course. He knew better than to get involved with anyone even remotely connected to a case. Besides, she was a civilian, and nearly eight years younger than he, according to her records.

A civilian, true, he thought then. *But since her brother is married to Jenny McAllister, Kate already knows all about the witch clans. Obviously, she knows how to keep a secret.*

Maybe so, but that didn't mean she wasn't still off-limits.

"The dead man's estranged wife," he said, the words coming out too harsh as he hardened his tone to make it sound as if he didn't care all that much, one way or another. "Is she in danger?"

"I can't say," Consuelo replied. "That is, it would be logical to assume that she must be in some kind of danger, if the killer is using civilian relatives of the McAllisters to strike at the clan. But all of this is conjecture. There might have been an entirely different reason why this victim was selected—he had offended the killer in some way, or owed him money. Without more information, it's very hard to even make an educated guess."

Jack knew that feeling all too well. This early in an investigation, a lot of what he ended up doing was making educated guesses, going with his gut and his intuition. Later, as more evidence began to accumulate, then he could put intuition aside and rely on good old deductive logic. Now, though….

Now he was starting to get a bad feeling. He'd sent Kate home with police escort, and though he knew she had a friend staying with her overnight, there was no guarantee that friend would stick around throughout the day. People had lives, had jobs and school, couldn't just drop everything to play babysitter.

Abruptly, he got up from his chair. "Thanks, Consuelo. You've been very helpful. If I have any other information come up that I need help with, may I contact you?"

"Of course," she said. She pushed herself to her feet, with considerably less agility than he had. Her eyes narrowed. "You are worried for this woman."

"Yes. It's probably nothing, but I feel as if I need to get back to Scottsdale."

"Then follow your feelings." Another smile and a sideways glance. "Even when you don't want to believe what they're telling you."

6

THE RIDE DOWN TO TEMPE WAS QUIET, TENSE. Kate stared out the car window and watched the businesses that lined the freeway pass by—big-box stores, furniture stores, bland office parks that all looked the same. In her opinion, the planners hadn't done that great a job in this part of the Valley of the Sun. They should have planted native vegetation along the edges of the highway, thus providing some visual relief along with some privacy for the businesses that bordered the freeway. They'd done better in other, newer parts of town, but this area was older, not nearly as scenic.

She hadn't told her mother about the reporters. Thank God they'd decamped by the time Lynda Campbell showed up in Scottsdale, and no one else had appeared to take their place. Maybe they'd decided that chasing after the dead man's wife was a non-story.

"It's almost noon," Kate's mother said, out of the blue. "Do you want to stop for lunch somewhere?"

At any other time, Kate wouldn't have passed up the chance for a free meal. Right then, though, she just wanted to get to her parents' house and hole up inside…and hope that no one would be able to track her down there. "No, I'm okay," she replied.

"Kate, you need to eat."

"I had breakfast."

"Hours ago."

"I'm really not that hungry."

Her mother's fingers tapped on the steering wheel. She was a pretty woman who looked younger than her fifty-nine years, hair expertly highlighted, fingernails with a neat French manicure. "It's not like you not to talk about things."

Valid point. While she and her mother were never best-buddy chums the way some of Kate's high school friends had been with their mothers, the two of them usually got along well enough. In fact, instead of being disapproving the way Kate had feared, Lynda had actually been quite supportive of the separation from Jeff, saying she'd worried the two of them had gotten married too young, and that she was sure Kate would find the right man in no time.

Which, translated from Lynda-speak, meant she was glad her daughter had left while she was still young and therefore had plenty of time to find a new husband and start a family with him. Kate couldn't even really argue with her mother over that assumption, because it wasn't as if she wanted to spend her life alone. Kids could wait—she was too focused on her career right now to even start thinking about having a family—but she did hope she could learn from her mistakes and find someone this time who was a far better match for her.

Assuming you don't scare them off the first time you tell them what happened to your former husband, she thought then, and grimaced.

"I can't talk about some of it, because of the investigation," she told her mother. "And there's a lot I just don't know. At this point, I'll be happy to get my car back anytime in the near future."

"Have you heard from the police?"

"Not yet." And it wasn't because she hadn't been checking her phone, thinking that she must have missed a call while in the bathroom, or that somehow those calls simply weren't getting through and were going straight to voicemail. So far, though, nothing. Did it really take that long to sweep a car for fingerprints or fiber evidence, or whatever else they might be doing? Maybe they had a backlog at the police department or something.

"It was on the news again this morning," Lynda said. "Still not a lot of details, although they gave a name, whereas last night they just said 'a Scottsdale man.' I assume that means they must have notified Nancy."

Her mother's tone was too neutral; she didn't have any more use for Nancy Nichols than Kate herself did. At the same time, though, she was probably trying to be sympathetic, trying to put herself in the shoes of a woman who'd lost her only child.

"I guess so," Kate said. "I certainly didn't call her. I suppose Detective Sandoval contacted her."

"He's the lead investigator?"

"Yes. I haven't heard anything from him, though, which I guess must mean that he doesn't have any new information for me. I suppose I should be glad he didn't have me locked up."

Lynda took her eyes off the road briefly to send her daughter a worried glance. "Surely they couldn't think you were a suspect."

"Maybe they did for a few minutes, but then it became pretty clear that I couldn't have been responsible for Jeff's death. The detective didn't even tell me I couldn't leave town, or whatever the standard line is in these situations."

No, Jack Sandoval had been kind to her, if somewhat distracted. She couldn't blame him; he had more important matters to attend to, once he'd determined that she wasn't a suspect. Still, she wished she could have talked to him a bit more. He was…

…*outrageously hot,* an entirely inappropriate part of her brain thought then, and she wanted to shake her head at herself. Yes, the guy was attractive, but come on. She should not be paying any attention to Detective Sandoval's looks. Not right now.

Her mother guided her Subaru Outback off the freeway and through a commercial area with shopping centers and medium-rise offices, and on into the residential neighborhood where their house was located. Her parents had lived here for more than five years, and yet Kate still experienced a weird cognitive dissonance every time she came down this street, as though her mind still expected to see the cul-de-sac down in Tucson where she'd grown up, rather than this newer and—although she didn't want to admit it to herself —nicer suburb of Phoenix.

The garage was empty as they pulled in, since her father was at work. Oh, he'd asked if he should take the day off to be with her, but Kate had told him she'd be fine, that she didn't want to throw off his schedule. Since her mother was semi-retired and had gone part-time after her fifty-fifth birthday, rearranging her day had been a much simpler proposition.

Kate had brought a weekender bag and toiletries case with her, figuring that would be enough to see her through the next little while. She'd packed for two days, even though she planned to get back to work tomorrow. Her department was in the final stages of submitting a traffic plan for a new shopping center, and she didn't want to be away at that crucial time, even though she knew the other people on her team —Tom and Jennifer and Ben—could manage to cover for her if circumstances should prevent her from going into the office.

The guest room at her parents' house was a neat, prim space, with a daybed covered in a quilt in typical Southwest colors, an armoire, and a side table. Who exactly they'd intended to have stay there, she didn't know, because the room could really only house one person. However, it suited her current solo status just fine—in fact, she'd slept in here when she'd visited at Christmas, since by then she and Jeff had already been separated for months.

Kate set down her luggage and her purse on the bed, looked around, and tried not to sigh. This was only temporary, after all. Sooner or later the reporters would find another story to chase down, and the detectives would catch the murderer, and life would go on. For now, though, she had to figure out the best way to keep deflecting her mother's questions. There really wasn't much to say, and Kate was reticent to reveal the more gruesome details of Jeff's death, fearing that doing so would only intensify Lynda's attempt to keep her daughter safely here in Tempe for as long as possible.

Her phone rang, and Kate hurried to take it out of her purse. With any luck, the caller would be someone from the Scottsdale police department, contacting her to let her know she could come get her car. If nothing else, the errand would kill at least an hour, even though she had to reflect on the irony of them calling just as she arrived here in Tempe.

When she looked down at the screen, she saw that the call had come from Jack Sandoval. She didn't know why he'd be handling that piece of routine office business, but she didn't mind too much. Actually, it was silly the way her heartbeat quickened slightly as she touched the screen to accept the call.

"Ms. Campbell, this is Detective Sandoval."

"Hi, detective," she replied. "Can I get my car now?"

A brief pause, and then he said, "Oh, to tell the truth, I don't know if they're finished with it yet. I'm on my way back from Tucson and was hoping I could speak with you."

Tucson? Something connected to the case? Either way, she'd be happy to talk to him. Probably a little too happy, if she was going to be honest with herself. "Of course," she said. "Actually, though, I'm at my parents' house in Tempe. Some reporters came around this morning, pestering me, and so I thought it would be better to get out of my apartment for a while."

"I'm sorry to hear that. However, it is probably better that you're with your parents. I'm about"—a pause while he apparently paused to calculate the distance—"twenty-five minutes out from where you are. Can you give me the address?"

"Fifty-two La Rosa Drive," Kate replied.

"Got it. I'll be there shortly."

"Thanks, detective."

He hung up, leaving Kate to stand there and stare down at the phone in her hand. Her stupid heart wouldn't stop its excited beating, which was ridiculous. All Jack Sandoval wanted to do was discuss the case with her, and she just happened to be conveniently on the way back to his office, so he could stop and talk to her here rather than all the way up in Scottsdale.

All very logical.

Even so, she took her purse with her into the bathroom so she could smooth her hair and make sure her lip gloss didn't need to be reapplied. She told herself the primping was only so the detective wouldn't look at her and see a frazzled mess, but she knew better.

You really need to reexamine your priorities, woman, she scolded herself as she went downstairs, purse dangling from one hand.

Lynda was in the kitchen, putting together a couple of ham and cheese sandwiches. She must have intercepted her daughter's sideways glance at the meal prep, because she said, her tone somewhat defensive, "You don't have to eat it right now. I can wrap it up and put it in the fridge in case you get hungry later."

The battle wasn't worth fighting. Kate said, "Sure, Mom. Um, I just got off the phone with Detective Sandoval. He's on his way back to Scottsdale and wants to stop here and talk to me."

Her mother's eyebrows lifted. "'Back to Scottsdale'?"

"I guess he was down in Tucson. He didn't say why. Anyway, he should be here in about twenty minutes."

"Should I make him a sandwich?"

"Um, no, I don't think that's necessary. This is an official call."

Lynda appeared somewhat deflated by that response. She never seemed to know quite what to do with herself if she wasn't bustling around, being the perfect hostess.

Before her mother could offer to make lemonade, or dream up some other refreshment for the visiting detective, Kate said, "I'll go wait for him in the living room. But go ahead and have your sandwich, Mom. I don't want to keep you from having your own lunch."

"I can wait."

"Really, you don't need to. I'm not hungry yet, and I don't know how long this is going to take." Deciding it was better to leave matters there, Kate offered her mother a smile and then went to take up her post in the living room, where she could sit on the couch and have a clear view of the detective as he came up the front walk. True, he wouldn't be here for another twenty minutes or so, but she could take that time to check her phone, to log in remotely to her work email and see if there was anything critical she'd missed. Yes, she was supposed to be out sick, but it never hurt to stay on top of things.

However, there weren't any dumpster fires waiting for her in her work inbox, and her own email account was suspiciously quiet. Maybe the local news agencies hadn't yet tracked down her email address or phone number, but she assumed it was only a matter of time before they ferreted out that information. She did have a ton of private messages on Facebook, all from friends wanting to know about Jeff, wanting to know what had happened. There was no way in hell she was going to answer all of those—and she had a feeling that Sam would help out when she got off work, quietly disseminating information on her own so the burden wouldn't fall to Kate—but she decided that posting a public status might keep some people off her back for a while.

Yes, it's true about Jeff. I don't know very much right now, any more than the rest of you do, so I don't have a lot to say yet. This is a very difficult time for me, so I'm asking everyone to respect my wishes and give me a chance to process what's happened.

She turned off comments for the post, because the last thing she wanted was to have everyone gossiping and speculating in the very place where she'd asked for a little space, a little privacy.

When she looked up from her phone, it was to see a black Jeep Wrangler with a hard top parking at the curb in front of the house. A moment later, Jack

Sandoval got out and began to head up the walkway that cut through the property's rather improbable front lawn, conspicuously green in a land that should have been desert. He wore a white shirt with the sleeves rolled up and dark khakis, and right then Kate thought he might possibly be the best-looking man she'd ever seen.

Just stop it, she told herself as she set down her phone and got up from the couch. *You're being utterly ridiculous. Okay, I can see why you might want to distract yourself from what happened to Jeff, but crushing on a cop is a damn stupid way to do it.*

She let him ring the doorbell before she answered the door, just because she didn't want him to know that she'd been sitting there, watching him come up the front walk. "Detective Sandoval," she said, praying to God she sounded calm and unruffled, and not at all like someone who'd just been ogling the hell out of him.

"Jack, please," he said with a smile, his white teeth flashing in contrast to his warm-toned skin.

"Come on in…Jack." She moved out of the way so he could enter the living room, which, because this was her mother's house, existed in a state of spotless perfection not often seen outside a model home. "Can I get you something? Water, iced tea?"

"I'm fine, thanks." A pause as he sent a quick glance around the room, accompanied by just the faintest of head tilts, as if he listened to see if anyone else was around.

"My mother's in the kitchen," Kate said, trying to keep her voice pitched low enough that it wouldn't be overheard, but not so low that Jack might think there was something strange about her need to keep things private.

"Ah. I'd rather speak to you about these matters alone, if that's possible."

"We could go out in the backyard—"

Even as he appeared to consider that proposition, Kate's phone rang. She murmured an apology and bent to pick it up, then brightened a little as she saw the incoming call was from the Scottsdale police department.

"Ms. Campbell?"

"Yes, I'm Kate Campbell."

"Your car is ready to be picked up. You can get it from the impound yard."

"'Impound'?" she repeated. "What, I have to pay to get it out of hock?"

"Yes, I'm sorry, that's just policy," the woman on the other end of the line said. "If you get it before six, then you won't have to pay any fees for housing it overnight. The address is 215 85th Place. Have a nice day."

The call ended, and Kate took the phone away from her ear and shook her head, directing her next words to the detective standing a few feet away. "So you took my car, but I have to pay to get it back?"

To Jack's credit, he did look slightly embarrassed. "That's how it works. But I can probably get them to waive the fees. In fact, this is the perfect chance for us to talk in private. How about I drive you up to get your car, and I try to get things straightened out for you?"

That sounded just about perfect to Kate. She could be in the car with him, far away from any chance of her mother trying to eavesdrop. And then she'd have her own vehicle back. She hadn't realized how off-putting it would be to be deprived of her car, but the Jetta had always been a symbol of autonomy for her, and she needed to have it returned.

"That sounds great," she replied. "Let me just tell my mother I'm going, and then we can head out."

"Sure." Another of those smiles. Did he have any idea how devastating they were?

Kate decided it probably wasn't a good idea to dwell on that question for very long. Instead, she hurried into the kitchen, where her mother had finished with her sandwich prep and now sat at the table in the nook, having her own lunch. "Mom, the Scottsdale P.D. just let me know I can pick up my car. Detective Sandoval offered to drive me, since he's headed back there anyway. So I'll be out for a little while."

Her mother frowned slightly. "Are you sure that's

all right with him? You don't want to cause him any extra trouble—"

"He offered. It's fine." Kate gave Lynda a reassuring smile and added, "It shouldn't take that long. I'll be back in an hour and a half at the most."

"You're all right with driving alone? You're sure you don't want me to come along?"

That was the very last thing Kate wanted, but she knew she needed to keep that particular thought to herself. "It's just a short hop to get back here. I doubt the reporters have tracked me down yet. You won't even notice I'm gone." She bent and gave her mother a quick kiss on the cheek, then hurried out of the kitchen before Lynda could offer any further protests.

Jack was waiting by the door, keys dangling from one hand. "All ready?"

"Yep, good to go." She picked up her purse from where she'd set it on the floor. "Lead on."

He let himself out and Kate followed, turning the bottom lock so it would be somewhat secure, even though she didn't have a key for the deadbolt. A warm wind caught in her hair, and she thought for a second how nice it would be if they were just headed out for a simple drive, maybe going for a drink.

Once again she scolded herself for being an inappropriate idiot, even as Jack unlocked the Jeep and opened the passenger-side door so she could climb inside. He went around the front of the vehicle and slid in behind the wheel, then started up the engine and pulled away from the curb.

For a long moment, neither one of them said anything. Kate began to wonder if she should mention picking up her own car, the weather, anything to break the silence, but then Jack Sandoval spoke.

"I didn't have a chance to talk to you about this last night, for obvious reasons, but when you mentioned that your brother lived in Jerome, and when I saw his name, I realized he must be connected to the McAllisters."

Kate froze. She didn't dare look over at Jack, because she knew he'd be able to see the shock that had just registered on her features. Why the hell would a detective with the Scottsdale police department know anything about the McAllister witches?

"It's all right," he went on quickly, obviously noting her unnerved state. "I'm not out to expose them or anything. How could I? I'm part of the de la Paz clan."

A startled breath escaped her lips. "You mean you're—?"

"A warlock, yes."

"But…you're a policeman."

He chuckled. "Yes. The people in my family don't have quite the same bohemian lifestyle as the McAllisters. We have doctors and lawyers and teachers and insurance adjusters…and cops. All of us doing our best to blend in."

A thousand chaotic thoughts whirled in Kate's mind. She wouldn't have to worry about hiding anything that involved her sister-in-law or her family, wouldn't have to worry about something inadvertently slipping out during a moment of stress. And this man, this gorgeous hunk of detective, wasn't some ordinary guy, but a warlock, someone born with powers she still didn't quite understand.

"So…what's your talent?"

His smile faded. "Defensive magic."

"Oh." Did she dare ask what that entailed? It did sound like a good talent for a police officer to have. And it sounded especially good for her to have someone with that particular power close to her. "Is that why you took this case?"

"No," he replied. "I was assigned to it. I didn't realize who you were until I saw the texts from your brother. Then I put two and two together. But this crime—it worries me. You saw what was painted on the walls."

She swallowed. "Yes."

"I recognized a few of the symbols. Not all. That's what I was doing down in Tucson today. I needed to talk to someone who's an expert in these things."

"What things?" Kate asked, even though she wasn't sure she wanted to know the answer. That horrific crime scene had terrified her enough. To discover the purpose behind those arcane symbols? It had to be something dark and terrible, something she didn't want to understand.

"Spells of summoning. Summoning demons."

Right then she was very glad she hadn't eaten anything at her mother's house, because Kate was fairly certain she would have been sick. Since her stomach was empty, all it could do was lurch and make her faintly queasy. "Summoning demons? Seriously?"

Even in profile, she could see the grim set of his jaw. "Oh, yes. Demons are real. Or rather, the entities that we think of as demons are real. They come from outside this world and can wield terrible powers."

"But…why would someone do something like that? And to Jeff, of all people? I mean, he was a district manager at a logistics company. He's not exactly the sort of person who should be the victim of a vicious murderer."

"That's just it," Jack replied. "I'm not sure his was a random murder. There's your connection to the McAllisters. A while back, the *prima* of that clan—"

"Angela," Kate supplied, just so Jack would know that she wasn't completely clueless when it came to the McAllister clan. She knew who Angela and Connor were, knew that their being together had caused a lot of changes in both the *prima's* clan and the Wilcoxes, Connor's family.

"Right. Well, two years ago, some pretty nasty

warlocks from the Southern California clan, the Santiagos, came here to Arizona and stirred up a lot of trouble."

"I know. They murdered Jenny's sister." How awful it felt to say such a thing so matter-of-factly. Yes, of course Kate had never known Roslyn, because she'd died before Colin and Jenny even met, but such tragedies left an indelible mark on all those involved. Jenny seemed happy enough now, especially with the baby on the way, but during the times they'd all been together, Kate couldn't help noticing the sadness in her sister-in-law's eyes, the way she'd sometimes look as if she wanted to cry before she visibly pulled herself together and pretended that nothing was wrong.

"And in consequence, Angela and Connor stripped the powers from the three warlocks involved. It was their right, but the Santiagos weren't happy about the way the matter was handled. So I can't help wondering whether they're attempting somehow to get their revenge on the McAllisters by striking out at civilians who are connected to them, easy targets who can't possibly fight back."

Maybe it was the cold air blowing from the Jeep's vents that made her whole body go chill, but Kate didn't think so. She tried to sound calm, though, as she asked, "Does that mean I'm the next target?"

This time he did glance over at her, worry clear in his face. "I don't know. There's a lot here I don't know yet. But this is why I wanted to talk to you in private.

I can't go mentioning demons and spells of summoning around the other people in my department who're involved in the investigation, or they'll send me off to the rubber room. Sure, they'll have to acknowledge the occult nature of the symbols painted on the walls of Jeff Nichols' condo, because that's the sort of thing you can find on the Internet with a little digging. But they'll pass it off as coming from a murderer who dabbles in Satanism, or is obsessed with the occult. They won't think it's real."

"But it is."

"Unfortunately, yes."

Kate clutched the strap of her purse and told herself she needed to stay calm, that she couldn't freak out. But how could she not freak out, when Jeff was dead, when Jack Sandoval was sitting there and talking about *demons,* of all things. Demons and spells and God knows what else. When she spoke, her voice sounded very small. "What am I supposed to do?"

"Well, for one thing, you need to know that I'll be looking out for you. I'm still trying to figure out who we're up against, but while I may not have faced down demons before, I have apprehended some pretty bad people, including Matías Escobar, Roslyn's murderer. It's also good that you've gone to stay with your parents."

Kate managed a tired smile. "What, is my mother a demon hunter who's been hiding her true identity?"

This time Jack chuckled, even as he shook his head. "No, she's just a regular mortal. But it's good that you're not alone in your apartment, that you're someplace where the murderer doesn't know to find you."

Was that even true, though? She knew that Jeff had her new address lying around his condo, because of course she'd had to give it to him after they'd separated—he'd sent her a few packets of letters and bills until she could get her mailing address updated with her bank and the student loan company, among other things. But did he have her parents' address down in Tempe? He knew where they lived, but she'd taken her address book with her; she was always the one who sent birthday cards and Christmas cards and kept up with the family stuff.

And did any of the normal ways of getting that sort of information even matter when you were talking about witches and warlocks and demons? Couldn't they just look in a crystal ball or something? It was really nerve-wracking when you didn't even know how any of this worked.

"If you say so," she said, her tone openly skeptical.

"I do. And beyond that, I'm going to stay with you as you get your car, and then I'm going to follow you back down to your parents' house. I'll make sure you get inside safely. And I'll draw my own signs of protection on the doorways so nothing can get in."

"Hopefully not with blood," Kate remarked, part

of her glad of the offer, the other part not sure that the help he wanted to give would do anything at all. "My mother might have a few things to say about that."

He didn't smile. "Only those who follow the left-hand path use blood. No, just spring water and rock salt. Your mother won't even know I've done it."

That sounded a lot better. And how could it hurt? Jack seemed confident that his symbols or spells or whatever they were would keep out the bad guys. She had to let herself trust him. She was completely out of her depth here. Anyway, he'd said his talent was defensive spells, so maybe his signs of protection were a lot stronger than those drawn by an ordinary witch or warlock.

An ordinary warlock. There was an oxymoron.

"All right," she said after a long pause. "If you think it will help."

"It should."

Not exactly the most stirring reassurance she'd ever heard, but she'd rather he was truthful than try to tell her it was all going to be okay. She hated that.

They got off the freeway a few exits earlier than they otherwise would have if going straight to the main police department headquarters. This was a more industrial area, no doubt chosen for its cheaper real estate. Jack pulled up to a fenced-in lot and parked in one of the spots next to a shabby-looking cinderblock building. On the side of the building were the words *All-City Towing*.

"Come on," he said. "I'll make sure you don't have to pay any damn fees."

Well, she'd believe it when she saw it. Not that she had any real doubt about Jack Sandoval's authority here, only that dealing with bureaucracy could be a real bitch sometimes.

But there he was, showing his badge to the hard-faced woman behind the counter, working that amazing smile of his. The woman's gaze flickered to Kate for a moment before returning to Jack. "I'll need to see her I.D."

Kate stepped up to the counter and fumbled to get her wallet out of her purse. Then she opened it so the woman could see her driver's license.

"Take it out."

No "please," but Kate wasn't going to quibble right then. She slid the license out of its little plastic-faced compartment and handed it over to the woman, who made something of a show of inspecting it minutely before turning to her computer and entering something on the screen she pulled up.

More typing, and then the printer off to one side of the woman's workstation started to spit out a series of pages. "Sign here," she said, pointing toward the line at the bottom of the first page of paperwork. "And initial here, here, and here."

Under other circumstances, Kate might have scrutinized what she was signing a bit more minutely. Right then, though, she just wanted to get her car back and get the hell out of there. Besides, if there had been anything questionable in what she was signing, she was sure Jack would have said something about it.

The woman picked up the signed documents, scanned them briefly, and nodded. "All right. Detective Sandoval, you go around back and let Arturo know the fee's been waived. He'll bring the car up to the front parking lot."

"Thanks, Mavis," Jack said. "I really appreciate you helping me out with this."

The woman didn't exactly smile, but one corner of her mouth lifted. "Just don't try to sweet-talk your way out of too many more of these impound fees, or I'll have to explain them to my supervisor."

"Oh, you know I'd never take advantage of you like that." Still wearing a smile of his own, Jack turned to Kate. "Just wait out front. I'll be around in a minute."

She nodded, offered a murmured thank-you to Mavis, and headed back out to the parking lot. Even though she knew everything had been handled, she couldn't help but experience a small stab of worry that something might still go wrong, that Arturo— whoever he was—wouldn't relinquish her Jetta without a receipt or something, despite Jack's assurances.

But no, there was her little white car pulling up,

and a heavyset Hispanic man squeezing himself out from behind the wheel. The car looked dusty, probably from sitting out all night when it was usually sheltered by a carport, but otherwise none the worse for wear.

"All yours," said the man, presumably Arturo.

"Thanks," she responded, and got into the driver's seat. She had to make a few minute adjustments to get the seat and her mirrors back to where they were supposed to be, but she didn't notice any other obvious signs of the inspection her car must have endured. It felt so good to sit in it again. Until she had it back in her possession, she hadn't realized how important the car was to her, how it provided her with a sense of autonomy, of freedom…even if that sense might not be completely accurate.

"Okay," Jack said, leaning down next to the driver-side window. "I'll follow you back to your parents' house, and then I'll handle…that other thing we discussed."

"Got it." She turned the key in the ignition, and sat there idling for a few seconds as the air conditioning spooled up and she watched Jack go back to his Jeep and get in. Once she saw his backup lights come on, she figured it was safe to ease her car out onto the street and head back to the freeway.

As she came out of the driveway and gave the car a little more gas, though, it suddenly leapt forward, the accelerator plummeting to the floor even though she'd barely applied any pressure. Startled, she lifted her foot, thinking that would bring the car to a halt, but instead the pedal remained glued to the floor mat, as if an invisible hand was holding it there.

Shit. *Shit.*

She jammed her foot on the brake, but that didn't do a damn thing. In fact, her speed only increased. Fifty-five…sixty-five….

Her phone started to ring from within her purse, but she ignored it, because she didn't dare take her eyes off the road. And oh, God, there was a big FedEx van looming ahead where it was stopped at the light, and there wasn't a thing she could do to stop the Jetta's headlong flight. She was going to crash into that thing, possibly hurt the person driving it, someone with the hideous misfortune to be in exactly the wrong place at the wrong time.

No time to think. She had to react, and there was only one thing she could do. Her body already clenching against the impact, Kate wrenched on the steering wheel so her car went up and over the curb, plowed across an empty parking lot, and careened into the vacant building there.

The airbag exploded in her face, and the world went dark.

7

JACK WATCHED THE WHOLE THING UNFOLD LIKE A slow-motion scene out of a horror movie—the car accelerating far past a speed that could be considered safe anywhere except the freeway, the way it turned sharply at the last minute and went plummeting across a parking lot and into the side of a defunct HVAC supply store. Dust from disintegrating concrete floated on the warm air.

He pulled into the empty lot and threw the Jeep into park, then hurried over to the sad, crumpled heap of metal that used to be a Volkswagen Jetta. Cursing under his breath, he grasped the door handle and wrenched it open. Inside, Kate was slumped over the steering wheel, blood pouring down her face from a gash in her forehead, the exploded airbag like a limp jellyfish beneath her body.

God. With frantic fingers, he undid her seatbelt

and pulled her out, reaching with one hand to snag the strap of her purse and retrieve it as well. Maybe he should have waited for the paramedics, but he knew this crash hadn't occurred because of any natural malfunction. If he'd had the opportunity to look, he had no doubt that he would have found a sigil of destruction somewhere in the vehicle, maybe painted inside one of the wheel wells. Now, though, he smelled gasoline, and knew he had to get Kate away as quickly as possible.

He carried her over to the Jeep and maneuvered her sagging form into the passenger seat, then fastened the seatbelt so it would hold her firmly in place. Once she was secured, he dropped her purse on the floor next to her feet. As he backed away from the totaled Volkswagen, he reached over with his right hand and placed two fingers against her throat.

A pulse. Thready, and weak, but it was there.

Jack knew what he had to do next.

He grabbed the portable emergency flasher from where it sat on the dashboard, and opened the window so he could mount the light to the roof of the Jeep. Then he floored it, tearing away from the scene of the crash.

Not to the hospital, though. Too many questions. Also, after what had just happened, he knew he didn't dare leave Kate alone. The hospital wouldn't be safe. All it would take was one orderly or nurse's aide to be compromised, and then the young woman's life would be at risk.

No, he would take her back to his apartment. Even as he reached that decision, he pulled the phone from his pocket and said, "Call Alba."

Thank God, she answered almost at once. "What is it, Jack?"

"I've got someone with a head and possibly neck or back injury. Car accident. I'm taking her to my place because the hospital isn't safe. How soon can you be over?"

"I'm leaving now," she replied, sounding completely unperturbed by the information he'd just provided. "I'll be there in fifteen minutes, twenty at the most."

"Thanks, Alba." He ended the call, cursing that the impound yard was basically on the opposite side of Scottsdale from his own apartment, which was located north and west of the downtown area. Well, it couldn't be helped. At least the flashing light on the roof of the Jeep helped to clear the way, allowed him to maneuver in and around traffic, to barely slow down for traffic signals, just in case some numbnuts ignored the blaring emergency beacon that currently sat on his roof.

Less than ten minutes later, though, he was pulling into the parking lot at his complex. At that point, he plucked the light off his roof and shut it down, because the last thing he wanted was to attract any more attention than was strictly necessary. Bad enough that he would have to carry a comatose woman up the steps to his place, although he knew all his immediate neighbors should be at work. With any luck, no one would be around to see what he was doing. Unfortunately, none of his defensive skills included making someone invisible, so he'd have to hope there wouldn't be any witnesses to his next few movements.

He shut off the engine and hurried around to the passenger door. When he pulled Kate out, he was relieved to see that the flow of blood from the cut on her forehead had slowed. However, the pale blue cotton top she wore was basically ruined.

Telling himself they had far more important things to worry about, Jack lifted her from the seat and grabbed her purse, then shut the door behind her. The briefest of pauses to engage the security system, and then he was half-jogging, half-walking the distance from the carport to the path that led to his building.

As he'd hoped, the grounds seemed to be deserted. A couple of black-feathered grackles jeered at him from the rooftop of his apartment, but they provided the only real sign of life. Then he all but ran up the steps, although he did his best not to jostle the woman he held. He was no healer; he didn't know the extent of Kate's injuries. But he'd seen Alba perform near-miracles of healing, especially when a wound was as fresh as Kate's were, and so he had to hope he hadn't caused any additional damage by bringing her here, even if he didn't have much choice.

Cool air wafted over him when he opened the door to his apartment; he always left the A/C on low on days that promised to be warm, as this one was. A few steps to cross over to the couch, and then he laid Kate down on the leather surface. A soft moan escaped her lips, the first real sign of life he'd seen from her, except her pulse, but it told him she was aware enough to note the change in her surroundings, even if she didn't have the strength to open her eyes.

Although he knew she wasn't in any shape to drink anything right away, he went ahead and got a glass of water from the kitchen, then brought it back and set it down on the coffee table. At least it would be there for her once Alba had performed her healing spells. Jack recalled how thirsty he'd been when Alba had healed him of a gunshot wound, one he didn't want to report to his superiors, since he knew he'd be sidelined for days. Anyway, it was something to do while he waited for the healer to arrive.

Which she did only a few minutes later. A soft knock at the door, and he let her in at once. Alba was a trim woman in her late fifties, with a no-nonsense air about her. She nodded at Jack but then immediately crossed the room and knelt down on the carpeted floor next to the couch. "A car accident, you said?"

"Yes," he replied, trying not to let the extreme pallor of Kate's complexion worry him, or the slack way one arm hung off the edge of the sofa. "Her car was hexed. She had to be going about fifty when she plowed into a vacant building. The airbag deployed, but…."

Alba nodded, then passed her hands over Kate's body, letting her gift tell her the locations of all the injuries the other woman had suffered, as well as their severity. Her dark brows drew together, but Jack knew that wasn't necessarily an indication of the harm Kate had suffered, since Alba often frowned in concentration as she worked. "A concussion," she said quietly, "three broken ribs, and a perforated spleen. No neck or back injuries, luckily. It's good she's unconscious, though…this is going to hurt a good deal."

"Do what you have to."

"Of course I will." Alba's eyes shut, and she pulled in a deep breath. Then she laid her hands on Kate's midsection, resting them lightly against the areas that had suffered the worst injuries. She remained that way for some time, as though she had to expend a lot of energy to repair the damaged ribs, and the wounded organ beneath them. At last, though, she lifted her hands and placed them against Kate's forehead, ignoring the dried blood there. After remaining that way for a moment, she nodded, then opened her eyes and got to her feet. "She is healed. But because her body suffered so much trauma, she will probably sleep for at least another hour. When she awakes, make sure she drinks plenty of water. Nothing heavy to eat. Soup would be best for this evening. Tomorrow she can probably manage solid foods again."

"Thank you, Alba." Jack didn't bother to hide the relief in his voice. Seeing Kate like that, so still and lifeless when she was normally such a vibrant young woman, had struck him harder than he wanted to acknowledge. Deep within him burned an anger that wouldn't go away anytime soon. Whoever had done this would pay. He'd make sure of it.

"You said her car was hexed? Who would do such a thing?"

"I don't know yet," he replied. "But I intend to find out. For now, though, we need to get the clean-up crew to take care of the evidence. I brought Kate here because I couldn't be sure that she'd be safe in the hospital, but as soon as someone I.D.'s her vehicle, I'm going to be left with way too many questions to answer."

"I'll make the calls," Alba said. "Or rather, I'll call Luz and have her handle it."

"That's not necessary—"

"Perhaps, but you need to keep watch over your patient. We'll make sure it's all taken care of." A pause, and then Alba slanted a speculative glance up at him through her lashes. "How long do you plan to keep her here?"

"As long as it takes," Jack replied. "Until I can

track down the person responsible. She was staying with her parents, but a couple of civilians are no match for whoever is behind all this. Right now, I'm her first and only line of defense."

"Understood. I'm sure Luz would never fault you for stepping in. Take care."

Alba picked up her purse from where she'd set it down next to the coffee table, then went ahead and let herself out. As soon as the door closed behind her, Jack turned the deadbolt. An automatic gesture, no more. That deadbolt couldn't protect Kate from whatever was stalking her. No, the defenses here were not as clearly obvious—the sigils he'd traced around the front door, the slider to the balcony, around every window and even the flue of the small fireplace—but those would do far more to keep her safe than any lock.

And if something got past any of those deterrents, well, he would be here. Because Jack knew he sure as hell wasn't letting Kate Campbell out of his sight for the foreseeable future.

Slowly, Kate opened her eyes. Her head ached, and something about her midsection didn't feel quite right, as though someone had punched her repeatedly in the stomach. The room that came into focus around her didn't look at all familiar—white walls…

black and white photos in black frames…a stainless steel torchiere lamp in one corner. Everything very clean and sleek and modern, and quite different from the pleasant jumble of colors and styles in her own apartment.

"Where…?" she began. "What?"

Jack Sandoval's face, leaning down over here. "How are you feeling?"

"Like dog shit," she replied honestly, and he chuckled.

"Well, I can understand that." She realized then that he was sitting on a metal folding chair that he'd placed next to the couch. "Do you remember anything of what happened?"

"I…." The words trailed off as she frowned, trying to see if she could recall what had taken place in the time between when she'd left the impound yard and when she'd ended up here, apparently on Jack Sandoval's couch. Bits and pieces began to trickle in —the accelerator pressed to the floor, no matter what she did. Yanking on the wheel so she wouldn't hit that FedEx van. An empty building with plate glass windows looming in front of her. "I crashed, didn't I?"

"Yes, but it wasn't your fault." For the first time she noticed how taut his mouth was, the way the laugh lines around his eyes now seemed to be creases of worry. "Someone put a hex on your car."

"A what?" Maybe if her brain didn't feel so foggy,

she'd have an easier time understanding what he was trying to say to her.

"A hex. A curse. A particularly nasty spell aimed just at you. I told the clean-up crew to look for it, and they did find a sigil drawn underneath the front bumper of your car."

Her head was spinning. Did she have a concussion? She must, if she'd crashed full-force into that empty building. But if that was really what had happened, shouldn't she be in far worse shape than she was right now? Why was she here, rather than at the hospital?

So many questions crowded her mind, she wasn't sure which one to ask first. Something Jack had said jumped out at her, though. "'Clean-up crew'?"

His mouth lost that tense look, and he even smiled slightly. "People with my clan. They went out and got rid of your car, made sure any evidence of the crash was removed. It would have raised far too many questions otherwise."

"My car is gone?"

Something about his expression shifted. Now he seemed to look down at her almost with pity. "Yes. I'm sorry. It was totaled. But the important thing is that you're all right. I had Alba, my clan's healer, come here and take care of your injuries. You're going to be fine. You just need to take it easy for a while."

Her car, gone. And somehow the de la Paz witches had someone who could patch you up after a car accident, good as new. It was all crazy. She blurted, "But if your people took my car away, how am I supposed to file a claim with the insurance company?"

"Don't worry about that," he told her. "One way or another, we'll take care of it."

Kate really didn't see how they'd manage such a thing. Then she remembered how Colin once mentioned that all the witch clans had a decent amount of wealth. Some more than others, but no one who was a witch or a warlock ever seemed to want for anything. No one had to worry about being able to afford a house, or to purchase a new car when they needed one. So were the de la Pazes going to buy her a new car when all this was over?

Then she told herself the car was the least of her worries right then. Someone had tried to kill her. Her fear that she might be the killer's next victim had apparently been an accurate one. What she should be focusing on now was her great good luck that she was alive at all—thanks to Jack Sandoval, who'd clearly saved her from the wreck and brought her to this place so she could be healed.

"I'm here because it wouldn't be safe in the hospital, aren't I?"

"Yes," he said. "It seemed the best solution. Until I can figure out who killed Jeff, who tried to kill you, I don't dare let you out of my sight. I know it's going to be inconvenient for you, and I apologize. But inconvenienced is better than dead."

All Kate could do was nod and murmur, "It's not a problem." There was no way in the world she would admit to being just the teeniest bit excited that apparently she was going to be trapped in Jack Sandoval's apartment with him. At least, she assumed this must be his apartment. Then she asked, "What am I supposed to tell my parents?"

"You don't need to tell them anything. I've already spoken with them."

"You have?" Kate stared at him, feeling slightly aghast, and then put her hand to her forehead. The skin there felt tender beneath her fingertips, although she couldn't detect any sign of a cut or bruise or bump. The de la Paz healer must be very good at what she did. "How long was I out?"

"A couple of hours. It was perfectly normal—your body was just doing its best to catch up with the healing spells Alba cast. During that time, though, the situation with your car was handled, and I called your parents to let them know an attempt had been made on your life, and that you were just fine but were being kept safe in an undisclosed location."

"My mother would never go for that," Kate protested. "She'd demand to know where I was."

That remark made Jack smile, albeit ruefully. He reached up with one hand to brush back his heavy dark hair, while Kate did her best not to stare and think about what it would feel like to run her own fingers through that hair. "Well, she was pretty adamant at first, but I eventually wore her down and convinced her it was safer for everyone involved that no one know anything about your current whereabouts. One of the guys from the clean-up crew went by—posing as my partner—and collected your travel bags, so you have a change of clothes and your other personal items. Anything else you need, just let me know, and I'll go get it for you."

"So I'm stuck in here," she said.

To her surprise, he lifted an eyebrow at her and grinned. "What, you're not thrilled to be trapped in an apartment with me?"

"Not exactly," Kate replied, although she knew those words were at least partially a lie. No way was she going to tell the truth to Jack Sandoval, though, that being in this close proximity to him for an extended period of time made her pulse speed up far more than it should. "What about work?"

"I'll contact them tomorrow morning. All official." He stopped there and seemed to take a closer look at her, as if seeing all too clearly the worry in her expression. "It'll be all right. You can't lose your job over this. I know people in the planning department. I'll handle it."

He sounded so certain that she didn't dare argue with him. And really, when it came right down to it, her life was far more important than any job, even if the job in question was something she'd worked toward for years. She had to trust Jack that he'd smooth everything out.

"Okay," she said. "I understand why you're doing this. But what are you going to do? I mean, how are you going to track down this killer if you're stuck here babysitting me?"

"I'll figure it out," he replied. "I can have people from my clan stay here and watch you if necessary."

Being handed from witch to witch like a problem child that no one wanted to claim didn't sound like a lot of fun. Besides…. "I thought you said you were the person in your clan who was best at defensive magic, though. What can these others do to protect me?"

"They can do something. All witches know basic protection spells, and those spells will be stronger during the daylight hours. I won't leave you alone at night."

Kate wanted to protest that her car had been hexed during the daytime…but had it really? After all, it had been sitting in the impound lot overnight. The killer probably would have had an easy enough time breaking into the lot and casting his nefarious spells without anyone around to see what he was doing. True, the impound yard must have had video surveillance, but she guessed that a sufficiently moti-vated warlock would be able to get around that minor bit of technology. A creepy-crawly sensation moved down her spine as she wondered just what else this warlock was capable of.

"All right. But what about your own work? Aren't they going to wonder what happened to me?"

Jack frowned briefly, but then he shrugged. "I'm the lead investigator on the case. I've already cleared you. We don't have any reason to call you back—or rather, I'll make sure there isn't a reason. And I'll annotate your file to show that you're currently staying with your parents, so if anyone thinks it strange that you're not at your apartment, there's a perfect explanation why."

It did sound as if he'd thought of pretty much everything. Except…. "What about my friend Samantha? With most of my other friends, we just get together once a month as our schedules allow, so if I go MIA for a little bit, no one's going to notice. But I can guarantee you that Sam will definitely notice if I slip off the radar."

"Let her think you're at your parents' house, that they're keeping you busy. You have your phone, so nothing much should change about the way you communicate."

That might work for a while. Sam knew all too well that Kate's mother wished she could spend more time with her daughter, so at first it might not seem all that suspicious if Lynda monopolized her time. The key words being "at first." Sooner or later, though, Kate knew her best friend would want to get together, and wouldn't take any specious excuses as to why that wasn't a possibility.

"All right," she said. "That'll buy me some time. Not an indefinite amount of it, though."

"We don't need an indefinite amount," Jack replied, eyes narrowed. "Just enough to catch this bastard. Anyway," he went on, his tone shifting, "are you hungry? Alba said you could eat soup, but nothing heavier."

Up until the moment he'd asked, Kate would have said food was the last thing on her mind. But she realized then that she was actually ravenously hungry. Maybe it was a side effect of the forced healing her body had been put through, or merely that it was now afternoon— or even later, since she really didn't know what time it was—and she hadn't eaten anything since eight o'clock that morning, but either way, she knew she needed to get something in her stomach.

"I think I could eat," she said cautiously.

"I don't have much in the house," Jack said, his tone almost apologetic. "I mostly live on takeout. Does egg drop soup sound good? There's a good Chinese place close by that delivers."

Actually, that sounded heavenly to her, if she was going to be deprived of anything more substantial than soup. "Yes, that would be perfect."

"Good." Jack got up from the chair where he'd been sitting and pulled his cell phone from his pants pocket. Kate did her best not to gawk at how good he looked even in ordinary khakis, but it was a lot more difficult than she thought it would be. Maybe that blow to her head had disrupted some of the logic centers in her brain. Now more than ever she should be casual and cool around him, no matter how good-looking he might be. Her almost-ex-husband was dead, and someone had just tried to kill her, and yet she was sitting here and trying to not-quite ogle Jack Sandoval while he was doing something as prosaic as ordering Chinese takeout.

She tore her gaze away and pushed against the cushion where she lay, maneuvering herself to an upright position. The room spun briefly, but she made herself breathe deeply until the bout of dizziness passed. Once she felt a little steadier, she slowly moved her feet so they were flat against the floor.

Jack, who had just ended his call, eyed her with sudden alarm. "Are you sure you should be doing that?"

"I'm okay," she said. "I'm going to have to sit up to eat. Besides," she added, her cheeks flushing, "I kind of need to use the bathroom. Where is it?"

"Down the hall. It's the only door on the right."

"Thanks."

Not quite looking at him, she got up from the couch and went in the direction he'd indicated. Her legs felt a little shaky under her, but as she walked, they slowly felt steadier. She could tell she'd suffered a shock to the system, and yet her body itself seemed to be okay. In fact, walking around helped dispel some of the weakness she'd felt while lying on the couch.

This must be a two-bedroom, two-bath apartment, bigger than her own. Directly opposite the door to the guest bath was another doorway, one that appeared to open on the second bedroom, although the brief glimpse she caught told her that Jack must use it as an office, since it had a desk and some bookcases inside, and not a bed in sight.

The guest bathroom was very clean, and looked as if it had never been used. Kate took care of business and then dried her hands on one of the dark gray towels hanging from the rack. In here were more of the black and white art prints—Ansel Adams, looked like—and not much else in the way of decor. Very much a bachelor pad, except for the extreme neatness. She remembered all too well how much of a mess her brother Colin's apartment could become when he'd been working too hard and not paying attention to his surroundings. Clearly, Jack Sandoval didn't share that problem.

Speaking of messes, though—her poor shirt was a disaster, blood spattered all over the front. Maybe a good soaking in cold water could get some of that stain out, but she didn't know if the blouse would ever be the same. She needed to change, get out of these clothes. Well, Jack had said one of his "people" had brought over her things from her parents' house, so she'd get into something clean before the takeout arrived.

The cut that had bled all over her blouse was now apparently a thing of the past. If she squinted hard enough, she could see a faint red mark up near her hairline, but that was the only evidence remaining of the wound. Alba must have wiped off all the blood from her face, because her skin was clean, although the makeup she'd applied so carefully earlier that morning was now long gone. Not that it mattered. She might have a problem with trying to ignore Jack Sandoval's obvious good looks, but clearly the attraction wasn't reciprocated. He was all business around her. And that was a good thing, right? Her world was crazy enough right now without dragging some kind of illicit romance into it.

Kate emerged from the bathroom and walked carefully back to the dining area, where Jack had pulled out one of the chairs and was frowning down at his phone.

"Everything okay?" she inquired.

"Oh, sure," he replied, and set it down on the table. The top was gray granite, the base black metal, to go with all the other black accents in the apartment. "I was just trying to make sure that no one had reported the accident. It looks like the FedEx guy called something in, but by the time a beat cop was sent around to investigate, my people had gotten everything cleared away."

"Efficient," Kate remarked, trying to sound casual. The loss of her car really shouldn't be bothering her so much. Or maybe it was simply that she'd rather fixate on the one material loss than on what had happened to Jeff, what had almost happened to her. "Um, you said you had my things brought over? I'd really like to change out of these clothes. The blood, you know?"

"Oh, right." Jack got up from the table and went to the little entry area, opened a door there that led into a coat closet. From the floor of the closet he retrieved her weekender bag and toiletries case. "Here you go."

"Thanks." She took the bags from him and returned to the bathroom, then stripped out of her soiled clothes and into a fresh pair of jeans and a sky-blue V-neck T-shirt. That seemed a better choice than the nice embroidered blouse she'd also packed, since she wasn't going anywhere tonight. Luckily, her flats seemed to have survived the crash without any visible damage, so she slid back into those once she was finished getting dressed. It would probably be too obvious if she reapplied her makeup, but she did pause to fish some gloss out of her toiletries case and quickly swipe it over her lips. That way, she wasn't completely bare-faced but didn't look as if she was trying too hard.

When she was done, she really didn't know what she should do with her bags. Leave them in the bathroom? Bring them out so they could go back in the closet? Jack hadn't mentioned where she would be sleeping. Clearly, the second bedroom was out of the question, since it didn't even have a bed.

She decided to set the bags on the floor just outside the bathroom. Over dinner, she'd try to bring up the sleeping arrangements.

Jack had been busy while she was changing—he'd set out two glasses of water, and plates and bowls and cutlery, and folded paper towels in half to serve as napkins. "Sorry," he said, turning as she approached. "Like I said, I don't eat here much. I don't have any real napkins."

"It's okay," Kate replied. "I do the same thing." Of course, in her case it was more because she didn't see the point in spending extra money on paper napkins when paper towels worked just as well. It wasn't like she would ever have her parents over for dinner in her cramped apartment. The dining nook there was just big enough for a bistro set with a small table and two chairs, and definitely not suitable for company.

A relieved grin, one that had a little more impact on her than she would have liked. "Well, that's good to hear." Right then there came a knock at the door, and he stiffened, even though of course it had to be the delivery person with their takeout. "Can you wait back in the office while I handle this? I don't want anyone to see you here."

It was on the tip of her tongue to ask, "Embarrassed?", but she knew embarrassment had nothing to do with his wanting to conceal her presence. There was probably only a one-percent chance that the delivery person was anything other than what he claimed to be, but they couldn't afford to take chances right now.

She nodded and hurried off down the short hallway, then stepped into the office. Like the rest of the apartment, it was spotless, but here she noticed the first signs of a little clutter—books stacked on one of the end tables, some papers left out on the glass-topped desk. It looked to her like he'd been in the middle of paying bills, and hadn't stopped to put everything away.

And she would not look. None of her business what his electric bill was, or where he had a credit card. Or whatever all those statements were about.

Voices came down the hallway toward her, a brief exchange that ended with the door closing. Then Jack called out, "Coast is clear."

Kate left the office and returned to the main room, where he was pulling cartons out of a plastic bag and setting them in the middle of the table. The warm aroma drifted to her nose, and she breathed it in. That smelled so good.

"I know Alba said you shouldn't have solid food," Jack commented as Kate pulled out the chair nearest her and sat down. "But I got an order of egg rolls anyway. One or two shouldn't do too much damage."

"I promise I won't tell. And I'm starving, so egg rolls sound perfect."

He smiled and set two of them on her plate, then poured half of the carton of egg drop soup into the bowl next to the plate. As she waited, he did the same for himself. She noticed that no other takeout containers were forthcoming, though, and frowned slightly.

"Didn't you get anything else for yourself?"

"I didn't think it would be fair to make you watch me gobble moo shu pork while you were consigned to soup, so I didn't order anything more. It's fine—I got a huge burrito on my way out of Tucson."

That revelation made her feel a little better, although she didn't like the idea of Jack depriving himself just because she wasn't ready to eat an entire meal of solid food. But she didn't know him well enough to argue about it, so she merely shrugged and picked up one of the egg rolls. After she'd taken a bite, she asked, "So where do I get to crash?"

"I need to change the sheets, but I figured you'd stay in the bedroom. The couch has a pull-out bed, so I'll sleep in here."

Oh, no, she didn't like the sound of that. The last thing she wanted was to drive him out of his room. "You really don't need to do that. I'm fine with sleeping on the sofa bed."

"Now, how chivalrous would it be for me to ask a guest to sleep on the couch?"

"But it's not just a couch. You said it was a bed. So it's not the same thing at all." Kate set down her partially eaten egg roll and gave him a pleading look. "I understand why I have to stay here, but I'm just going to be crashing, while you still have to get up and go to work and function. Please—I don't want to kick you out of your bedroom."

For a minute, he didn't say anything. His fingers tapped against the glass of water by his place setting, but he didn't lift it to take a drink. Then he gave a very small shrug and said, "All right. If it matters that much to you."

"It does."

Again he seemed to hesitate. Then he reached for his glass of water and drank, and went on to say that he'd need her to make a list of what else she needed from her apartment, so he could fetch everything the next day. Kate told him that wouldn't be a problem, and the conversation moved a little more easily after that.

The whole time, though, she had to keep herself from gazing too long at his mouth, or those dark, dark eyes with their heavy sweep of lashes, or the way the rolled-up sleeves of his dress shirt showed off the hard muscles of his forearms. And she was supposed to be crashing here with him indefinitely?

Kate had no idea how she was going to survive that.

8

JUDGING BY THE DEAD SILENCE EMANATING FROM
the living room, Kate was already passed out. Jack
couldn't blame her—she'd been through hell today,
and even though she wouldn't suffer any permanent
damage from the accident, he knew she needed to
sleep, to let her body finish the healing process Alba
had begun. He'd actually been surprised by how
recovered Kate had seemed already, enough to sit up
at dinner and eat with a healthy appetite, and to help
him with pulling out the sofa bed and getting it set up
with sheets and a blanket. This was actually the first
time he'd ever used the damn thing; in the past, when
a woman had slept over, she sure as hell wasn't
sleeping on the couch.

Which led him to his current conundrum. It was
absolutely imperative that Kate stay here until the
killer was caught and dealt with, and yet Jack knew

such ongoing cohabitation was going to make for a serious test of his willpower. He shouldn't even be thinking of her in such a way, and yet he couldn't help noticing the way her jeans showed off her long, slim legs and firm ass, or how the T-shirt she'd changed into revealed a small yet tantalizing glimpse of the shadow between her breasts.

She really was beautiful.

And too young for him. And a civilian. And technically a brand-new widow, even if she and Jeff Nichols had been estranged at the time of his death. There were probably a few more "ands" Jack could have thrown in there, but he thought that was enough to tell him he needed to stay far, far away.

Maybe he should have had Kate stay with Luz and her husband David. There was certainly enough room at the big house that had once been Maya's, especially with Luz's daughter Alicia attending school down in Tucson at the University of Arizona. But something told him that wasn't a good idea, that he was better-equipped to protect Kate than even Luz would be.

Problem was, he still had to go to work, had to pretend as though Kate was staying with her parents and nothing strange had happened the day before. What he really should do was ask for a leave of absence until all this was settled, but then he wouldn't have the resources of the department to assist him while he was tracking down the killer.

Can they really help all that much? he thought as

he turned over for what felt like the tenth time that night. Normally his bed was comfortable enough, but he couldn't stop thinking about Kate out in the living room, not so very far away at all. Maybe it would be better to take some leave. This case would only be solved by using his own abilities and the resources of the clan, and he might as well admit that fact right now. Even the world's best criminal databases wouldn't help much when it came to finding a murderer who also happened to be a warlock.

Not that he was sure he'd even be granted a leave of absence, should he ask for one. Taking off in the middle of a murder investigation, especially one so fresh, wouldn't exactly endear him to his superiors. And yes, when it came right down to it, he didn't need the job, could up and quit if he wanted to, but the de la Paz clan needed people on the inside, just to help ensure that they stayed safely anonymous. He shuddered to think what would have happened if he hadn't been around to help clean up the mess his niece Zoe had left behind when she'd summoned her "creature" last year.

Damn it. Well, he'd wait and see how tomorrow went until he made any rash decisions, especially since he'd already reached out to Luz and asked if she could have her son Alex and his wife Caitlin come over and keep an eye on Kate. Alex's unique talent of being able to cast a field of protection around himself and anyone in close proximity seemed the best line of defense when Jack himself wasn't around, and Caitlin —well, she was a seer. Maybe she'd be able to catch a glimpse of the killer, provide a few much-needed clues. True, while her visions were almost always accurate, she couldn't summon them on cue, so her being able to offer any tangible help was a more remote possibility. Anyway, the couple was close to Kate's age, and the three of them should be able to keep themselves amused while he was gone for part of the day. And after that…well, he'd just have to play it by ear, decide how best to handle things at work once he had a better idea of how everyone had fared today. Yes, he knew he couldn't rely on Alex and Caitlin indefinitely, since Alex had a job of his own to worry about. He'd taken the day off from his position at a local television station down in Tucson, but he couldn't keep doing that. Caitlin's schedule was more flexible, as she'd just finished college and was now working from home full-time, but Caitlin's gifts on their own—formidable as they might be—weren't enough to protect Kate.

And so he went, thoughts going around and around, as he worried at every detail, every contingency, sure he must have forgotten something, left some hole unplugged. It was his way, and one of the reasons he'd flourished in his field, but his ever-racing brain sure played hell with his attempts to fall asleep. At last, though, he let go enough to fall into slumber, even as he thought of the empty space in the bed next to him, and how much better he would feel if Kate was lying there right now.

Sun slipping through the cracks in the vertical blinds woke her, and for a minute Kate couldn't quite think of where she was, why the walls were so plain and bare, compared to the ones in her apartment, covered with all the prints that Jeff hadn't liked and which she'd taken away from the much bigger townhouse they'd once shared. Her back was stiff, and she had a serious crick in her neck. From the bed?

No, from crashing your car into an empty building, she reminded herself. *I don't care how good your witch healer is—that sort of thing is going to leave some kind of a mark.*

She sat up and glanced around. No sign of Jack, although she thought she heard the faint whispery sound of a shower running way off at the other end of the apartment. Made sense, since it seemed the second bathroom was *en suite* in the master bedroom.

And no, she sure as hell was not going to let herself think about what Jack might look like in the shower, water sluicing over the hard muscles of his body, black hair slicked back with moisture.

Of course, the more she tried not to think about it, the more that image seemed to crowd itself into her brain. God, she needed coffee.

She pushed back the covers and got out of bed. Yes, now she could feel the various aches and pains all over her body, from outraged muscles that had been subjected to some serious abuse the day before, but a lot of that would probably go away with a long, hot shower. Since she'd slept in leggings and an oversized T-shirt, she wasn't too worried about Jack finding her wandering around his apartment in a state of undress. What she was worried about was whether it would be too huge an imposition to make some coffee now, before he was out of the shower. Her body was practically screaming for caffeine.

When she flicked on the overhead light for the kitchen, she saw that he had a Keurig coffeemaker, and one of those little racks that displayed all the various flavored cups. Surely it would be okay if she popped one in—it wasn't like she'd have to go rummaging through his cupboards, looking for coffee and filters and whatnot. All right, she'd still have to locate a mug, but first things first.

Kate pulled out the carafe and got some water from the tap, then selected some mocha java and started the coffeemaker on its cycle. As it began to heat the water, she tentatively opened a cupboard door, hoping she wouldn't have to dig around too much to find a mug. Luck appeared to be with her, because she located plates and bowls and matching cups on the first try, and got two out. There, that would make it look as if she was thinking of Jack, getting things ready for when he wanted some coffee, too.

Actually, that was true enough. She was thinking about Jack, only not in a way that involved his caffeine intake.

She'd just poured the coffee into her mug when he appeared. Giving the lie to her fantasies, he was completely dressed, although his tie hung limply around his neck, as if he wasn't going to bother to knot it until the very last minute.

"I see you found the coffeemaker," he remarked as he came into the kitchen and began inspecting the rack of Keurig cups.

Her cheeks colored. "I hope you don't mind. I was just dying for some coffee, and—"

"It's fine," he cut in, wearing that familiar grin, the one that probably would have made her knees feel weak even if she hadn't just been in a car accident the day before. "Everything was sitting out on the counter, after all. I don't usually eat breakfast, though, so there isn't much here for you. I'll try to get something at the store while I'm out today, if you let me know what you like."

There was something totally adorable about the way he peered worriedly down at her, as though he was afraid he must be the world's worst host. Kate lifted her shoulders and said, "Mostly I just have yogurt. Chobani, the Greek stuff. And fruit. But I skip breakfast more often than not, so going without today isn't that big a deal."

"It is a big deal," he told her. "Your body needs to keep working on recovering, and that's going to be harder if you don't have anything to eat. Let me see what I've got."

He went over to the pantry and started moving things around. Kate couldn't get a very good look inside, but it seemed he mostly had a lot of canned stuff, as if he'd once thought it would be a good idea to have a bunch of things on hand that wouldn't spoil easily, and then ignored all of it in favor of going out to eat or bringing home takeout. At last, though, he turned around to face her, a mini-box of cereal in each hand—one Frosted Flakes, and the other Rice Krispies.

"From when a couple of my nephews stayed here a while back," he said, sounding sheepish. "I know it's not the best, but it's something. And I do have milk… because coffee."

"Cereal would be awesome," Kate said. "Thanks." She hesitated, then asked, "So you have nieces and nephews?"

"Tons of 'em," Jack replied as he got down a bowl from the cupboard. "I have four older brothers, and they all have at least three kids each. They like to take turns coming over to trash Uncle Jack's apartment, although most of them are getting a little old for that, thank God."

"That is a lot." She reflected on her own fairly small family, fewer than five first cousins combined. Well, it did make keeping track of everyone a lot easier. And then she wondered why Jack, who was handsome and intelligent and had a good job, was so obviously single. Their limited acquaintance wouldn't allow her to ask the question, though. The last thing she wanted to do was give him the wrong impression, cause him to think that she was making those inquiries for personal reasons. Which of course she would be, even if she didn't want to admit it to herself.

"Catholics, huh?" His expression was deadpan, and she wasn't exactly sure how she was supposed to react to that comment. Then he chuckled and said, "It's okay, Kate. I don't take us too seriously, so you don't have to, either."

"So your family is Catholic, even though you're...." Her words trailed off there, and she realized she was blushing again.

"A bunch of witches and warlocks? Yes, that's how the de la Paz clan rolls. Our family goes way, way back here, back to when the Spaniards first came to these lands. Of course, we weren't called 'de la Paz' then. I don't even know what the family name was before we mingled with the Spanish and took on their religion and their language. But we're definitely not like the McAllisters, all New Age and Wiccan."

"Oh." It would take a little processing to understand how different this clan must be from the one her brother had married into. To her, the McAllisters seemed to be much more what you'd expect from a modern-day witch or warlock, sort of artsy-fartsy and with collections of crystals and houses that smelled of incense or patchouli, although she had to admit that her sister-in-law Jenny wasn't exactly your typical crystal-bedecked witch, and Colin was not a big fan of incense, since it made him sneeze. Still....

"Milk?" Jack asked as he reached into the refrigerator, then extended a small container of two-percent milk to her so she could take it with her free hand.

"Yes, thanks." Realizing that her coffee was getting cold, she took a few sips before she set the mug down on the counter. Ah, that was better. She poured the milk into the bowl of Rice Krispies, then drank some more coffee, leaning up against the counter opposite from Jack as he poured coffee into his own mug before he reached over to reclaim the milk so he could doctor his morning drink.

"I didn't ask if you wanted sugar."

"No, I drink it plain."

"Hardcore."

She couldn't help smiling, the twinkle in his eye was so infectious. For the first time, she realized she was standing there with her hair a mess from sleeping and not a speck of makeup on her face, and she hadn't even stopped to think about it. There was something about Jack that made her feel at ease, even though she knew there was absolutely nothing easy about their current situation.

"So who's babysitting me today?" she inquired.

A pained expression crossed his features at the term "babysitting," but he only said, "My cousin Alex and his wife Caitlin. She's actually a McAllister, so I guess you can say you're cousins by marriage."

Of course Kate had heard of Caitlin, although she hadn't actually met her. Going against her clan's wishes, Jenny and Colin had had a very small wedding in Sedona, just the immediate family on either side, and so there really hadn't been an opportunity for Kate's and Caitlin's paths to cross before now. Kate's work prevented her from going up to visit Jerome more than two or three times a year, and it sounded as if Caitlin and Alex didn't get out of Tucson all that often.

"Aren't we all sort of related, then?" she asked, and Jack lifted an eyebrow. "I mean, since Caitlin is Jenny's cousin and is married to Alex, who's a member of the de la Paz clan."

"I guess you could say that." Jack shrugged and sipped some more of his coffee. "That's how it works with witch clans—a lot of people distantly related or related only by marriage. But yes, my oldest brother Luis is married to Luz's sister Andrea, so that makes me Alex's uncle-in-law. Or something along those lines. Most of the time we just say 'cousins' and leave it at that. It's simpler."

"Jenny told me pretty much the same thing about the McAllisters. Does anyone keep track of everything?" What she really wanted to know was whether there were designated record-keepers in the witch clans to make sure no one got involved with a cousin who was too closely related, but asking that sort of question veered a little too close to those thorny topics of marriage and relationships, so Kate decided to let it pass.

"In my clan, my cousin Rosalie handles all that. She set up a huge database on her computer that tracks all the various relationships and how closely connected everyone is. I don't know what the McAllisters do—their clan isn't nearly as big as mine. But I have a feeling the Wilcoxes must have something similar, since there are a lot of them, too."

Yes, Kate had gotten that impression, although she had yet to meet any of the fabled Wilcox witches or warlocks. Since she knew she'd better eat her cereal before it turned into a total soggy mess, she picked up the bowl and dutifully started to work on it, having flashbacks to slumber parties when she was a kid and her friends' parents had provided big packs of the little cereal boxes so they wouldn't have to make a real breakfast for a whole gang of little girls.

Jack's phone buzzed, and he pulled it out of his pocket and peered down at the screen. "Alex and Caitlin are on their way."

"Which means I should probably get in the shower." Kate scooped the last spoonful of cereal out of her bowl and ate it. That had gone quickly. Then again, those little boxes were intended to feed small children, not grown women.

"I put out fresh towels for you." Jack's tone was almost too casual, as though he didn't really want to dwell on the thought of her taking a shower in his apartment. Or maybe she was reading way too much into the innocuous comment, just because she wanted him to be having the same inappropriate thoughts about her that she was about him.

Better not to dwell on it too long. If Caitlin and Alex were just leaving Tucson now, that meant she had a good hour and a half before they appeared, but still, she might as well go and get herself put together. "Thanks," Kate said. "I'll get moving. What time do you have to be at work?"

"Not until ten. Alex and Caitlin should be here by then. If they're not, I'll manufacture an excuse for being late."

The unspoken intimation being that he wasn't going to leave her alone, not even for ten or fifteen minutes. While Kate appreciated the solicitude, it also made her realize how dire her situation truly was. For a few minutes there, she'd almost forgotten why she was here, had allowed herself to relax and enjoy a chat about coffee and family and other innocuous topics that didn't involve being the target of a murderous warlock.

"Well, hopefully it won't come to that," she said lightly, then headed off to the bathroom.

The shower did feel good. Jack had decent water pressure in his apartment, unlike hers, which could be temperamental if anyone else on her side of the building also decided to shower at the same time she did. Even so, she didn't linger for very long, just made sure her hair and body and face were clean, and then got out and dried off.

Since she didn't have to be anywhere, and in fact was probably going to be stuck in the apartment all day, Kate didn't bother with the blow dryer, once again working serum through her hair to keep it from frizzing as it air-dried. Quick makeup of a little blush and mascara and gloss, not a full face like she'd put on if she was going to work. Then her jeans and the short-sleeved embroidered blouse she'd brought, reminding her that she really needed to put together a list of things to get from her apartment. Her cheeks heated as she thought of Jack rummaging through her underwear drawer to fetch her more bras and panties. She only had enough to get through another day, however, which meant he'd have to fetch those items for her, no matter how embarrassing it might be.

When she came back to the living room, it was to find him sitting on the couch, talking to someone named Larry. His boss? Possibly.

Jack gave a brief nod to acknowledge her presence, but clearly he was going to be occupied for the next few minutes. Well, that would give her a chance to compile the list of things she needed from her apartment. Since he'd already called her and she therefore had his number stored in her phone, she could simply text the list to him and be done with it.

She pecked away at the screen on her phone, the list getting longer than she'd first imagined it would. Problem was, she really didn't know how long she was going to be here, how many days she'd have to make her wardrobe last. Of course there must be a laundry room here at the complex, but she had a feeling she wouldn't be allowed outside alone to handle even that menial task. It seemed safest to have him bring enough items to get her through a week. She prayed that this situation wouldn't take any longer than that to sort itself out—no matter what Jack said, she couldn't see how they'd be so forbearing at her job as to let her take a whole week off without some kind of repercussions. Anyway, she'd be completely stir-crazy by then, even if Jack would have retrieved her laptop from her apartment by then.

You'll probably have jumped Jack's bones out of desperation by that point, she thought as she went back over the list. Sexual tension could be a real bitch. Or at least, she was just discovering that fun little fact. With Jeff, she hadn't waited long enough for any tension to even build. They'd met at a party when they were both going to ASU, and back then he'd been much trimmer, although thick with muscle because of being on the football team. She'd thought him handsome, and very different from the skinny, not-quite-nerdy guys she'd preferred up until that point, and they'd progressed from dating to sleeping together to moving in together in a scant six months. Too bad she hadn't stuck with her previous type, though. Several of those semi-nerdy dates of hers had later become geologists and engineers, people with whom she'd have had much more in common.

She'd never thought she'd ever be attracted to a cop, either, but here she was. Then again, Jack Sandoval wasn't your ordinary garden-variety beat cop. She doubted there were too many homicide detectives who also happened to be warlocks.

He ended the call and looked over at her, one eyebrow slightly tilted, as if asking what she'd just been typing on her phone.

"I'm putting together the list of things I'll need from my apartment," she said. "Actually, I think I've got it all figured out. Okay if I text it to you?"

"Sure," he replied, although he didn't sound too thrilled.

"Is something wrong?"

"No," he said at once, and offered her a smile. "Yes, send it over. I'm just irritated with Larry, my department head. He got the brilliant idea last night that I should be interviewing every scumbag who's gotten caught in the last eighteen months painting satanic graffiti or who's been involved in any kind of a crime that had some sort of occult element to it. Total waste of time."

"You're sure it couldn't be anyone like that?" Even as she asked the question, she realized it was a foolish one. No high school kid dabbling in black magic had caused her car to crash. Trying not to sigh, she touched the screen on her phone to send the list to Jack.

"Positive. We're dealing with real magic here, not some punk who looked up *The Satanic Bible* on the Internet and now thinks he's some kind of bad-ass." His phone binged, and he glanced down at it where it sat on the coffee table. "Got your list. I'm not sure when I'll be able to swing by, but I'll figure it out. Hopefully I won't have to waste my day interviewing kids who got a little too carried away playing *Call of Cthulhu.*"

Despite the situation, Kate couldn't help grinning at that remark. She could just see Jack looming over some high school kid who thought he'd score some cool points by drawing pentagrams in the bathroom of the local AMC Theatre or something, his impatience ratcheting up with every moment he had to spend on that sort of nonsense rather than trying to find the real killer.

"Hopefully not," she agreed.

Someone knocked at the door then, and Jack was on his feet at once to answer it. Kate got up from the chair where she'd been sitting and slid her phone into the pocket of her jeans, even though it was really too big to fit properly, and she'd have to take it out before she sat down again.

On the landing outside were a man and a woman Kate had never seen before but guessed must be Caitlin and Alex. He looked to be around Kate's age, or close to it, while she guessed that Caitlin was probably a few years younger. Her bright, coppery hair had been pulled back into a loose French braid, and she was casually dressed, in a T-shirt and jeans and flats. Alex also wore jeans, but with a polo shirt and running shoes. They both looked as if they were on their way to a shopping expedition at Costco or something, rather than providing protection to someone who was being stalked by a murderous warlock.

"Kate, this is Alex and Caitlin," Jack said, somewhat unnecessarily, since she couldn't think who else it might be. Still, Kate supposed it was a good thing that he'd made some sort of introduction.

"Hi," Kate said, as the couple also offered their greetings.

They came inside, and Jack shut the door behind them. "I need to get going," he went on, very crisp and businesslike. "Just a couple of rules. Stick together, no matter what. It's better if you stay here and order in lunch—there are a bunch of menus in the drawer in the kitchen next to the fridge—but if you do go out, don't get separated, and don't go any farther than the shopping center down on the corner.

Keep the windows shut. If it gets too hot, turn up the air."

Alex, who was darkly handsome like his cousin Jack, raised an eyebrow. "You're not fooling around, are you?"

"No," Jack said, his tone just this side of curt. "And neither should any of you. I still don't know exactly what we're up against, but so far, he—or she, or it—makes Matías Escobar look like Mr. Rogers. This apartment is safe. Your car should be safe. But don't pretend that anything else is."

Caitlin, who had the fair complexion of a redhead to begin with, looked even paler. "We understand, Jack. We'll be careful."

"Good. I'm off shift at seven, but if I have an opportunity to swing by during the day, I will. If anything looks or feels or even smells weird to you, call me." His gaze traveled from Caitlin to Alex and finally to Kate, who did her best not to flush under that piercing regard. Something about the hard set of his mouth softened slightly, and he went on, "I'm sure it'll be fine. I'm just being careful. I do need to get going, though."

"We'll be fine, Jack," Kate told him. "You go and do what you have to."

He nodded, looked over at Caitlin and Alex, and said, "Thanks," and then grabbed his suit jacket from where it had been draped over the arm of the couch and put it on, concealing the shoulder holster he wore. A final "be careful," and he was gone.

Kate and Alex and Caitlin looked at one another, and for a few seconds, no one said anything at all. Then Caitlin gave a lopsided grin. "Well, I don't know about you, but I could use some more coffee. Then we can all sit down and get acquainted. Okay?"

"Okay," Kate said. Anything to get the ball rolling. Even so, as she had them come into the kitchen for her so they could make their selections from the rack of Keurig cups, she had a feeling this was going to be a *very* long day.

9

JACK WAS ALREADY IN A FOUL MOOD THAT morning, and it didn't improve when he saw the group of misfits Larry had pulled in for questioning. While he knew that Alex and Caitlin were both capable, and that probably the worst thing any of them, including Kate, would be subjected to was unfortunate choices in their Netflix binge-watching that day, he still felt on edge, worrying that he had missed something, that despite his efforts to reassure himself everything would be fine, something awful would happen while he was stuck here at the station, talking to some of Scottsdale's worst dregs.

A lot of people might have been surprised to learn that Scottsdale had dregs at all, but even the most affluent communities had their fringe dwellers, and that was who Jack would have to deal with today. Six of them in all, ranging from nineteen to thirty-nine.

Each one had priors—vandalism, or minor dealing, or, in the case of Bret Harkins, the oldest of the bunch, breaking and entering, which had led to an eighteen-month stint in the state prison in Florence.

The kids—the ones under twenty-two—Jack spoke with briefly and then had released, since they had alibis that matched the time frame of Jeff Nichols' murder. A couple of the older ones were definitely shifty, but even they passed the sniff test when it came to the timing of the crime, so after a bit more in-depth questioning, they, too got released back into the wild.

Harkins, though…of course he wasn't a warlock, any more than Jack was the star of the latest *Fast and the Furious* movie, but he'd done time in Florence, which just happened to be the same prison where Matías Escobar had been sentenced to life without the possibility of parole. Now, it was most likely that a two-bit criminal like Harkins had never crossed paths with Escobar, a lifer, but if he had, well, there was a connection that needed to be explored. Especially since Harkins' last run-in with the police had been out of character, for a domestic disturbance during which his girlfriend claimed he'd gotten violent after she threw out some "devil books" she'd found in their apartment.

At first glance, Bret Harkins wasn't terribly impressive. A good six inches shorter than Jack, with a lined face that belied his thirty-nine years, he slouched into the interview room and gave some serious side-eye to the deputy who'd escorted him there before transferring his baleful, pale stare to Jack.

"I didn't do nothing," Harkins said.

Which, if Jack wanted to get snarky about grammar, meant that presumably he had done *something*. However, pointing out that detail would only get this interview started off on the wrong foot, so he decided it was best to take the high road. "I just wanted to talk to you, Mr. Harkins," he said, his tone pleasantly neutral. "Once you settle my mind on a few points, you'll be free to go."

"What points?" Harkins asked, eyes narrowing.

"Can you tell me where you were on the evening of April fourth?"

"I was home. Damn parole doesn't let me do anything except go to and from my job."

"Ah." Jack opened the file in front of him and scanned its contents. "So you're working for Arroyo Waste Management?"

"Yeah. It was the only thing I could get."

Harkins was actually lucky to get that job. While waste management wasn't exactly most people's dream career, it actually paid decently and offered benefits. The ex-con could have done a lot worse. "Is there someone who can vouch for your being at home? Your girlfriend?"

The other man's scowl creased itself further into his lined forehead. "She bailed last month. I'm by myself, unless you count the cat. She left the damn cat because she couldn't take it with her to her new place."

Poor cat. Harkins didn't look the type who was much into cuddling fluffy animals. "So you don't have anyone to verify that you were actually home between six-thirty and seven-thirty on the evening of April fourth?"

"No. Except...." The man paused there and scratched behind his left ear, his gaze sliding away from Jack's.

"Except what, Mr. Harkins?"

"I was online. On my computer," he added, as if that phrase needed some kind of clarification.

Probably watching porn, Jack thought wryly, but he didn't mention that possibility, only waited in silence. People tended to hate quiet, would do whatever it took to fill it.

Clearly, Bret Harkins was typical in that regard, because he shifted uneasily in his chair and then said, "I was in a chat room. Sometimes that's the best way to meet people, you know?"

By "people," Jack assumed Harkins meant women. No doubt he'd told whoever he was chatting with that he was a six-foot-two lawyer, or something along those lines. Anything to make himself more appealing. Usually, Jack wouldn't care one way or another what kind of lies people told each other online, since eventually they'd be found out if the decision was ever made for them to meet in person.

"No, I wouldn't know," Jack said. "I don't hang out much online."

Harkins frowned, his eyes narrowing as he took in the detective who confronted him. His nostrils flared slightly, as though he wished he could come up with a satisfying rejoinder but knew he was outmatched. "Anyway, I should be able to prove that, right? Time stamps or whatever?"

That sort of thing should be easy enough to follow up. Jack doubted it would be necessary, though; the ex-con's offer of information that could be verified without too much trouble pretty much guaranteed he was telling the truth. He could be bluffing, but his attitude didn't have that particular smell about it. "Yes, the chat program would show when you logged in and logged out. I'll let you know if we need to follow up on that." Jack opened the file in front of him and pretended to read its contents, although he already knew what it contained—and which questions he wanted to ask. "Can you tell me something about your arrest on December fifteenth?"

The scowl was back, this time digging itself so deeply into Harkins' forehead that Jack was sure it must be creating new lines in addition to worsening the ones which were already there. "Ellen and I got in an argument. That's all. She blew things way out of proportion."

"In what way?"

Harkins crossed his arms and settled back in his chair. "Why you asking me about this? The cops questioned me and let me go, since they could tell I hadn't touched Ellen, that everything was fine in our apartment."

"Because it's relevant information, Mr. Harkins. Or would you prefer that I make a note that you're being uncooperative? It's something your parole officer might want to hear about."

"Fine." The ex-con might as well have spat the word. "Ellen was getting on my case anyway—she got into all that Jesus stuff while I was in Florence, tried to make it sound as if her praying every day was why I got out with only half my time served." A crooked smile touched Harkins' thin lips as he added, "Maybe Jesus had something to do with all the overcrowding, which was the real reason I got let out early. But I didn't have the energy to argue with her about it."

"So she was getting on your case about going to church?"

A crafty look entered the other man's eyes, and he glanced away for a second. Then he lifted his shoulders, but the shrug looked too practiced, as if he was doing his best to appear as if he wasn't truly concerned about the current topic of conversation. "Sort of. I'd never been into that kind of thing anyway, and I learned a few things while I was inside that told me how much of a waste of time it really was."

"Such as?"

"Just things."

Jack tapped his pen against the file folder in front of him. "When you were in Florence, did you ever meet a man named Matías Escobar?"

At once Harkins went rigid. He'd already given every indication of being a shitty liar, but this tell was even worse than some of the others Jack had observed. "Who?"

"Come on, Bret. You'll need to do better than that. When I said Escobar's name just then, it looked as if someone had goosed you."

That same wary gleam came and went in Bret Harkins' eyes. "I heard of him," he said after a discernible pause. "Doesn't mean I met him, or knew him."

A lie, but Jack decided to go with it for now, to see how much he could get out of Harkins by going at this by an oblique angle. "So you heard of him. What did you hear?"

"Things. He was in for killing a girl. Some kind of satanic crap, I guess. I heard about it on the news not too long before they sent me away. I guess he shanked a guy while he was in there, but his posse covered it up."

Posse? It was Jack's turn to frown, although he did his best to smooth his expression as soon as he could. The last thing he wanted was for Bret Harkins to see that he'd struck a nerve. Still, it bothered him that

Escobar had insinuated himself with one of the prison's gangs. His talent for bending everyone around him to his will had been stripped from him, but apparently he still possessed enough native charisma —and toughness—to get close to some of those who wielded their own power while behind bars. Right then, Jack wished he'd done more to keep track of the disgraced warlock, because maybe then he would have gotten word of his doings in prison, would have had a better idea of exactly what he was up to.

"So you heard these things, but you didn't have any actual dealings with him."

"No."

But again came that sideways look. Liar. Good thing Harkins had never decided to try the professional poker circuit. He would have been doomed to failure before he even got started. "So what made you start reading material that your girlfriend"—Jack glanced down at the file before him—"referred to as 'devil books'?"

Sweat was actually beading on Harkins' forehead, even though, like most public buildings in Arizona, the temperature in the room was set to something just slightly above "meat locker." "Can't a guy even choose what he wants to read?"

"Of course he can, Mr. Harkins," Jack responded, his tone smoothly casual. "I just find it interesting that you were reading 'devil books,' to use your ex-girlfriend's phrase, while by your own admission you knew that Matías Escobar was guilty of a crime that involved satanic rituals. Escobar can be a very persuasive guy. Maybe he was looking to have someone on the outside to do his dirty work, since he knew he himself wasn't getting out for a very long time, while you were up for early release on a minor conviction."

"No—no, it's not like that," Harkins stammered. He reached up to pass a hand over his damp brow before continuing, "He just said I might want to read some of this stuff, that it might open my mind. That's all."

"Ah." Jack leaned back in his chair and allowed himself a very small smile. "So you do admit to speaking with Matías Escobar."

"No, I—" The other man stopped dead right there, as if he'd just realized that Jack had neatly maneuvered him into a trap. "That's not what I said."

"But it is what you said. You've admitted to at least a social relationship with a convicted murderer. And two nights ago, a murder was committed here in Scottsdale, one that had all the earmarks of an occult ritual killing. Do you recognize any of these symbols?" From underneath the file folder, Jack drew out one of the photos of the blood-smeared walls of Jeff Nichols' apartment and laid it flat on the table in front of Bret Harkins.

The ex-con went pale under his weather-beaten tan. "Is that…?"

"Blood? Yes. A lot of it, in fact. Satanic symbols.

You've just admitted that you were reading this sort of material after fraternizing with Matías Escobar while behind bars. So unless you want to be booked on suspicion of first-degree murder with special circumstances, you'd better start talking."

"I—I didn't do that. I was home, I swear!" Harkins' agitation was so extreme that he started to launch himself up out of his chair. Immediately, the deputy who'd been keeping watch in the corner the whole time began to move toward the man. Jack shook his head almost imperceptibly, and the deputy backed away. "I was. I had nothing to do with it. But...."

"But what?"

"But the last time I saw Escobar, he said he needed foot soldiers on the outside, that something big was coming, and anyone who was loyal would get their reward. He wouldn't give me any details, though, said I'd know when the time came."

Most people would have dismissed that confession as the babbling of someone who was just telling his interrogator what he wanted to hear, but Jack knew better. Something in his gut told him that Bret Harkins wasn't just talking out of his ass. Who exactly had been talking to the felon, Jack didn't know yet, but the murder of Jeff Nichols and the tampering with Kate McAllister's car couldn't be dismissed that easily.

Something big was coming. Cold inched its way down Jack Sandoval's spine.

"You have any contact with Matías Escobar after you were released? I don't have to remind you that any such contact is a violation of your parole."

"No, I haven't talked to him," Harkins replied, naked fear on his sharp features. "I know better than that."

"But you're doing your assigned reading. Getting prepared."

"I guess."

"Prepared for what?"

"I said I don't know. Escobar wouldn't tell me any more than that."

Which Jack did believe. Say what you wanted about the rogue warlock, but Matías Escobar was not stupid. He wouldn't have given any details to the stooge who sat in the interrogation room now. All he'd done was puff him up, give him a reason to think that he might have a chance to become someone other than the nobody he was now. Asking any further questions would be a waste of time. Even so, he'd still request a warrant to check Harkins' computer, just to make sure, even if he didn't for a minute believe that the petty criminal was capable of the sort of brutality he'd witnessed in Jeff Nichols' apartment.

"All right, Mr. Harkins, you're free to go," Jack said, ignoring the visible relief on the other man's face.

"We will want to take a look at your computer, just to confirm your story."

"Sure, absolutely." He didn't look dismayed at all by Jack's comment, which meant there was probably nothing to be found. Still, it didn't hurt to be thorough.

Jack nodded at the deputy, who stepped forward so he could escort Harkins from the interrogation room. Once he was alone, Jack stared down at the file in front of him, at the crime scene photo from Nichols' apartment.

Foot soldiers. Something big coming.

What the hell was going on?

10

THE THREE OF THEM ALL LOOKED AT ONE
another rather awkwardly, and Kate fought back a
grimace. Yes, getting coffee had taken up some time,
but right then, seven o'clock and Jack's return felt
eons away.

"So…." Kate said at last. "Do you get a lot of jobs
babysitting civilians?"

"Not really," Caitlin replied. She smiled somewhat
lopsidedly. "Most of the time we probably seem like
normal people. Our neighbors have no idea."

"Thank God," Alex said. "Sometimes I think it
would be easier up in Jerome, with witches on
every side."

"Are there?" Kate asked, somewhat confused. "My
brother made it sound as if only about half the people
in Jerome are actually McAllisters."

"Your brother's right," Caitlin said, giving her

husband a mock-severe look. "But all the civilians who live there know who we are, so it's a lot more relaxed than living down in Tucson or here in the Phoenix area, where we have to pretend every second of the day that we're something we're not."

"Not every second," Alex protested. "Once we're home, it's a different story."

"As long as we're not having a barbecue with the neighbors or something."

"Well, true."

Kate sipped her coffee, weighing their words. That all sounded very normal and suburban, and a far cry from how Colin had described day-to-day life in Jerome.

"It's not so bad," Caitlin said. "I just had a little adjustment period. Luckily, though, my talent isn't the sort of thing that's flashy, you know? It's not like Jenny's dad, who can throw fireballs."

"He can?" Kate asked, impressed. She knew that Jenny's father was a warlock while her mother was a civilian, but Colin hadn't gone into any details about his father-in-law's talents.

"Yes. It's a fun trick, but not something you really want to mess around with during fire season."

"I guess not."

Another silence as they all drank some coffee. Alex didn't let it last very long, though, because he said, "Has Jack told you much about what he thinks is going on?"

Damn it—for a few seconds there, Kate realized she'd almost forgotten the reason why Caitlin and Alex were here. "Demons," she replied, and the witch's eyes widened.

"'Demons'?" she repeated, managing to sound frightened and disbelieving at the same time.

"Well, I don't know if that was who—what—was responsible for Jeff's murder," Kate said. "Jack thinks it was a warlock who summoned the demons to do his bidding. Problem is, we're not really sure what that bidding was. Jack has a theory that it might be an oblique way of getting back at the McAllisters, that striking at civilians connected to the family was this warlock's way of getting revenge."

"'Revenge'?" Alex echoed. "The only people I can think of who'd want revenge are Matías Escobar and his two cousins, and since all three of them had their powers taken away, I don't think they're much of a threat."

"That's what Jack said. But maybe they have family members who aren't happy with the current situation?"

Caitlin and Alex exchanged a glance. Kate didn't know them very well, but it was easy enough to tell that her question troubled them.

"Maybe," Caitlin allowed. "Although Matías himself was kind of adopted into the Santiago clan and didn't seem to have any immediate family other than his sister, who's a *nunca*—"

"What's a *nunca?*" The word meant "never," if Kate remembered her three years of high school and college Spanish correctly, but it didn't seem to make much sense when applied to a person.

"It means someone who was born of a witch clan but never developed any real powers," Alex explained. "So Matías' sister Olivia definitely wouldn't have anything to do with it, and from what I was able to gather, his mother is dead, so that doesn't leave many other possibilities."

"What about his father?"

Alex shrugged. "I don't know. He must be still in El Salvador, if he's even still alive. Matías' mother came to California when her two children were little, from what we've been able to gather, but we don't really know anything more about their history besides that."

"I could ask Lucinda," Caitlin offered.

"Lucinda?" Kate asked, somewhat bewildered. Yes, she'd had a lot of de la Paz and McAllister names thrown at her over the past couple of days, but she didn't recognize that one.

"Simón Santiago's daughter," Alex said. "Old Santiago doesn't want to have anything to do with us, but luckily, he's also not the most technologically savvy guy in the world. Caitlin and Lucinda keep in touch by private messaging on Facebook—it's something her father wouldn't even think to check. He does watch her emails, though."

"Does he really keep that close an eye on her?" Kate asked, reflecting that she had it easier than she'd thought back when she was in high school. "How old is she?"

"Late twenties," Caitlin replied. "But Simón doesn't care about that. She disgraced him, and so he's going to keep her locked up in their house like Rapunzel in the tower or something until he drops dead."

As she spoke, Caitlin's blue eyes flashed angry fire, and her pretty features hardened. Obviously, the man running the Santiago clan was not a favorite with her. Since her previous response had only prompted more questions, Kate asked, "What did Lucinda do to disgrace her father?"

"Slept with Matías Escobar," Alex said, adding quickly, "Not her fault—Matías' talent was to make everyone around him do whatever he wanted. Or at least, he could get *most* people to do what he wanted. There were a few exceptions, like my cousin Jack. But Simón Santiago was one of the few people Matías couldn't wrap around his little finger, and so when he found out that Matías had despoiled his only daughter, Simón banished Matías from Santiago territory."

"Which was why we ended up with him here in Arizona," Caitlin put in. "Just our luck. Anyway, I've kept in touch with Lucinda. She's really lonely, since none of the other Santiagos want to have much to do with her. I keep having fantasies of going to California and busting her out of there, hooking her up with a nice McAllister guy."

"What's wrong with a nice de la Paz guy?" Alex asked, feigning wounded pride for his clan.

"Nothing at all, only it just seems like it would be safer to have her up in Jerome. The farther away from her father, the better."

"In which case you might as well hook her up with a Wilcox. Flagstaff would be the best solution, if that's your take on it."

Caitlin sent Alex a sly smile. "Maybe you're right. There are a *lot* of good-looking Wilcoxes."

Alex appeared so offended by that remark that Kate couldn't help chuckling. "That's what I've heard, too," she said, knowing she was only adding fuel to the fire. But it was good to deflect the conversation toward Wilcox men. The last thing she wanted was to admit that she thought de la Paz men were pretty hot…or at least, one of them was.

"I feel outnumbered," Alex complained.

"We're just making an observation," Caitlin said. As she spoke, though, she was rummaging around in her purse, which sat next to her on the floor. After a minute, she retrieved her phone and unlocked the screen so she could navigate to the Facebook app. Still looking down at the phone, she went on, "Lucinda spends a lot of time on her computer, if she isn't tending to her parents. It sounds like Simón is pretty demanding, and with her mother confined to a wheelchair—"

"The *prima* of the Santiagos is in a wheelchair?" Kate cut in. "Their clan doesn't have a healer?"

"They do," Alex replied. "But not every clan is lucky enough to have someone who's particularly strong. It's sort of a roll of the dice when it comes to that sort of thing. I guess when the Santiago *prima* had her accident, their healer was able to save her life, but couldn't fix her up enough to keep her out of the wheelchair. But that's why Simón basically runs the clan, even though the Santiagos don't believe in having a *primus* the way the Wilcoxes do."

"Ah," Kate said. It all sounded very complicated to her, although she supposed she could see why having a *prima* who wasn't on top of her game could cause issues in her clan. Big, messy issues like Matías Escobar, although it sounded as if he'd been pretty well handled.

Letting out a small sigh, Caitlin set her phone down on the coffee table. "Well, I sent her a PM. It didn't look like she was online, so I guess she's off doing something else right now. But usually she gets back to me within an hour or so. We'll just have to wait."

Waiting was the last thing Kate felt like doing right then. She'd tried to resign herself to being confined to this apartment all day, but Jack had said they could go out for food or something, as long as the three of them stuck together. The digital clock on the cable box across the room said it was now ten-thirty. Great. Kind of late for breakfast, but definitely too early for lunch.

Or maybe not. By the time they chose a place and went out and actually had food served to them, it would probably be closer to eleven. "Are you hungry?" she asked.

Both Caitlin and Alex looked at her as though she'd just sprouted horns. "We ate on the way up," Caitlin responded. "Why…are you?"

"I'm running on a kid's box of Rice Krispies," Kate said. "Your cousin doesn't exactly have a well-stocked pantry. I'd kill for a breakfast burrito. Or a burger. I'm not picky."

"Do you really think it's that good an idea to go out?" Alex wore a dubious expression, and she couldn't really blame him. The safest thing would be to stay here, although Jack had said they could go out as long as they didn't venture very far.

And really, would ordering in even be the safest thing? After all, that meant having someone come straight to the apartment. If the killer had known where Jeff lived, and probably knew where she lived, then it wasn't too much of a stretch to imagine he'd also pinned down this apartment as being Jack's. It would be pretty easy to tamper with any food sent here, whereas if they all went out, and took a circuitous route to whichever restaurant they chose, then the odds of the killer—or his demon servants—catching up with them seemed much more remote.

She explained this reasoning to Caitlin and Alex, and, to her relief, neither of them shot her down immediately.

"She does have sort of a point," Caitlin said, to which Alex lifted his shoulders.

"Maybe. But we still need to stay on our guard."

"Of course," Kate said. "And if any of us feels like something is off, we'll come straight back. But come on," she added frankly, "wouldn't you rather get out for a bit instead of sitting here and staring at each other for the next eight hours?"

Alex grinned, a flash of white teeth that went a long way in showing exactly why Caitlin might have fallen for him. "Okay, you've convinced me."

"I'll text Jack once we're on the road, just to let him know what we're doing," Kate said. "But I won't tell him which restaurant we're going to…just in case."

"You think his phone is compromised?" Caitlin asked then, one russet eyebrow lifting in obvious skepticism. "I thought we were dealing with demon-summoners here, not the NSA."

"I don't know what we're dealing with," Kate said frankly. "So I figure it's better to be as careful as possible."

"Can't argue with that," Alex remarked. "Well, let me check to make sure the coast is clear, and then we can head out." He paused and sent an inquiring glance at his wife. "You feeling anything about this?"

"Other than an odd spike of hunger? No. I'm not getting any bad vibes. But you know my visions don't always work that way."

"True."

Caitlin got her phone and deposited it back in her purse, while Kate rose from the couch and went to fetch her own bag, which she'd slung over the back of one of the dining room chairs. At the same time, Alex sidled up to the vertical blinds that covered the sliding glass doors, then carefully pushed one of them aside so he could look down onto the walkway that wound its way past the building.

"I don't see anything," he said, after watching in silence for a moment. "I mean, I just saw a guy go past with a couple of Trader Joe's bags, but he didn't give me the impression of being a demon in disguise."

Would any of them be able to recognize a demon, if it had taken on human form? Could demons even do such a thing? Kate had to admit that when it came to demonology, she was pretty clueless. And for all she knew, it wasn't even a demon they should be looking out for, but the killer himself. Except, didn't witches and warlocks have the ability to sense when they were around one of their own? She seemed to recall Jenny making a comment to that effect at one point, but now Kate couldn't remember for sure.

"Then I guess we're good to go," Caitlin said.

"We're out in one of the guest parking spots at the front of the complex."

"Okay."

She got out the spare key Jack had left for her, and locked up while Alex and Caitlin waited on the landing. Even just stepping outside felt better to her—a warm wind ruffled her hair, and the sky overhead was bright, bright blue, with only a few high cirrus clouds to break up the sapphire expanse. It was good to know that the world still existed out there, that for most people, life was continuing just as it always had.

It was a bit of a hike to the guest parking lot, just because the apartment complex was large, a good bit bigger than the one where she lived. Newer, too, everything clean and bright and shiny. Well, she supposed detectives who'd been with the Scottsdale P.D. for a while probably earned a bit more than junior designers in the city's planning department, even those who had master's degrees. And that didn't even take into account the money all witches and warlocks seemed to have at their disposal. She remembered how shocked she'd been at the casual way Jenny and Colin had purchased a home at the foot of the hill in Clarkdale. The flat where Jenny had been living was not really suited for children, so almost as soon as the pregnancy had been confirmed, the couple bought a brand-new four-bedroom, three-bath house in a new community just down the hill from Jerome. Kate knew there was no way they could have afforded such a place on Colin's salary at the *Verde Valley News*, which meant most of the money had to have come from her sister-in-law.

Alex had a shiny newish Pathfinder, which only seemed to confirm her musings about the relative affluence of witches and warlocks. Kate climbed into the back seat, while Caitlin and Alex took their places up front.

"Any preferences?" Caitlin asked as they pulled out of the parking lot. She already had her phone out.

"Not really," Kate replied. "I guess check to see what's in the shopping center down the street? Jack didn't want us going any farther than that."

Caitlin bent her head over the phone and entered a few characters, then started scrolling. "There's a diner that looks like it has both American and Mexican food, and it has four and a half stars. Sound okay?"

"Sounds great. Do I need to have it give directions?"

"Not if we're only going down the street," Alex said wryly as he backed the Pathfinder out of its parking space. "I think I can manage that much."

There was some traffic, but not too much, since they were past rush hour but not yet into the noontime crush when people would be trying to cram their meal into the one hour given them by their work. They drove for a few minutes, and then Alex pulled the Pathfinder into the shopping center's parking lot.

Their destination appeared to be at the far end. There were plenty of spaces, so they parked almost at the front door and headed in.

Although Kate couldn't help giving everyone around them the side-eye, wondering if anyone was a demon in disguise, the crowd seemed fairly innocuous, mostly retirees who could afford to be out at that hour of the morning, and a few harassed-looking mothers with their children.

"Nothing from Lucinda," Caitlin said after they'd slid into a booth in the corner. She still had her phone in her hand, and apparently had checked her Messenger app as they were walking in.

"Well, it's only been a half hour," Alex told her, his tone soothing. "She could have gone to the store, or out for a walk. Yeah, she's on the computer a lot, but it's not like every second of every day."

"I know." She went quiet as the waitress came up and asked if anyone wanted coffee.

By that point, Kate had had enough coffee, so she asked for iced tea. The other two followed suit, and the waitress went off to fill their drink orders as the three of them opened their menus.

"But still…." Caitlin continued, once their waitress was out of earshot. "I'm just…."

"Getting a vision?"

"No. Just a prickling of my thumbs. Something isn't right."

That comment did nothing to soothe Kate's

unease, and apparently it rattled a little of Alex's confidence as well, because he said, "Maybe it isn't, but there isn't much we can do about it from here. We'll just have to wait and hope she gets back to you."

The waitress returned with their drinks and asked if they'd made up their minds about what they wanted to order. Of course, Kate had barely glanced at the menu she held, but a quick scan told her that huevos rancheros actually sounded better than a breakfast burrito, so she ordered that, while Alex asked for a burger and Caitlin requested a grilled cheese sandwich.

While they waited, they talked about innocuous subjects—whether the McAllisters and Wilcoxes were going to combine their big family gatherings that summer, and, if so, where they would hold the event. Alex's family's plans for when his little sister graduated from the University of Arizona that May. Things like that. It all sounded very normal, which Kate supposed was the whole point. Anyone trying to eavesdrop on their conversation wouldn't hear anything terribly out of the ordinary.

The food came, and they all plowed in, even Caitlin, who supposedly hadn't been all that hungry. With each bite, Kate felt slightly better. It was entirely possible that she'd made matters worse by eating that little bit of cereal earlier rather than just waiting until she could have something more substantial. Now, though, she felt more restored, better able to face whatever happened next. After this, they could all go back to the apartment and digest, hang out and watch Netflix or whatever. And soon enough Jack would be home, and Caitlin and Alex could go back to Tucson and their own lives. Yes, Kate would have to deal with once again trying to hide her growing attraction to Jack, but she'd still rather be with him.

Despite her improved outlook on the world, she couldn't help but notice the way Caitlin kept glancing surreptitiously at her phone when she thought Alex wasn't paying attention. Even though Kate had never met this Lucinda person, it sounded as if she'd already had enough crap to deal with in her life, and she hoped that everything was okay, that Lucinda had, as Alex said, simply gone out shopping or on some other errand. Surely her father couldn't prevent her from doing something so completely mundane?

Eventually they finished their meal, just as more people began to show up for lunch. Kate pulled out her own phone to check the time. Eleven fifty-six. Well, they'd managed to get out and kill an hour or so, which was better than nothing.

When the check came, Alex pounced on it, and no amount of arguing would convince him to let her chip in for the meal.

"I'll bill my cousin Jack," he said with a grin. "After all, it's his fault that there isn't anything decent to eat at his place."

"I think you should," Kate replied, all seriousness.

"Maybe that'll shock him into going grocery shopping."

"Doubtful," Caitlin put in as she grimly shoved her phone back in her purse. "Jack loves his takeout. When they have de la Paz get-togethers, he always shows up with egg rolls or won tons or something, which of course makes all the purists in the family gasp in horror. Can't say as I blame them, though— why anyone would want takeout when people like Alex's cousin Liza make such sublime tamales, I have no idea."

Homemade tamales. Even though Kate was almost full to bursting after her brunch, she could still feel her mouth water at the thought. Someone had brought a huge batch to the office Christmas party this past December, and she could still remember how amazing they had been—pork, and chicken, and beef, and cheese with green chile.

They were all smiling, sharing the joke at Jack's expense, as they headed back out to the parking lot and Alex's SUV. While he was backing out of their parking space, Kate wished she could come up with an excuse for why they needed to stay out longer, maybe a TJ's run to get some snacks for later this afternoon, after the meal they'd just consumed had begun to wear off. Was there even a Trader Joe's around here? She wasn't super-familiar with this part of Scottsdale, since she lived at nearly the opposite end. She thought there were three in the city altogether, but she couldn't remember for sure. Too late, though, because now they were back on the road and headed toward Jack's apartment complex.

All of a sudden, Caitlin said, "Oh, my God!"—so sharply that Alex swerved and then quickly recovered. He probably thought that she'd seen something in the road, but actually, her head was bent down over her phone.

"What is it?" he asked, his voice sharp with worry.

"I just got a PM from Lucinda. She said, 'Help me—she's gone. They're both gone.'"

Kate's meal seemed to congeal into a heavy lump at the bottom of her gut. "'She'? 'They'? Who's gone? Who's she talking about?"

"I don't know!" Caitlin replied, clearly distraught. Her face was pale. "I—"

And she stopped there, the phone falling from her fingers onto the seat.

"Caitlin!" Alex twisted in his seat, turning to see what the problem was. "Oh, shit—she's having a vision. I'm going to pull over."

All Kate could do was nod as Alex turned sharply into the parking lot of a small business complex, one with computer repair places and a mailbox store. At the edge of the lot were a number of empty spaces, and he pulled into one of them and put the vehicle in park.

During all this, Caitlin had gone stock still, her

blue eyes wide and staring, although they didn't seem to be fixed on any one thing in particular.

"Is she okay?" Kate whispered from the back seat. "Is there anything we should do?"

"Just wait it out," Alex said in a low tone. "Once she comes out of it, she'll be able to tell us what she saw."

"How long will it last?"

His shoulders lifted. "Depends. Sometimes her visions hit and are over with in just a few seconds. Other times, it can be a few minutes."

That sounded awful, to have such a thing come over you with no way of controlling it. For the first time, Kate realized that having supernatural powers wasn't all excitement, that they could have negative consequences on living one's life.

Then Caitlin let out a horrible rattling gasp, and she reached up to grab the "Jesus" handle above her head. "Oh, God," she moaned.

"Water?" Alex asked gently, lifting a plastic bottle from one of the cup holders in the center console.

She shook her head. "I'm all right. It's just—I *saw* it. I saw what was happening to Lucinda. They were all at their house in Pasadena—her and her parents' house, I mean. A man came in through the front door without knocking, just walked in like he owned the place."

"What man? Did you recognize him?"

"No. He was older. Not as old as Simón. Maybe

in his late forties? Dark…Hispanic, I'm pretty sure. He went up to Simón, took him by the throat, and—and *lifted* him. Straight up in the air, like, like Darth Vader or something. Broke his neck." Caitlin paused there and put a hand to her throat, as if she could feel the echoes of the killing blow in her own neck. Her breath came and went, harsh. She sounded like she'd just run a mile, rather than sitting stock still in the passenger seat of an SUV.

"It's okay," Alex began, his tone reassuring, but she only shook her head again.

"No, it's not okay. Because next he, he…." She stopped there, eyes nearly as wide and strained as they had been while she was suffering the vision. "He went up to the *prima* and snapped her neck as well. Just like that. She slumped over in her wheelchair, and then he went up the stairs, like he was going to look for Lucinda. That's where it ended. I couldn't see what happened next."

"Wait," Kate said. She hated to interrupt, despite the horrors that Caitlin had described, and yet she couldn't quite figure out what the young witch was getting at. "I thought the *prima* was, like, all-powerful or something. How could this man just go up to the Santiagos' *prima* and attack her like that? Why didn't she stop him?"

Caitlin shook her head. "I don't know. I don't *know*. How could any of this happen?" She picked up her phone and opened the Messenger app, but clearly there wasn't anything new from Lucinda, because Caitlin let out a hiccupy little noise that sounded like a barely repressed sob and dropped it into her lap.

Alex reached over to touch her shoulder, offering what comfort he could, even as he said, "Beatriz Santiago was weak from spending years as an invalid. We're not talking about a *prima* like Angela, or my mother. Beatriz might not have been able to react quickly enough to even try to defend herself. But this is bad…really bad. I need to call my mother. And Kate, you'd better call Jack, see if we can all meet at my mother's house to talk about this."

"Sure," she said, and got her own phone out of her purse. With shaking fingers, she navigated to her "recent calls" list and found the number for Jack's cell phone, then pressed the little phone icon. As it rang, she listened to Alex make his own call, while at the same time maneuvering the Pathfinder out of its parking space so he could head for home.

No, not home. She didn't think Alex had ever lived in the house where Luz now held sway as the *prima* of the de la Paz clan, and he certainly didn't live there now.

Her own call rolled into Jack's voicemail. Shit. Voice shaking, she left him a brief message, saying only that Caitlin had just had a terrible vision about the Santiago clan's *prima,* that she had been killed, and that the three of them were now headed up to

Luz's place and he should join them there as soon as he could.

There. Kate knew she couldn't do much more than that. She didn't put her phone away, though, but held it clutched in both hands, as though the contact might somehow make Jack call her back more quickly. In the front seat, both Alex and Caitlin were silent. She was bent over her phone, typing away, probably trying to send another message to Lucinda, even though Kate had a feeling it was a wasted effort. Was there anyone else they could call? She was kind of hazy on how that worked, because in general it seemed as if the clans here in Arizona didn't have much to do with the Santiagos.

Alex drove fast, faster than Kate would have considered safe, but she sure wasn't going to say anything about it. His driving wasn't reckless, and maybe he had a "get out of jail free" card because his cousin was with the Scottsdale P.D. She sure couldn't fault him for wanting to get to his mother's house as quickly as possible.

Problem was, Kate really didn't see what Luz—or Jack, or anyone else—could do to change the tragedy that had already occurred, what might still be occurring. And that was the worst feeling of all.

Being helpless.

11

Jack could feel his phone buzz in his pocket, but he ignored it because right then he was getting an ass-chewing from his supervisor.

"You let them go?" Larry asked, his normally ruddy complexion redder than ever at the moment because of his irritation.

"They all had alibis, Larry," Jack replied. Even Bret Harkins, who was probably guilty of a lot of things, but not, unfortunately, Jeff Nichols' murder. "You think I don't want to get this thing buttoned up as soon as I can? I get why you had them brought in for a closer look, but none of them were our guy."

"You sure spent a lot of time talking to Harkins, though."

"Because I thought he might have some information. No," Jack went on quickly, when it looked as if Larry intended to interject some kind of comment, "not because he actually committed the crime—Harkins is no saint, but I don't think he's capable of the kind of violence we saw in Nichols' murder—but because he said a few things that made my spider sense tingle. Unfortunately, it was all a dead end. I'm pretty sure our murderer is someone who's not on the radar at all, someone without a record."

"Great," Larry groused. "Because right now we have shit-all when it comes to leads. The killer didn't leave behind a single shred of physical evidence, so we have nothing to go on from that angle. No witnesses. No nothing."

All Jack could do was give a sympathy shrug, because Larry only spoke the truth. Of course, Jack did have slightly more to work with, just because he had the whole warlock angle to explore, but he couldn't mention that to his boss. He walked a fine line here and he knew it, but at the end of the day, his loyalty was to his clan and to the witching world as a whole, not the Scottsdale police department. Most of the time, those loyalties weren't in conflict. This time…well, his path was clear enough when it came to either obliging his supervisor or making sure nothing about the de la Paz clan or any other witches or warlocks ever saw the light of day.

"Something will turn up," he said, trying to sound as reassuring as possible. "It's early days yet. You know how sometimes these things break wide open, seemingly out of nowhere."

"Sometimes," Larry said. "On the other hand, sometimes they just add to the cold case files that keep stacking up. Anyway, what's the word on the widow? You think you need to talk to her again?"

"I doubt it," Jack replied. One thing he had to do was make sure that Kate was absolutely cleared of any suspicion. Some might have wanted to make her the bad guy, just because that was the easiest route, but he would not allow that to happen. No matter what. "She had nothing to do with any of it. Just bad luck that she went by that particular day to drop off her divorce papers. It's clear from Jeff Nichols' phone records that the last time they'd spoken before that night was nearly a week earlier. She was doing her best to maintain her distance. Anyway, she's down at her parents' house in Tempe, lying low. She let me know that she got harassed by some reporters and didn't want to stick around her apartment, and so decided to get out for a while."

"Well, as long as she's around," Larry grumbled, clearly not thrilled by the situation, but not annoyed enough that he would require Kate to return home. After all, Tempe wasn't that far away. It wasn't as if she'd taken her passport and made a run for Mexico or something.

"Trust me, she's not going anywhere," Jack said. In his pocket, his phone buzzed again, reminding him that he had a voicemail he needed to listen to. "If that was all you needed?"

"Until I think of something else."

Deciding to ignore that somewhat ominous response, Jack nodded and then headed out of Larry's office and down the hall to his own. As he walked, he pulled the phone from his pocket and checked his missed calls. Kate's number. Damn it.

He went into his office, although he didn't close the door behind him. Larry didn't like closed doors. He was all about transparency. Jack shuddered to think what his boss would do if he ever found out that one of his top detectives also happened to be a warlock. As secrets went, that was kind of a biggie.

As soon as he sat down, he tapped his phone's screen to listen to Kate's voicemail.

The Santiagos. The *prima* killed. What did that mean? Had Beatriz Santiago died in an accident? Had she been murdered? With everything that had been going on, Jack suspected the worst.

Jesus Christ.

At once he got back up from his chair, shoved the phone in his pocket, and began hurrying for the exit to the parking lot. In the hallway, he passed Grace Pedersen, who lifted an inquiring eyebrow at him.

"Going somewhere?"

"Uh, yeah—a possible lead in the Nichols case. I shouldn't be gone long."

"A new witness?"

"Something like that." He hated lying to her, but he sure as hell couldn't tell her the truth.

"I hope it pans out," Grace said. "Because when it comes to physical evidence, we're pretty much screwed. Ian and I went back to Nichols' apartment and did another pass, and we still found bupkis."

"I'll keep you posted," Jack responded, and then offered a smile and kept going. He didn't have time to hang around the station and hold her hand. Yes, it was frustrating to be completely stymied like that, but it was also part of the job.

Since he didn't know how long he was going to be gone, or what might happen next, he took his own vehicle rather than the unmarked car assigned to him. Gunning the Jeep and racing out of the parking lot would only attract attention, so he did his best to drive with care—at least until he was a few blocks away from the station. Then he sped up, although not to excess. Luckily, Luz's home was only about a half-mile away from his work. He'd be at his destination in a couple of minutes.

When he stopped in front of the gracious hacienda-style home, he saw Alex's black Pathfinder parked in the driveway. Good. He wouldn't have to wait on Alex and Caitlin and Kate, but, more importantly, they'd gotten here safely, hadn't been blindsided the way Kate had been when she'd tried to drive away from the impound lot.

Jack got out of his vehicle and all but ran up to the gate that opened into the courtyard. Since he was family, he let himself in, ignoring the buzzer mounted into the stucco wall next to the gate. He did knock at the front door, simply because he knew Luz always kept it locked, and he knew better than to use his powers to waltz right in, no matter how urgent the situation might be.

She answered his knock right away, almost as though she'd been standing next to the door, waiting for him. Although she looked, as usual, like she'd just come from lunch at the country club or something, in her linen sheath dress and low-heeled sandals, he didn't miss the tension in her posture, or the strained expression in her eyes.

"Thank God," she said, closing the door behind him. "I was just about to try calling you again, even though Kate said she left a message."

"I was talking to my supervisor when she called," he explained. "I retrieved the voicemail as soon as I could, and then came straight over here."

"Everyone's waiting in the living room. And I've tried to call the number I have for Beatriz and Simón Santiago, but it just rings and rings. It doesn't even go to voicemail."

As Jack gave the *prima* a grim nod, Luz led him out of the foyer and to the room in question, where Kate and Alex and Caitlin sat on the couch. A pitcher of iced tea and matching blue-rimmed glasses sat on the coffee table, but it didn't look as if anyone had helped themselves to the beverage yet.

Jack did what he could to prevent himself from

looking at Kate first, but it was difficult. He still needed to reassure himself that she was okay, that she hadn't suffered any lasting harm from the car accident the day before. Although she appeared paler than usual, and her wide, friendly mouth was set in tense lines, she otherwise seemed to be just fine.

Alex and Caitlin held hands, and sat very close to one another. Well, Jack could see why the seer would need as much reassurance as possible, after witnessing something like what Kate had mentioned in her voicemail.

After nodding at all of them, Jack took a seat in one of the empty armchairs that faced the couch, while Luz settled herself in the one remaining chair. "Caitlin," he said, and she startled slightly, and grasped Alex's hand even tighter, as though she feared what Jack was about to say. "Was this a real-time vision, or a glimpse of the future?"

"Real time," she replied, her voice shaky, although she hadn't hesitated before answering him. "That is, the text I got from Lucinda came through just a minute before the vision did. She must have been hiding in her room when it happened."

Damn it. Jack ran a hand through his hair. He'd been hoping against hope that the horrors Caitlin had seen were something which could be prevented. No such luck, though.

"What are we supposed to do now?" Alex asked. His eyes went to his mother, who sat still as a statue on her leather chair. "Has anything like this ever happened before?"

Luz moistened her lips, then shook her head. "No. At least, not in any of the history of our clan, which goes back more than three hundred years. I suppose it's possible that in less civilized times, these sorts of coups against a *prima* and her family might have been attempted, but I've never heard of such a thing. To murder a *prima*—it goes against everything that witch society is built on."

"Well, clearly this person didn't have any scruples about committing such a crime," Jack said grimly. He shifted his attention back to Caitlin, who looked as if she was in need of a much stiffer drink than iced tea. "Caitlin, were you able to tell whether Simón or Beatriz tried to defend themselves?"

A small silence as the seer frowned, clearly trying to wring every detail out of the horrible vision she'd just endured. "I—I think I saw Simón lift his hands, as though he was trying to cast some sort of spell, but nothing happened. And afterward, the man who killed him took him by the neck and lifted him right off the ground. That's when his neck snapped. Beatriz was sitting across the room in her wheelchair, and again, it looked like she was trying to do something— her lips were moving—but it didn't seem to have any effect." Caitlin stopped there, fear and worry twisting her pretty features. "I don't understand how that could happen. I mean, I know that as far as *primas* go,

Beatriz Santiago wasn't all that powerful. But she still should have been able to stop that man from killing her husband, or herself. It was almost as though none of their magic was having any effect."

Listening to those words, Jack felt a chill go through his body. A terrible suspicion began to form, although he wasn't sure he wanted to acknowledge it. Doing so would mean they'd all have to confront the fact that this murderer possessed a magical gift which hadn't been seen in generations, one that could do terrible harm if the person born with it didn't do everything in his power to curb his talent.

Ignoring the problem wouldn't make it go away, however. Better to face it head on, and try to come up with some way to solve it.

"It sounds like the attacker is a null," he said.

"A what?" Alex asked, his brows pulling together. Obviously, he'd never heard the term before. And, judging by the equally bewildered expression Caitlin wore, neither had she. Kate also looked mystified, but that was to be expected. She knew a little of the witch world, just because her brother had married into the McAllisters, but she certainly wouldn't possess this kind of knowledge. Nearly forgotten concepts such as a null would never have been mentioned to her, because so few people knew of them.

But Luz obviously understood. Her body went stiff, even as she gave an almost imperceptible shake of her head, as though she didn't want to acknowledge what Jack had just said. Her hands knotted together in her lap as she twisted the gold wedding band on her ring finger. "A null," she said, in a clear, precise voice, as if discussing the topic in a nuts-and-bolts fashion would make it a little less difficult to deal with, "is a witch or a warlock whose talent is suppressing all other magic around them. It's very likely that both Simón and Beatriz did try to defend themselves, but were unsuccessful because the null's gift—if you can call it that—canceled them out."

"A null is powerful enough to defeat even a *prima's* magic?" Alex asked, his tone clearly skeptical.

"Oh, yes," Jack said. Across from him, sitting quietly on the sofa, Kate straightened, her worried hazel eyes meeting his for just a second before she glanced away. What he saw in those eyes...well, he didn't want to acknowledge it. Especially not right then, with Luz and Caitlin and Alex watching him. "A null is sort of like a black hole, except what he pulls into himself is magic. Other people's magic. You can't defeat that. It doesn't matter how strong your own gift might be. Now, if the null is an honorable person, a good person, then they won't use their talent to harm or take advantage of others. The problem is when you get someone like the man Caitlin saw in her vision." He shifted in his chair, directing his next words to Luz. "Have you ever heard of a null in Santiago territory?"

"No," she replied. "Not that our clans ever had

that much communication—you know as well as I do that we tend to keep to ourselves. But such a thing… such a terrible talent…that might have come out. I have heard of no such person, though, not from the Santiagos, certainly not from any of the Arizona clans, and not from the Castillos in New Mexico, either. Wherever this man came from, it is nowhere around here. The question we must ask is, why did he attack the Santiagos now? To what purpose?"

"Well, wouldn't he be trying to take over?" Kate asked then, prompting everyone else to send a curious look in her direction, as though they were surprised she would comment at all on a subject so far outside her own experience. "I mean, that sounds like the most logical explanation for his crimes. Didn't Matías Escobar try basically the same thing, by attempting to kidnap your *prima*-in waiting?"

"And eliminating my mother through the use of vile blood magic," Luz said, the bitterness clear in her tone. "Yes, you are right, Kate. No doubt that is his goal, although I am not sure what he plans to do with the Santiagos' *prima*-in-waiting. She is young—in her middle twenties—but still, she has been bonded with her consort for several years. It is not as though this interloper will be able to have a true consort bond with her."

"But he doesn't have to," Alex pointed out. "Matías knew he probably wouldn't have the bond with Zoe, either, but it would be enough to be with her, to control her. He'd still have the power he wanted."

"Who is the *prima*-in-waiting for the Santiagos?" Jack asked then. Already he worried that they were too late, but they had to do their best to try to contact her…if there was any time left at all.

"Marisol Valdez," Luz replied. "She is Beatriz's niece, and also lives in Pasadena. But I don't know if I have her contact information."

"Check anyway."

A nod, and Luz got up from her chair and headed down the hallway toward the secondary bedroom that Jack knew she used as her office. After she was gone, Alex said, "Is contacting her really going to do any good? I mean, if what you said about a null's power is true…."

"It would give her a chance to run," Jack told him. "That's about all she could do. But she could leave, and come take refuge with us."

"Could we protect her, though?" Caitlin asked then. She still looked far too pale, but her gaze was steady enough as she met Jack's eyes. "Could *anyone* help her?"

"I'm not sure," he said truthfully. "Even a null might think twice about facing down a large number of witches and warlocks. But I don't really know. It's been so long since we've had to deal with this kind of magic that we don't have any real data."

That reply certainly didn't reassure her; she

shrank up against Alex, who let go of her hand and dropped an arm around her shoulders. That shifting of her position made Kate look even more alone as she sat at one end of the couch, back straight, hands folded in her lap. Right then, Jack had a foolish but nearly overwhelming urge to go to her and hold her the way Alex held Caitlin, just so she'd know someone was here to look out for her, but he could only imagine Kate's reaction—not to mention the reactions of his family members—if he were to do such a thing.

Luz returned then, a small address book in one hand and the handset for a cordless phone in the other. "I actually do have her number. But I just tried to call, and it went through to her voicemail."

Of course it did. Anxious tension knotted the muscles of his neck and shoulders, but Jack kept his voice calm as he said, "Try again. She might just be out running errands, or picking up her kids from school."

"She doesn't have any children," Luz said.

Right. Luz had told him that when they were discussing the Santiago clan just the day before. "Grocery store, then. Whatever. Just try."

Her expression dubious, Luz entered a number into the keypad of the phone, then held it up to her ear. Even from where he sat, Jack could hear the phone ring and ring, and then a cheerful woman's voice say, "Hi, this is Marisol. Tony and I can't take your call right now, but if you'd like to leave a message…."

Jack shook his head at Luz, and she took the phone away from her ear and pressed the button to end the call. As she set the handset down on the coffee table, she shot him an inquiring glance.

"If the null has already gotten to her, the last thing we want is for him to know that we know what he's up to. We have to hope he doesn't know anything about Caitlin's powers, that we have the ability to see what he's done, even though he's hundreds of miles away from us."

"I saw one thing," Caitlin said, her voice gloomy. "Just one thing. This is what I *hate* about this damn talent of mine. It shows me what it wants to show me. Life would be so much easier if I could just make it show me things on command. Then I would be able to see what this bastard is doing right now."

"I know it's frustrating," Jack said, as Alex hugged his wife a little tighter. "But even that one vision gave us a whole lot of information. We could be flying completely blind in terms of this coup within the Santiago clan. Thanks to you, though, we do know something. Don't sell yourself short."

"But…." Caitlin stopped there, her body going rigid within Alex's embrace. A strangled-sounding gasp emerged from her throat, and she stared at Jack with white-rimmed eyes that reminded him of a startled horse.

"Oh, shit," Alex said. "Another one." He continued to hold Caitlin, as though he knew she would fall over if he didn't prop her up. "They don't usually come this close together."

"Let's be glad they have this time," Luz said. "Perhaps she will be able to give us more information so we can help Marisol."

Jack agreed, although he had to admit it was unnerving to watch Caitlin while she was in the grip of one of her visions. This was the first time for him, and there was something very disconcerting about seeing the way she completely lost contact with the world around her, as though her body was still there but her mind was ranging someplace very far away.

And he could also tell that it upset Kate, though she didn't move from where she sat, made herself remain quiet and still, clearly worried that any movement on her part would knock Caitlin loose from her vision. Once again her eyes met his, only this time they were wide and frightened, seeking some form of reassurance in a world that must have felt as if it had gone completely mad.

Then Caitlin gasped, and sat bolt upright. She looked around, as if she needed to remind herself where she was. Her chest heaved, and tears stood out in her eyes. "Tea?" she whispered, voice hoarse.

At once Alex reached for the glass that sat before her on the coffee table, then placed it gently in both hands and wrapped her fingers around it, as though he worried that she might drop the iced tea if she didn't have a firm grip on it. "What is it?" he asked, soft but urgent. "What did you see?"

A teardrop slipped from the corner of one eye and ran down her cheek. "We can't help her," she replied. She raised the glass of iced tea to her lips and took a large swallow, then another. "He has her."

"The null?" Jack said.

She nodded. "He—he went to her house. Walked in just like he did at Simón and Beatriz's home. Marisol was sitting on the couch, crying. I guess—I guess it must have been because she sensed her aunt's death, felt the *prima* powers come to her?"

"Probably," Luz put in, her voice quiet and calm, although Jack could see the way the muscles in her neck tensed as she swallowed. "The *prima*-in-waiting can always feel it, even if she doesn't have the privilege of being at the *prima*'s side as she dies."

"There was a man with Marisol," Caitlin continued. "He was comforting her, and had a set of car keys in his hand. It looked like they were about to leave and go find out what had happened. But then...."

Alex pushed a lock of fiery hair away from his wife's face. "Then the null came?"

"Yes. He walked right in, just as he did at Beatriz and Simón's house. Marisol started to get up, to ask him what the hell he thought he was doing, but the null ignored her and went to the man with her. Dragged him away, and broke his neck just like he did to Simón. Marisol screamed, and the null went to her and pulled her close. She struggled, but he whispered something in her ear, and for some reason, she stopped fighting, went limp in his arms. Then he picked her up and carried her down the hall, away from the living room. The vision ended there."

Thank God, Jack thought grimly. *Caitlin is traumatized enough already without having to watch some monster rape the Santiagos' new* prima.

Dead silence. Everyone knew exactly what must have happened next, but there was no way in hell any of them were going to say it out loud.

Luz spoke first, her usually warm-toned voice taut, strained. "So the Santiagos have fallen. What do we do next?"

"You should contact Connor and Angela," Jack said. "They need to know what's going on, because it may come down to all of us presenting a united front in order to defeat this bastard."

"Of course. What else?"

There was a damn good question. Everything Caitlin had just related sickened him, even though, because of his work, he was used to seeing the worst that humanity had to offer. At the same time, his brain started picking through the facts at hand, trying to find the connections. What did the horrifying events in Southern California have to do with Jeff Nichols' murder, or the hex on Kate's car? Maybe nothing. Maybe they were all just a hideous coincidence.

He didn't believe that, though. If he could just figure out which thread to pull, then he might be able to unravel the whole sordid tapestry. In the meantime, the de la Paz clan had to hunker down and prepare for the worst—as did the McAllisters and the Wilcoxes. Jack supposed it was possible that, having accomplished his terrible goal, the null might rest on his laurels, would leave them all alone. He doubted it, however. The man had shown a ruthlessness on a level that even Jack hadn't encountered before. There was something going on here, something he couldn't yet figure out.

Which meant Kate was still in danger. No, she didn't have any magical talents that the null would wish to usurp, but, as her estranged husband's death had proved, dark warlocks had uses for ordinary humans, uses conjured from their very blood and pain. If the null was seeking some strange form of revenge against the McAllisters or those close to them, then she still could be the next target. Which meant he had to do everything he could to keep her safe.

How, though? Jack had the impression that the null—and anyone who might be working for him—possessed far more knowledge about his targets than he should. There was that hex on Kate's car. How could they have known where it was being kept? It was as though they were being watched.

Another seer? Maybe, but every single seer he'd met or known of experienced much the same problems as Caitlin in terms of controlling what they saw. This type of surveillance felt far more comprehensive.

Everyone was watching him, waiting for him to answer Luz. The weight of their combined gazes, of their hope that he would offer a solution, was almost a palpable thing. Problem was, he didn't have any answers right now. Just more and more questions. He wiped his damp palms on the knees of his khakis and said, "Well, for one thing, no one goes anywhere alone. Luz, call David and have him come here to be with you. Caitlin and Alex, make sure you're never separated."

Alex stirred uneasily on the couch. "What am I supposed to tell them at work?"

"Tell them whatever you want. Family emergency. I don't care."

"Are you going to do the same thing?"

There was a faintly challenging note to Alex's question. Clearly, he didn't appear too eager to follow instructions from someone who wouldn't take his own advice.

"Yes, I am," Jack said firmly. "I'll take a leave of absence."

"What about the investigation?" Kate asked. She was still huddled into a corner of the couch, clearly scared out of her mind, even though she was doing her best to look calm. But her hand shook slightly as she pushed back a lock of hair that had fallen over her shoulder, and her voice was too tight, too controlled.

"Anything I would have been doing at the station would have been busywork. The real investigation is the stuff I'd have to follow up on after hours, because it would involve the witch world, not the civilian one."

She nodded at that reply, and went quiet. Good. Not that he didn't want to speak to her, but they didn't have time right now for arguments. Clearly, she understood what was at stake.

"He cannot come after all of us," Luz said then, her chin up and her eyes fierce. "The only way he could do so would be to rally all the Santiagos to follow him, and I don't see that happening, not when he is responsible for the deaths of their *prima* and her consort, and the consort of the *prima*-in-waiting as well."

"Even if he threatens them with taking their magic away?" Kate asked in a small voice.

"He cannot do such a thing. The null's power only affects those in his immediate range. Yes, he is obviously a cold and practiced killer, but it is not as if he can reach across the miles and burn the magic out of a person. Even Connor and Angela had to have Matías Escobar and his cousins in their immediate presence to take away their powers. I am not saying that it would be easy to take out the null, because anyone who approached him would lose their own powers, but at least it would be a temporary loss."

"Where's this house in Pasadena?" Kate sounded a little more in control now, possibly because she was trying to come up with a way to defeat the null, rather than sitting back and worrying that he was going to come after all of them. "Maybe the best thing to do would be to drop a bomb on it or something."

Jack studied her face. She was dead serious. On the surface, her suggestion did sound like a plausible solution. After all, a null's powers were formidable, but even he probably wouldn't survive a strike by a couple of carefully targeted missiles.

A shake of the head, and Alex said, "We're a witch clan, not the army. And even if we had the resources to do such a thing, we still wouldn't risk it because of the collateral damage. Marisol lives in a house in Pasadena, not out in the middle of the desert somewhere. We'd be putting innocent civilians at risk."

"Oh, I knew you really wouldn't do something like that. It's just…if this guy can render all your magical powers ineffective, how are you supposed to get rid of him?"

"I don't know." Alex glanced over at his mother, and then at Jack. "Do either of you?"

"Not yet," Jack said. "But we'll figure it out. In the meantime, be careful. At least Caitlin knows what this man looks like. Can you give us some more details, Cate?"

She knotted her fingers together and gave an uneasy swallow. Obviously, she wasn't too keen to go back and study her memories of the null's features in any detail, and Jack couldn't really blame her. But she was the only one who'd seen his face.

When she spoke, it was slowly, as if she needed to make sure of every detail before she passed it on to her watching audience. "Like I said, he looked as though he was in his middle or late forties. Hispanic. Dark wavy hair, sort of slicked back from his face. He was…." Her mouth twisted. "I hate to say it, but I guess, objectively speaking, you'd say he was attractive, for an older guy."

As someone who was only a decade away from being in his middle forties, Jack had to keep from smiling at Caitlin's "older guy" comment. "Anything else?" he asked, doing his best to sound neutral.

"Tallish but not super-tall. He has interesting eyes…sort of a diagonal crease over his eyelids, if you know what I mean. Deep-set dark eyes. His clothes were pretty plain—he had on khaki pants and a light-colored shirt, although I couldn't tell if it was ivory or white." She sighed, and tucked a strand of hair behind her ear. "And that's about all I can remember."

"It's very good. It'll help a lot," Jack told her, even as he wished he could bring her to the station so she could go over her description of the null with one of the sketch artists there. Subjecting her recollections to that kind of rigor would probably give them a much better picture of the dark warlock. Unfortunately, Jack knew that taking Caitlin to the police station would only raise a lot of questions he didn't want to answer, and so he put that notion aside. The information she'd provided was still enough to let them know who—or what—to avoid.

The small shrug she gave in reply to his words told him that she wasn't so sure, even though she didn't look like she wanted to argue the point.

"Well, then," Luz said. "We know something of who this criminal is. I'll call Connor and Angela. Alex, you might as well take Caitlin home—and go get your sister Alicia when you're back in Tucson. I don't feel comfortable having her alone in that dorm. She can stay in your spare bedroom."

"She's not going to like that," Alex remarked, to which his mother raised her eyebrows.

"It's not a matter of what she does or doesn't like. If she doesn't want to stay at your house, then you can tell her to come up here and stay with her father and me."

"Good one," Alex said, smiling despite the seriousness of the situation. "Because I know she'd have a fit if she had to miss any classes when she was so close to graduating."

"My thoughts exactly. And since getting into veterinary school depends on her completing her undergraduate work, well, I am sure she will find herself sufficiently motivated to stay with you."

Jack couldn't help but be impressed by the way his cousin managed that situation. If the null decided to go after Alicia for some reason, she might be safer with her brother. Yes, his protective magic wouldn't work, but the kid was in good shape. He might be able to prevail physically, if not magically.

"And I," Jack said, "am going to take Kate back to my place and try to see if there's a connection we've been missing."

Tilting her head to one side, Kate asked, "Aren't you supposed to be on shift until seven?"

So she'd made a careful note of that. Had she been counting the hours until he got off work? No, he'd better not flatter himself. "I am," he said calmly. "But I was going to have to take off anyway. I'll say it's a family emergency, that a relative in California has been murdered. That's both serious enough to warrant a leave of absence, but conveniently well out of the Scottsdale P.D.'s jurisdiction." And, he thought, it was only a bit of a stretch. Someone had been murdered in California—three people, actually—and one might say that all witches and warlocks were connected in a way. Not family exactly, but close enough.

His response appeared to satisfy Kate, because she nodded but didn't say anything else.

"All right," Luz said. "I'll start spreading the word, let everyone know what's happened and what this null looks like. I have a feeling that Angela and Connor will probably want to discuss this in person. I'll let you know, Jack, if they want to speak to you as well."

"Sounds good." He got up from his chair and looked over at Kate, and a second later, she stood as well. Caitlin and Alex followed suit, and soon after that, everyone was moving for the front door. Jack paused at the gate and looked up and down the street, but he didn't see anything more suspicious than someone driving by in one of those reverse-trike-style motorcycles.

Kate said her goodbyes to the couple, and Jack waved as they headed to the Pathfinder and got in. Then he turned to the woman who stood a few feet away, clutching her purse and looking both frightened and somehow shy, like she'd just realized that she was going to be left alone with him again and didn't know what the hell to do about it.

Well, that made two of them.

12

––––––––

KATE STARED OUT THE WINDOW AS JACK DROVE them away from Luz's house and to the northwest part of Scottsdale, where his apartment was located. Her heart kept giving odd little nervous thumps, although she honestly didn't know whether that was because of the dreadful news she'd just heard, or because Jack Sandoval was sitting only a foot or so away from her.

Which was really the dumbest damn thing to be focusing on. All this death, all these horrors, and yet her stupid brain kept obsessing over details like the fine outline of his profile, the strength of his hands as they gripped the steering wheel. Maybe it was only a way to distract herself…and Jack was pretty damn distracting. Kate thought it much better to fixate on the muscles under his dress shirt, rather than mentally go over the terrible things Caitlin had seen in her vision. All those people dead. A young woman forced to bend to the null's will. And an entire clan with their leadership gone. A coup for sure, but definitely not a bloodless one.

"Are you okay?" Jack asked after a while, casting a worried sideways glance in her direction before returning his attention to the road. Although it was barely midafternoon by that point, traffic had begun to thicken. Maybe there were a lot of parents on the road, heading out to pick up their kids from school.

For some reason, that thought made Kate's throat tighten. All these people going about their business, about their ordinary lives, with absolutely no knowledge of the evil that might lurk under the surface.

Her brunch had to have been mostly digested by then, and yet she suddenly felt queasy. She wished she didn't know about any of these things, either. She wished the world would go back to the way it had been two days ago, when the biggest worry in her life had been how Jeff would react when she finally did show up with the divorce papers.

"I'm…." She let the words trail off, then shook her head and forced herself to start over. "Well, I can't say I'm okay, because that would be a lie. But I'm holding it together. I think."

"I understand," he said. And he did sound understanding, his voice calm and somehow soothing. Was that how he talked to the survivors at a crime scene? She couldn't remember exactly how he'd sounded when he spoke to her. Too many upheavals must have rattled her brain. "It's a lot to take in. Hell, I'm having a hard time with it, and I'm—" He stopped then, as if he wasn't quite sure what he'd meant to say.

"You're a warlock?" Kate asked. "You should be used to this kind of stuff?"

"Well, I don't know about 'used to it.' What happened in California…that's unprecedented. Like we said, we can't think of anything like this ever happening before, such a targeted strike at a *prima* and her family. Maybe back in the dark ages or something, when we were all killing each other with axes and swords and the deadliest spells we could cook up, but…."

She shifted in her seat so she could get a better look at the expression he currently wore. Jack looked serious enough, but there was the slightest lift at the corner of his mouth, as though he might be joking just a little.

Maybe.

"How far back do your witch families go?" Kate asked.

"As far back as we can remember. The de la Paz clan has been here in southern Arizona for hundreds of years, long before it was part of the United States. I don't know as much about the Wilcoxes and McAllisters, but I'm pretty sure they had a long history in England and Scotland before their families immigrated to America."

She thought about that for a moment. It made sense, of course—everyone had to have come from somewhere. Her father's family had also immigrated to America from Scotland, whereas her mother was sort of a mutt, a mixture of German and Irish and English and a tiny bit of Welsh. "And you weren't always as peaceful as you are now?"

His shoulders lifted. "Actually, I was joking about throwing spells at each other…mostly. Back then, just like now, most witch-folk just wanted to fly low and avoid the radar. It's never a good idea to let other people know that you possess magical powers. Nowadays we'd just get poked and prodded by doctors and scientists, I suppose—and possibly questioned by the NSA—but back then when the consequences of being found out included getting burned at the stake, well, our ancestors kind of wanted to keep things on the down-low." He turned off Scottsdale Road and continued west before adding, "So anyway, witch clans tend to be respectful of one another's territory, because the last thing any of us can afford is the sort of all-out war that would attract notice."

"How many clans are there?"

"I have no idea," he replied. Although he wasn't looking at her, he seemed to register her surprise at his reply, because he went on, "There are people in my clan who keep track of all the families and all their territories and such, but that's never been something I paid a lot of attention to. We all stay where we come from, pretty much. Here in Arizona there's some mixing of the clans, now more than there used to be, thanks to Angela and Connor joining the McAllisters and the Wilcoxes. In general, though we don't cross state lines without permission. The Wilcoxes have been on friendly terms with the Castillos in New Mexico for more than a hundred years, though, so I think there must have been some travel involved between the two of them. Because we're so territorial, it means we don't have a lot of need to know everything about clans in states on the other side of the country…or the other side of the world."

"So you're everywhere."

"Oh, yeah, witches are global. Everyone has their own particular flavor of magic, from what I've heard, but some things are universal, like the basic spells we all can do, and certain talents, like being a seer or a healer or someone like me, someone whose strength is defensive magic. Then you get the odd talents like Alex's, or your sister-in-law's overwhelming mind reading, some of which seem to be unique, and some which can skip generations before they crop up again."

"Like the null."

The small hint of a smile Jack had worn during the previous discussion disappeared immediately. "Yes, like him. I think a lot of people were probably hoping that particular talent had died out. Even when the person who was born with it was a decent human being, the null 'gift' still had so much potential to be misused."

Kate could see that. The temptation to use that talent to get back at your enemies, or to exert a little leverage on a business partner, or a spouse…she could see why it would have been much better to be consigned to the ash heap of history. It certainly seemed as if the null who had just gone on his killing spree in Southern California was on some sort of vendetta.

"Anyway," Jack said, "there are a lot of us, probably hundreds of thousands worldwide. And since we don't know much about other witch clans, except the ones that directly border our own lands, we have a real problem now trying to figure out where this guy came from. He literally could be from anywhere."

Caitlin had said he looked Hispanic, though. Which meant he could be from Southern California…or New Mexico…Texas…or Mexico itself. Or South America, or Spain or Portugal. Who knew? But they'd have to find out, or else they would have no way of discovering what it was that had driven him on this mission of revenge against the Santiagos. Or was it revenge at all? Maybe the null had been looking for an opening for a long time, and finally struck because he deemed Beatriz Santiago weak enough. There was just so much they didn't know.

Jack pulled into the parking lot of his apartment complex and then went easy on the speed bumps until they got to the carport closest to his building. After he turned off the ignition, he said, "Let me come around and open the door for you. Don't get out of the car until I'm there."

In another world, she might have thought he was merely being chivalrous. Now she knew that he wanted to make sure he was right there in case the worst happened. But would the person who'd hexed her car really be so brazen as to attack the two of them in broad daylight in a parking lot in Scottsdale?

Well, someone had been brazen enough to murder three people in the late morning in Pasadena, so anything was possible.

As instructed, Kate stayed in her seat until Jack came around. After he opened the door, he extended a hand to help her out. Although she tried to stay as cool and unflustered as possible, she couldn't quite prevent a thrill from going through her as she slid her hand into Jack's and felt his strong fingers close around hers.

All too soon, though, he'd let go and pressed the remote to lock the vehicle. He stood next to her for a few seconds, scanning the parking lot, but apparently he didn't see anything suspicious, because a moment later he said, "Come on. Everything looks clear."

She followed him along the walkway that led to his building, and then up the stairs to his apartment. He already had his keys out, so within another minute, they were safely inside, with Jack locking the door behind them.

Only…the apartment clearly wasn't safe, because instead of the orderly, somewhat austere interior she'd expected to see, it appeared as if a whirlwind had hit the place. The leather furniture was slashed, the stuffing strewn everywhere. The TV looked as if someone had put a foot through it.

"Oh, my God," Kate said, a hand going to her mouth. A second later, a terrible thought went through her mind. Had she somehow bungled locking the front door? Was this all her fault?

But no, she'd seen Jack unlock the door just a minute earlier. Both the deadbolt and the lower lock had been engaged. Anyway, an unlocked apartment was more an invitation to theft, not the utter destruction she saw around her.

He stood a few paces away from her, mouth grim. Then he said, "I need to check the rest of it out. Stick close to me." And he drew the gun from his shoulder holster, clicking off the safety as he did so.

She nodded, mouth too dry for her to give a verbal reply. More than anything, she wished she could reach out and take his hand in hers, more for reassurance than anything else, but she didn't want to distract him.

They moved farther back into the apartment, encountering much the same destruction—the bookcases in the study toppled, the laptop hurled to the floor and stomped on repeatedly. In the master bedroom, the bedclothes had been torn to shreds, the lamps smashed, the mirror hanging above the dresser broken into a thousand glittering pieces.

Seven years of bad luck, Kate thought then. But bad luck for whom? Jack, or the person who caused all this destruction?

He peered into the bathroom and Kate followed suit. The mirror there had been broken as well, the toiletries from the medicine cabinet and the drawers strewn all over the floor.

"Don't think I'm getting my security deposit back," he said with a grim chuckle.

"I'm sorry," she murmured.

"It's fine. I'm just thanking God right now that you and Caitlin and Alex had decided to go out, and weren't here when this…person…did all this."

He headed out of the bedroom and back toward the front of the apartment. As Kate looked on, he reached up with his free hand to trace around the lintel of the door, then shook his head.

"They're gone," he told her. "I put sigils of protection all around this door, and around the windows and sliding glass door as well. But they've been erased."

"So this wasn't an ordinary burglar."

"Oh, no. I have a feeling this is the handiwork of the same person who put the hex on your car."

"So whoever that is, they can't be the same as the null."

"I doubt it, unless he also possesses the power to teleport himself hundreds of miles. I suppose there's the remotest chance that he could have caught a flight to Phoenix immediately after he committed those murders in Pasadena, but from what Caitlin said, it sounded as if he was going to be occupied for a while."

Kate shuddered. Yes, the vision had ended before things could get too explicit, but she had no doubt as to what had happened next. And why hadn't the new *prima* fought back? Kate knew if she'd been placed in similar horrifying circumstances, she would have clawed and kicked and done everything she could to keep herself from being taken by the monster who'd just killed her husband. But Marisol had fallen into the null's arms as if he'd been whispering sweet nothings in her ear.

She'd need to ask Jack about that at some point. Could witches and warlocks have more than one prominent talent? Maybe the null could also control people's minds, the way that Matías Escobar apparently had been able to.

Still almost expressionless, Jack turned away from the front door. "Well, whoever did this, it's obvious we can't stay here. Let's check to see if any of your things were damaged."

Kate nodded and went back to the spare

bedroom, where she'd stashed her overnight bag on the floor of the closet. She had to step around the books that had been hurled all over the floor, but when she got to the closet and opened it, her weekender bag was still sitting there, apparently untouched. It didn't look as if the intruder had gone into the closet at all.

"Let me see it," Jack instructed her, and she handed the bag over to him.

He ran his hands over its surface, then said, "It's clean. I was worried that the intruder might have put a hex on it—sort of a witchy tracking device—but I can't feel anything. I think it's okay." After making one last pass, clearly trying to reassure himself, Jack gave the bag back to her.

"My other stuff is still in the guest bath," she pointed out.

"We'll check that, too."

However, when she retrieved her toiletries case from underneath the sink where she'd stowed it, Jack couldn't find anything off about that, either. This bathroom appeared completely untouched, as though the person who'd come here and wreaked all this havoc had decided the guest bath wasn't worth their time. Maybe it didn't have enough of Jack's imprint on it, or something like that. Whatever the reason, Kate couldn't help but let out a relieved breath. Yes, she had a ton more important things to worry about, but it still felt good to know that she wouldn't have to replace all her makeup and toiletries.

Jack headed into the destruction of his bedroom, his expression once again giving no indication of what he was thinking. With quick, efficient movements, he went to the closet and retrieved a leather overnight bag from the top shelf, then started throwing clothes into it. Kate couldn't help but notice that he wasn't packing any "work" clothes—she saw jeans and T-shirts and a couple more casual long-sleeved shirts, but nothing like the button-down and khakis he currently had on.

She turned away and pretended to be inspecting the damage in the bathroom as he began to collect some of the underwear that had been pulled out of the dresser drawers and flung on the floor, but she hadn't moved quite fast enough. Apparently, Jack Sandoval was a boxer-briefs kind of guy.

At last, though, he was done, zipping up the bag and throwing it over one shoulder. "Let's get going."

"Where are we going?"

"A place where we'll be safe."

While she had no reason not to trust him, she didn't really like the idea of taking off into the blue without any idea of where she was going. "You want to be more specific?"

"Not really. I don't have time to inspect every square inch of this apartment, so I don't know if the intruder left listening hexes here. Until I know it's okay to talk openly, I'm not saying anything that might give away our destination."

Those words didn't exactly reassure her. Kate glanced around the room, even though she knew that hexes could be nearly invisible. It wasn't like she was going to see speakers suddenly sprouting from the ceiling or something.

"They can do that?"

"Obviously, 'they' can do a lot of things. So we need to be cautious. Let's go."

She nodded, and followed him out of the bedroom and through the apartment. Jack didn't even glance at the mayhem around him; clearly, he'd catalogued it, and saw no further reason to waste time on inspecting everything. However, he was careful about locking up, although she didn't know what he was trying to protect.

In silence, they went down the stairs and back to where he'd parked his Jeep. It wasn't until he'd pulled away from the apartment complex that he said, "We'll swing by your place first."

"Really?" she asked, somewhat startled. "Why?"

"Well, you said you'd only packed things for two days. I was going to head over there after work to pick up some extra clothes for you, but clearly, circumstances have intervened. Anyway, this will also give us a chance to see whether your apartment has been hit as well."

"And if it has?" Kate was relieved that she sounded

calm enough as she asked the question, but even so, her gut clenched at the thought of that same destruction being visited on her own apartment. Unlike Jack, she didn't have the unlimited resources of a witch clan to help her replace any items that had been wrecked or broken, let alone the money to pay for all the damage to the apartment itself.

As they drove south, back toward her complex, she found herself continually glancing into the rearview mirror, worried that one of the cars behind them might be occupied by the intruder, that he might be following them back to her apartment. Yes, she trusted Jack to protect her, but this unknown person seemed so…so…implacable. As if it didn't matter what they did, because he would keep coming after them.

"No one's following us," Jack said, and she startled.

"What?"

"I can see the way you keep checking the mirror. It's okay. Whoever broke into my place, they're not on our tail."

"Oh," she responded, slumping against the seat. Was it possible to feel foolish and relieved at the same time?

He seemed to note her discomfiture, because he glanced over and offered her a reassuring smile. "It's all right. It's a logical thing to be worried about. But I think we're okay for now."

She hoped so. Right then, all her nerves were jangling, and she didn't know if she'd ever be able to relax again. Everything was beginning to pile up on her—Jeff's death, the wreck of her car, the crisis in California. And now the mayhem in Jack's apartment. When would it all end?

Another light, and then they turned down the side street where her complex was located, and pulled into the parking lot. This time, knowing the drill, Kate waited for Jack to come around and open the door for her before she got out. Even though he'd said no one had followed them, she couldn't help giving a quick look around, just in case.

But the parking lot was empty, except for a lone pickup truck moving away from them and toward the exit onto the street. The driver didn't even glance in their direction as he passed by

"It's fine," Jack said. "Let's go."

"Okay."

She hurried down the pathway that led to her building, then went quickly up the stairs, Jack sticking behind her the whole time. When she reached the landing, she pulled her keys out of her purse and murmured a silent prayer that everything would be okay. Her world had already been thrown topsy-turvy, and the thought of facing the same destruction that she'd just seen at Jack's apartment made her entire body tense. She told herself she could handle whatever might be waiting for her behind that door, but…could she?

The door swung inward after she unlocked the deadbolt. For just the briefest second, Kate wanted to shut her eyes, in case her worst fears were borne out.

But she didn't close her eyes. She looked inside, and let out a breath.

Everything was fine. The air inside felt stale and warm, because she'd now been gone for more than twenty-four hours, and she hadn't left the A/C running, but the apartment itself appeared to be untouched.

"Let me go in first," Jack said. "Just in case."

Kate couldn't really argue with that request. She nodded and stepped out of the way so he could enter the apartment. His hands were outstretched, as though he wanted to feel the currents of the air inside.

"Seems all right," he told her. "But stay close."

Like that was a problem. She planned to stick to him like glue.

He paused right inside the door and looked up to inspect the lintel, just as he had with the doorway at his own apartment. "Nothing. That's good."

"No sigils?"

"None that I can detect. The place feels like it's undisturbed. So let's go and get anything else you need, and then get out of here."

"Got it."

Kate hurried back to her bedroom and dug her

little rolling suitcase out from under her bed. It felt weird to have Jack follow her, then pause in the doorway while she hurriedly packed the things she thought she might need. Yes, she understood why he didn't want to let her out of his sight, but she could have done without having him stand there and watch while she retrieved panties and bras and a couple of the long tanks she liked to sleep in. And then, following the example of what he had packed for himself, jeans and T-shirts and one or two nicer tops.

"Should I bring a jacket? Sweater?"

"Couldn't hurt. The desert can get cold at night."

The desert. That remark in and of itself didn't really tell her that much—after all, Phoenix was surrounded by desert. They could be going anywhere.

She didn't comment, though, only packed a few more items she thought would be useful, including a pair of trail shoes. Just in case. Jack didn't really seem like the hiking type, but the shoes could come in handy if they did need to move through rough terrain.

Her toiletries were already stowed in the Jeep, so Kate didn't have to worry about packing any of those items. In a remarkably short time, she was done, the little suitcase completely full.

"I'll take that," Jack said, and came into the room so he could lift the suitcase from the bed and take it back into the living room. "Anything else you need?"

"Just my laptop." It had been sitting on the dining

room table this whole time, charging, and Kate unplugged the charger and took both it and the laptop and shoved them into her oversized purse. It bulged a little but fit well enough—one of the reasons why she'd gone for a model with a smaller screen. "I think that's it, though."

"All right." He paused then and looked around. Trying to make sure she hadn't missed anything? Kate couldn't really tell, because he still wore that inscrutable expression. "Don't suppose you have a timer for one of these lamps."

"No, sorry." Once upon a time, she had. Or rather, Jeff had bought a couple of the devices for the times they went out of town. The one time, actually. They'd taken a trip to San Francisco about a year and a half after the wedding, mostly because Kate had just finished a grueling semester and needed to get out and away, even if only for a few days. Anyway, if the timers were still around, they'd be in with Jeff's stuff. She experienced a sudden pang at the thought of the detritus from their marriage being packed away in storage, and how Jeff's mother would probably have to deal with sorting through all of it.

"Just a thought," Jack said. He paused, and looked more closely at her. "You okay?"

"Yes," she replied. Was it the truth? She didn't know for sure. The only thing she did know was that she had far more pressing things to worry about at the moment. "Let's go."

13

A QUICK STOP TO FILL UP THE TANK, AND THEN they were headed south on I-10. Kate stirred in the passenger seat and glanced over at him. "Can you tell me now where we're going?"

Well, he'd made her wait long enough. There was no point in keeping it a secret any longer. "I have a place in the desert outside Tucson," Jack said. "I bought it a few years ago as an investment property, but the tenants moved out last year, and I've been using it for an Airbnb rental until I decided what I wanted to do with it. Anyway, because I bought it as an investment, I set up a corporation to handle the transaction. The corporation is listed on the deed, not me, so even if the person who's responsible for all this has done some digging into my background, they're not going to find this property. I have an agent in Tucson who handles it for me, and I let him know to have it cleaned up and ready. He thinks it's been rented out to a couple of tourists. No point in tipping our hand by telling him that I was actually the one who'd be staying there."

"That's handy," Kate said. Something about her posture seemed to relax slightly, and he could tell she was relieved that he'd appeared to have considered all the angles. "How far outside Tucson?"

"About a half hour. The place is secluded, and the way the property is set up, we'll be able to easily see if anyone is approaching. It's safe."

She nodded, but he saw how her brows drew together, as if she wasn't quite as thrilled by that particular piece of information as she should be. Was she worried about being alone with him, out in the middle of nowhere?

Jack couldn't really blame her—he knew he was slightly on edge at the prospect. Not because he thought they had much chance of being attacked out there, but because he didn't know how he'd handle himself, alone with a beautiful woman, with not much to occupy their time.

You will be a perfect gentleman, he thought. *The woman just lost her husband.*

Almost ex-husband. Someone she was no longer in love with.

Damn it.

"I think you'll like the place," he said. "It has a lot of fun touches. Homey. The people I bought it from put a lot of work into it. And the stars at night are incredible. There's a telescope."

That comment made her smile. "Really? That would be fun. I always wanted a telescope, but they're expensive. Anyway, the light pollution in Phoenix makes it hard to get a good look at the stars."

True enough. "Well, you won't have to worry about light pollution where we're going."

A nod, and the smile she wore began to fade. "I really need to call my work, though. If I'm disappearing into the desert for lord knows how long, I'm going to have to tell them something."

Just as he was going to have to make his excuses very soon as well. The story he'd told Grace would work to cover him for most of this afternoon, but he'd have to hand over the "death of a relative" story in the very near future.

"Tell them the truth," he said, and Kate lifted an eyebrow.

"Excuse me?"

"All right, part of the truth. They'll certainly know by now that your estranged husband was murdered. Say you're going through a difficult time and that you need to take some time off to handle things. No one can argue with that."

From the way she frowned, he could tell she wasn't entirely convinced. And he could understand her worry—unlike him, she was new on the job, without any real seniority. In that kind of situation, you generally wanted to be careful. But what was going on here—it was much more important than a mere job.

Easy for you to say, he told himself. *If the Scottsdale P.D. dumps your ass for going AWOL, it won't be the end of the world. You don't need the money. But Kate....*

He glanced over at her, and surprised himself by experiencing a strange surge of protectiveness...of tenderness. Right then, he wished he could take her in his arms and tell her that it was going to be okay. That no matter what happened, he'd take care of her.

Where the hell had that come from? It wasn't like him to go all alpha male. He was a curiosity among his clan, a man who'd made it to his mid-thirties without ever encumbering himself with a wife or family. No one had ever tempted him enough to give up his freedom, even though most witches and warlocks tended to marry young. But with Kate, all he could think about right then was how much he wanted to keep her close to him.

Crazy. Then again, all of this was crazy.

"I'm going to have to do the same thing," he went on. "Well, make excuses to my work, I mean. Do you want me to go first?"

She managed a tired smile. "Are you teasing me?"

"No." And he wasn't. He just wanted to provide a little moral support. "I know it's hard. But you'll get through this. Okay?"

For a few seconds, she didn't respond. Then she said, "Okay. I'll go ahead and call. Best to get it over with. But it's not just work—my family will need to know I'm all right, and so will my friend Samantha."

Right. He'd almost forgotten about Kate's friend, the one who'd stayed with her that first terrible night after the murder, but of course she'd need to be contacted, too, just to put her mind at ease…or at least, as much ease as possible, considering that Kate couldn't provide any details, could only say she was going out of town for a few days.

He hoped it would be a few days. Right then, he really didn't have any idea how all this was going to play out. The most important thing was to get Kate out of harm's way, but then they'd also have to get to the bottom of who had been committing all the crimes here in the Phoenix area, not to mention the identity of the null who was currently orchestrating a particularly nasty coup out in Southern California.

"Well, first things first," Jack said. "At least your parents and Samantha know you're with me, so that can wait a little bit. But you might as well call work now—we're coming up on Casa Grande, which means you'll have a decent cell signal for a few minutes. After that, it's going to get dicier until we reach the outskirts of Tucson."

Kate nodded and pulled her phone out of her purse, then unlocked it and went to her contacts list. For a moment she paused, finger hovering over the phone icon on the screen. Then she took a breath and pushed it to connect the call.

After that, Jack made sure he kept his eyes fixed forward on the road. This was hard enough for Kate without him staring at her while she made the phone call. He couldn't do much about being able to hear the whole thing, but at least he didn't have to appear as if he was hanging on her every word.

"Hi, um, Christopher? It's Kate Campbell. I—" A pause, probably because the person on the other end of the call had interrupted her. "Yes, and…thank you. It's been…well, I guess you can imagine how it's been. Anyway, I was really hoping that I'd be able to come back in tomorrow, but this has all been a lot tougher than I could have ever imagined. I need to take some more time off." Another pause, and she shook her head, even though of course the person on the other end of the line couldn't have seen the gesture. "I'm not sure yet. Can I just say through the end of the week for now, and then we'll see how it goes?" She paused, the fingers of her free hand twisting in the strap of her purse as it sat in her lap. "Sure. Yes, I can do that. Thanks—I'll be in touch."

She ended the call there and released a little huff of breath.

"So it's okay?" Jack inquired.

"Yes, I think so. Christopher—my boss—was really understanding. He told me to take as much time as I needed, and he'd work it out with HR. I guess if you miss more than a week for something unscheduled like this, you have to take an unofficial leave. But he said I shouldn't worry, that it's just standard and he'll do whatever is necessary to get me reinstated when I come back."

"That sounds like it's going to be fine, then."

"I think so." She'd been looking out the passenger-side window as she spoke, but then she shifted in her seat so she could face him as best she could. Even though it seemed as if the conversation with her supervisor had gone well, Jack didn't miss the worry in her wide hazel eyes, or the tension in her fine jaw and throat. "For some reason, though, it doesn't feel fine. It feels…I don't know if I can even explain it. Like everything should be worked out, but it isn't. Like I won't ever be going back to that job."

He wished more than ever that he could reach over and pull her into his arms. Something about the tone of her voice sounded lost, full of fear that nothing would ever be the same again. And the problem was—it wouldn't. Yes, he supposed they could catch her estranged husband's killer and somehow do something to mend the situation in California, but even accomplishing those worthy goals wouldn't bring Jeff Nichols back, or Simón Santiago and all the others the null had killed. Something about the fabric of the world had been twisted out of true, and Jack knew it would never go back to the way it was. Not completely.

Trying to sound reassuring, he said, "It will be fine. Yes, things are up in the air right now, but they're not going to stay that way." Pausing, he tried to think of a way to distract her. "I don't suppose you cook."

"'Cook'?" she repeated, looking startled. "Why?"

"It's just that the house is kind of isolated, so driving into town for dinner every night isn't really an option. I can barbecue, but...."

She smiled then. "Yes, Jack Sandoval, I can cook. Actually cook, because for a while I was trying to be a good little wifey, even while going to school and working as a T.A. So you don't need to worry about starving to death while we hide from our demon-conjuring warlock."

Even though it was a relief to hear her say that, he didn't want her to think that he was trying to take advantage of her. "I didn't think we'd starve. Get bored of eating steaks and hamburgers...probably. Anyway, I don't cook, but I'm very good at chopping things up. So I can take over the drudge part of the meal prep."

"And the dishes?"

He liked the dancing light in her eyes, liked the way the afternoon sun streamed in through the window and turned the warmer streaks in her brown hair almost to gold. "I would never ask you to do the dishes."

"Then I think we'll be just fine."

"Good," he said. "We'll stop in Tucson and get

some groceries and whatever else we think we might need. There's a convenience store off the freeway on the way out to the house, but that won't do us much good unless you want to subsist on energy drinks and Slim Jims."

An actual grin, with none of the worry and doubt he'd seen just a few minutes earlier. "I'll pass on that."

He smiled, too, and they drove in silence for a while. Not a tense one, though; Jack could tell she'd relaxed slightly, now that she'd handled the dreaded call to work, which had turned out to be not as bad as she'd feared. Yes, she still needed to contact her parents and her friend Samantha, but that could wait until they got to Tucson.

And after all that…well, he'd have to see what happened.

Jack stopped at a Trader Joe's, and they loaded up on supplies there, and afterward went to a Safeway to get all the things they might need to fill in the gaps. Kate thought his idea of barbecuing at least some of their meals was a good one—less work in the kitchen, and the weather was certainly mild enough that they'd be able to linger on the patio he'd described, cooking the main part of their dinners there, maybe even eating outside, too, if the temperatures didn't drop too quickly once the sun went down.

Having those thoughts run through her mind, though, just made her want to shake her head at herself. This wasn't some vacation getaway. She and Jack weren't going down to his house outside Tucson just to have a romantic weekend together. There shouldn't be anything romantic about this at all—they were hiding from a malevolent force or person who'd somehow managed to circumvent all the safeguards that Jack had put in place at his apartment. The only reason why they had any chance at refuge in the place they were headed was that no one appeared to know about it. So she definitely shouldn't be treating this as some kind of a spa retreat.

Even so, she realized something as they made their selections at the various stores and then loaded up everything in the back of his Jeep. Despite the underlying sexual tension—something she really couldn't deny any longer—she felt easy around Jack. Yes, she thought he was hotter than hell, but she also liked him, liked the way they interacted, enjoyed the way he never seemed to get too ruffled about anything. Not like Jeff, who tended to be phlegmatic in the extreme until something didn't go his way, but more because Jack was comfortable with himself, with who he was and his place in the world. Maybe that was a function of age. Of course he wasn't old, wasn't even ten years older than she, but he'd still had time to settle into his work, his routine.

Whereas she'd thought she'd known where she was

going, only to upend everything when she realized she just couldn't stay married to Jeff. And then when things had felt as if they were maybe going in a good direction, that she'd been able to land her dream job and could start moving forward again, all this had happened.

Right then she really had no idea where it would end.

But once they were on the road again, she got out her phone and left a message for Samantha, which was about what she'd been expecting. Her friend's schedule was so hectic that about all you could do was leave a voicemail and then hope she'd have the opportunity to return the call in a somewhat reasonable amount of time.

It was basically the same situation when she tried to contact Colin, although Kate guessed that he might be at the doctor's with Jenny. Apparently, the McAllisters didn't have a healer in their clan, so they went to see a regular doctor just like ordinary civilians. She left a message saying that she was all right, that she was with Jack Santiago, but the cell reception wasn't very good where she was going, so she'd get in contact when she could.

The call to Kate's mother was more difficult, because of course Lynda had two more questions for every answer Kate provided, but she eventually managed to extricate herself when the phone started glitching as they got farther away from the cell towers of Tucson. Would they have any reception at all at Jack's house?

"Okay, I guess I'm a free woman," she said as she tucked her now mostly useless phone back in her purse.

"Feels good, doesn't it?"

Actually, it did. Maybe it was just the bright sunshine outside the car windows, or the friendly wildflowers blooming along the borders of the highway, but right then she did feel good. Not great, because she couldn't forget what had happened to Jeff, what might be happening even now in California, but she could accept "good." Good was better than the opposite.

She nodded. "For a minute I wished I could tell my mother what was really going on, and then I realized that would be the very worst thing of all. Jeff's murder—that's terrible, but it's something she can try to accept. I don't know how she'd handle finding out about witches and warlocks and demon-summoning and all the rest of it."

Jack sent Kate a speculative sideways glance. "So Colin never discussed Jenny's family with your parents?"

"God, no." She risked a quick look over at Jack. His expression was still pleasant, but that could have been merely a mask he wore to hide his displeasure. Maybe he thought Colin was a coward for not telling his own mother and father that he was married to a witch. "Colin and I talked about it. I talked to Jenny, too. And it just seemed…it seemed like too much of a risk. Even if Colin could have gotten them to believe him, he didn't want to have to worry about either of my parents saying the wrong thing in front of the wrong people." Kate paused, because she knew that painted her parents in a poor light, and she didn't want Jack believing they were blabbermouths who couldn't be discreet. "That is, they wouldn't say anything intentionally, but when my mother gets going when she's with her friends, sometimes her mouth engages before her brain does. I guess some civilians have told their families about the witch clan their relatives have married into, and that's great. In our case, though, we all agreed it was better to let it go, especially with Colin and Jenny up in Jerome where my parents wouldn't be crossing paths with them all that often."

"That was probably wise," Jack said. "We usually don't talk about it, either. It's a similar situation with Alex's older brother Diego—he married a civilian, and of course Letty knows, but she wasn't about to tell her parents, from what I've heard. Too much can go wrong."

Those words reassured Kate more than she wanted to admit. She hadn't wanted Jack to think Colin wasn't up to the task of explaining witch clans to his own family. But it had been so much easier to just keep quiet on the subject.

They continued south on I-19, until Jack pulled off the highway in Tubac. This was an area Kate didn't know very well; she'd driven through once while going down to Nogales with some friends when she was on spring break years ago, but she'd never had much of an opportunity to explore. It was a small town, but she was surprised to see how many shops and art galleries it boasted in the part of downtown they passed through before heading out into the open desert.

"I thought you said there weren't many restaurants here," she said, her tone faintly accusing.

"There aren't. There are some," Jack confessed. "But it's also safer if we're not seen too much."

"You think the warlock could have followed us here?" Despite the sun beating through the window, Kate was suddenly chilled, even though the air conditioning in the Jeep wasn't turned up that high.

"No," he said. "But the thing is, I don't know for sure. Keeping a low profile just seems like the smart thing to do."

She couldn't argue with that, so she didn't try. Instead, she gave a faint nod and then turned to look out the window, watching as the countryside opened around them, an expanse of rolling high desert, studded with mesquite and manzanita, and the occasional saguaro cactus. Wildflowers bloomed here, too, along with the warm-toned desert broom. Well, if they had to go into hiding, they'd definitely chosen the right time of year for it. In a few months, this area would be baking in the upper nineties or low one hundreds, but right now the digital thermometer on the dashboard said it was a balmy seventy-eight degrees outside.

They followed a winding two-lane road for a few more miles, then turned off onto a dirt lane, clouds of dust billowing out behind them as they headed for the house. Kate could just barely see it now, a multilevel structure built into the hillside, part of it painted the same deep purple as the mountains on the horizon. It grew closer, and then they were pulling up to the garage.

"Remote's in the glove compartment," Jack said. "Can you get it out and push the button for me?"

Kate did as he requested, and a moment later they were inside and the garage door closing behind them. It was very clean in here, empty except for a storage rack to one side filled with neatly labeled cardboard boxes. Well, she supposed Jack wouldn't have much reason to clutter up the place if he didn't actually live here. Anyway, his apartment had been equally clutter-free. Unlike a lot of people she knew, he didn't seem to be all that into "stuff."

They got out of the Jeep and retrieved the groceries from the storage compartment in the back, leaving their luggage there for later. As they came up the stairs into the main part of the house, she could see what he'd meant about the home having a lot of nice touches—a lovely mural of the mountains had been painted along the stairwell, and the floors were gleaming red Saltillo tile. Off to one side she saw an "Arizona room," or enclosed porch, perfect for enjoying those desert sunsets, while ahead was the kitchen, which clearly had been updated in the recent past, with its stainless appliances and mica countertops.

"This is kind of amazing," Kate remarked while pulling their various purchases out of the shopping bags and setting them on the counter. "When you said you rented it out as an Airbnb, I guess I was expecting something smaller."

"Well, like I said, I first bought it as an investment property." He picked up several packages of meat and stowed them in the refrigerator, then did the same thing with the fruit and vegetables they'd purchased. "And I was thinking about maybe retiring here."

"'Retiring'?" she repeated, eyebrows lifting in surprise. Jack Sandoval certainly didn't look like a candidate for retirement.

He grinned, as if all too aware of what she'd just been thinking. "I can retire with full benefits at fifty."

"That's still a ways off, isn't it?"

"Fourteen years. I guess I just like to think ahead."

So he was eight years older than she. Kate had guessed their age gap was somewhere around there. It wasn't that big a deal. Hardly worth mentioning.

And hardly worth thinking about, she told herself,

since nothing is going on here. Time to get a grip on reality.

"There are three bedrooms," he said as he closed the refrigerator door for the final time, all the groceries now put away. "You can pick which one you want."

"I don't want to take yours away from you—"

"None of them are really 'mine,'" he cut in. "I've only stayed here a handful of times, and I've used all three of them. So don't worry about that."

Because Kate could tell he didn't want to argue about it, she just said, "All right. I'll go take a look."

Despite what Jack had said, she saw right away that one of the rooms was clearly intended as the master, since it was bigger and had an *en suite* bathroom, while the other two bedrooms shared a bath down one hall. She decided she wouldn't take the master bedroom, but instead the larger of the two rooms that were left, with the warm terra-cotta-colored paint on the walls and a spectacular view of the Atascosa Mountains.

"This one's great," she said, while Jack stood in the hall and gave her a quizzical look.

"You can have the master. It's fine."

"And this one is fine, too," she replied. "I'm good."

At that point he shrugged and said, "All right. Let's get our bags."

She followed him back down to the Jeep, where

she waited as he handed over her weekender bag and toiletries case, and the rolling suitcase she'd filled with items from her apartment. Jack retrieved his own bags, and not too long after that, they were back upstairs, where they each went to the rooms they'd claimed and began to unpack.

This was weird. It was weird, wasn't it, to be staying in this house in the middle of nowhere with Jack Sandoval?

Probably.

But...strange as the circumstances were, at the moment she couldn't think of anywhere she'd rather be.

14

It took longer for Kate to unpack than it did Jack, probably because she'd brought a few more things than he had. He took advantage of the extra time to call work and offer his own carefully manufactured lie as to why he'd have to take an indefinite leave of absence. Larry had been less than thrilled, but, as Jack had surmised, he really couldn't protest too much when the excuse involved a murdered relative in California.

"I'm sorry to hear of your loss," Larry said, sounding uncharacteristically subdued. A second later, though, he continued with, "But it's going to be a hell of a problem continuing with our own investigation here while you're out of state."

"Grace and Ian can handle it," Jack replied, which was no more than the truth. His assistants were both extremely capable people. No, they wouldn't be able to make much progress with this particular case, but that was only because they simply weren't equipped to track down a malevolent warlock with a desire for revenge. About all he could hope was that, once this was all over with, there would be some way to pass on the information about what had happened to Jeff Nichols' murderer, so there would be some closure to the investigation and it wouldn't end up as yet another cold case file.

"Yeah. Maybe. Well, take care, Jack. Again, sorry to hear about what happened to your cousin."

At that moment, Jack couldn't help feeling guilty over the lies he'd told, even though he knew they were necessary. "Thanks, Larry. I appreciate it. I'll try to be in touch."

He ended the call then as Kate emerged from the room she'd claimed as her own. Once again he was struck by her casual beauty, somehow perfectly at home in this place of warm handmade tile and desert vistas, of how lovely she was in her jeans and embroidered top and flat-heeled sandals. When he'd first met her, of course she'd been shaken and horrified by what she'd just seen, but he'd also realized that she looked slightly out of place in her buttoned-up work clothes, like she was playing a part rather than being the person she truly was.

Or maybe that was a load of horseshit. Maybe he just wanted to think about how at home she looked here because he wanted her to be a part of this house, a part of his life.

He cleared his throat. "Well, I'm set with work now, too, so I guess we're both free agents. Let me show you the rest of the place. Do you want some water?"

If Kate was a little put off by these seemingly disjointed questions, she didn't show it. "Sure, water would be great."

They went into the kitchen, where he got two plastic bottles of water from the fridge and handed one to her. "This way."

The covered patio and adjacent courtyard were, in their way, the most striking parts of the house, and so Jack took her there first, letting her smile at the cobalt blue paint of the walls along the covered patio, the star-shaped lights of pierced Mexican tin that hung from the roof. The switch for the pond fountain was hidden behind a potted palm, and Jack reached over and flicked it on so the soothing sound of bubbling water soon filled the space.

"It's absolutely gorgeous," Kate said. "Like a little oasis. I'm surprised it wasn't rented out."

"Well, we're just past spring break for most places around here. It had been full up until about a week ago." He took her to the covered area where the built-in gas barbecue and sink were located, along with the brick pizza oven.

As soon as she caught sight of the pizza oven, her

face lit up. "Now I see why you wanted me to get those pizza crusts at Trader Joe's. Although you could've told me you had your own gourmet setup here. I thought I was going to have to wrangle pizza in a regular oven."

"Well, I didn't want to give all my secrets away at once," Jack replied.

In response, her mouth quirked. "Do you have all that many secrets?"

"Not really. You already know the biggest one."

"That you're a warlock?"

"That's the one. It's not exactly the sort of thing I can just drop casually at the water cooler at the office."

For a moment, she didn't reply, only gazed up at him, brows knitted slightly. In the subdued light out here, with the sun filtered through the overhanging palms, her eyes looked almost pure green. "Is it hard?" she asked at last. "I mean, I know what it's been like to keep the secret about Jenny's family, about the McAllisters, but that has to be nothing compared to what you go through every day."

He hadn't really been expecting the compassion, the realization that being a warlock in a world of civilians wasn't always a bed of roses. Clearly, Kate had done some thinking on the subject, and the unlooked-for perception only made him warm to her that much more. "It can be hard sometimes," he said, although his casual tone belied the words he had just spoken. "But it's something I'm used to. The de la Paz clan has always been one that mixed in with the regular population. We learn from a very early age how to conduct ourselves, since we know that one day we'll have to 'pass,' for lack of a better word, in the real world. It's not as big a deal as you might think."

From her expression, Kate didn't appear entirely convinced, but she didn't contradict him. Instead, she moved out to the edge of the patio, where a low stucco wall separated this small sanctuary from the rest of the yard. Not that it was a real yard, in the suburban sense, just a span of mesquite trees and artfully placed rocks and succulents that eventually gave way to the open desert. The true property line was actually quite far from the spot where they stood, since the lot comprised a good six acres.

"And we're really safe here?" she asked, studying the outline of the Atascosa Mountains, now starting to grow hazy as sunset approached.

How was he supposed to answer that question? Right now, Jack wasn't sure if any place was entirely safe, no matter what precautions he might have taken to make it that way. He said, "Much safer than being back in Scottsdale."

"That's not what I asked." Her gaze was level, unwavering. It was the sort of look that expected the truth.

So he'd give it to her. "Can I guarantee that it's

safe? No, because the events of the past few days have proved that nothing is guaranteed. But our warlock would also have to be a gifted hacker to know that I own this place, so…I'd say it's pretty safe."

"No one in your family knows about it?"

"My brothers know I bought an income property somewhere near Tucson. That's all." And really, forty-five minutes away wasn't all that "near," when you got right down to it. The obfuscation had been a harmless one, but it could also help him and Kate now.

"Why didn't you tell them more details about it?"

"And have all my nieces and nephews come down here and trash the place?" he returned in mock horror.

That reply made her smile. "Okay, I think I see your point. But…what if the warlock has some other way of tracking us down?"

It was a question that had worried Jack, too, but he'd also taken precautions against that sort of thing as well. "This whole place," he said, indicating with a sweep of his arm the expanse of the property, "has been warded. Every couple of months I come down here and walk the perimeter, refresh the sigils I've inscribed on the stones, repeat the spells. Not," he went on, as Kate opened her mouth to speak, "because I ever thought this place would actually be under attack, but because it's what I do. This is my magic. Performing these spells helped me to keep in practice, if you know what I mean. And it doesn't hurt to have the house protected, even if it's just being rented out to civilians. Those spells of protection can also prevent mishaps in the microwave or stopped-up toilets."

She actually chuckled. "Okay, I can see how that might come in handy."

"So do you feel safe enough to eat something? It's getting around that time."

"Sure. I'm dying to try out that pizza oven."

They went back into the house, where they assembled the ingredients on the counter. Since Kate announced that she wanted to make a concoction with goat cheese and sun-dried tomatoes and olives, there wasn't a lot of work for Jack to do, although he dutifully shredded lettuce and spinach leaves, getting the salad ready while she worked.

Afterward they went back out to the patio, where he fired up the oven, then plugged in the strings of round, clear party bulbs that hung over the space. By then it wasn't quite dark yet, a warm orange sunset lingering in the west, but the lights were still needed as the shadows grew on every side.

He'd also brought out the plastic plates and cups he kept in the house for patio dining, and set the table as Kate planted herself in front of the pizza oven and kept an eagle eye on their meal. Last was a bottle of Sangiovese from one of the local vineyards; she arched an eyebrow at the bottle as he pulled out the cork and poured a measure into each of their glasses, but she didn't say anything.

And then it was time to get out the pizza, which Kate let him handle, maneuvering the wooden peel so it wouldn't get scorched as he carefully drew the pie, all dripping with melted cheese, the crust a perfect golden brown, from within the brick oven. He put it down on the table, and watched as Kate sat down, her eyes shining. Right then, he could tell she was only thrilled by the novelty of the experience, wasn't thinking about her estranged husband's death or all the tragedies that had followed. And Jack was glad of that. He wanted her to forget.

He wanted…her.

"To the desert," he said quickly, raising a glass. Across the table from him, Kate appeared somewhat nonplussed by the toast, but she lifted her glass as well.

"Why the desert?"

"Why not? It's a good place to shelter, in a lot of ways. Anyway, you won't be asking that question when we go look at the stars after dinner."

"Oh, right…the telescope."

"It's a good time of year for star watching," he went on, knowing he spoke too quickly, trying to cover up the unwanted surge of desire he'd just experienced as he gazed across the table at her. "During the winter, you can't see the Milky Way because of the orientation of the Earth on its axis, but now we're enough into the spring that you'll be able to see it in all its glory."

She swallowed some of her wine, then said, "Really? I've never seen it. In person, that is. On Facebook I follow this photographer in Tucson who takes amazing night-sky shots of the desert, but I've never been able to see for myself the things he's talking about."

"Well, you will soon enough, although we have to wait for it to be full dark."

"Then I guess we'd better eat."

That sounded like a good idea, especially now that enough time had elapsed for the pizza to cool a little and the cheese to congeal somewhat. Jack cut the pie into eight slices, then put one on Kate's plate, and another on his own. She dished salad, and for a moment neither of them spoke, since they were too busy eating.

No, she hadn't been joking when she'd said she could cook. True, the pizza they were eating had been assembled from simple enough components, but she'd still needed to know which ones would work best together, and how much of each one to use.

At length, though, she set down her half-eaten slice of pizza and picked up her glass of Sangiovese, then said, "You told me this property was warded, but...didn't you do the same thing with your apartment in Scottsdale? No offense, but it doesn't seem as if the wards you put up there did what you wanted them to."

He'd been wondering if she was going to ask that question. To fortify himself, he drank some of his wine, then responded, "Yes, I had signs of protection up in my apartment, and yes, an intruder still got in, but their real purpose was to protect whoever might be inside, not the property there. Since you and Caitlin and Alex were gone when the warlock showed up, the wards weren't really needed. And actually," he went on, as Kate took a swallow of wine and regarded him with a slightly skeptical expression, "who's to say you didn't all get the notion to leave because the spells I cast compelled you to do so? They would be protecting you by making sure you weren't there."

At that explanation, she actually chuckled. "Well…that's putting a spin on it."

Jack wasn't offended. He knew he might have reacted in the same way if he'd been told something similar. "Magic is…well, it's magic. It's not science. It can have a mind of its own. The wards I have here"— with his free hand, he gestured out toward the open land surrounding the house, now all a sea of darkness, since the moon hadn't risen yet—"they're meant to serve as a warning as much as anything else. If someone I haven't given permission to be here crosses them, I'll know."

"How? Does an alarm go off or something?"

"Not exactly. More like…I'll feel it, like someone

poking me in the middle of the back. A twinge. And that will give me time to prepare."

For a few seconds, she didn't reply, but swirled the wine in her glass, watching the ruby glints reflecting from the lights overhead. "If you feel that twinge, what will you do?"

"To be honest?" he replied. "We pack everything in the Jeep and get the hell out of here."

"Well, that's…brave."

Since the ironic inflection in her voice told him she was teasing…at least partially…he didn't take offense. "This person is a killer, Kate. I'm not going to take chances with you. Yes, I know a number of spells to drive back a magical attack—and I know how to shoot straight, too. But since I don't know exactly what we're up against, it's very likely that it would be safer to hightail it out of here and drive up to Tucson. Alex's powers would come in very handy in a situation like that."

"I guess so." She looked at him directly then, all traces of amusement gone from her face. Now she only seemed tense, and worried, and all too vulnerable. "But…am I always going to be running?"

"No," he said, his voice firm. "This is just temporary. Luz texted me to let me know that she was going to be meeting with Connor and Angela tomorrow, and I'm sure they'll come up a plan to deal with the person who's been causing all this mayhem. The *prima* and her *primus* working together are pretty formidable, and if they can figure out a way to connect their powers with Luz's, then I have no doubt that they'll take care of our problem."

"And what about the null in California?"

"I'm sure they're working on that, too. The most immediate matter, though, is the warlock here in Arizona. What we really need to do is relax and sit tight, and let some of the powers-that-be do the heavy lifting for a little while."

"Relax." Kate shook her head and drank some more wine, finishing off what was in her glass. Jack picked up the bottle and poured more for her; she didn't protest. "I think relaxing is about the last thing on my mind right now."

"Maybe so, but I've already told you that we're fine here." He refilled his own glass and then put the bottle back down on the tiled surface of the table. "Now, drink up. We've got about an hour before the moon rises, which means this is the best time to get a good luck at the stars. Once the moon's up, it'll overpower a lot of the smaller constellations."

"I had no idea you were such an expert," she remarked. She didn't argue, though, but swallowed some more wine, and then went to work on finishing the last few bites of the pizza on her plate.

"I wouldn't say I'm an expert, but I like to keep track of these things. In my line of work, it helps to know when the moon is full, when it's going to rise."

"Full moon…all the crazies come out?"

"Something like that."

Once again she nearly smiled, but it faded almost as soon as it had come. "It was a full moon when Jeff was killed, wasn't it? That was important, right?"

"There are a lot of rituals that require a full moon. But there are just as many that need the moon to be dark, so I honestly don't know how much bearing it had on your husband's death."

Her mouth opened, as though she wanted to protest that Jeff hadn't really been her husband anymore, at least in anything more than name. But she appeared to stop herself, and instead drank another mouthful of wine.

Watching her, Jack couldn't help being somewhat encouraged. He'd already gotten the impression that she'd removed herself emotionally from her estranged spouse a long time ago. In the eyes of the law, yes, they were still husband and wife when he died. But her heart and mind had divorced themselves many months earlier.

There were so many things he wanted to ask her, although he knew that they hadn't yet crossed over into any kind of real intimacy. They'd spoken of the matters that tied them together—Jeff Nichols' murder, the tangled complexities of inter-clan relations—but he still had no true idea of what was in her heart. She seemed open and friendly enough, and yet there seemed to be something at her core that was known only to her. Which was as it should be…if they were going to continue as they had so far.

He wanted more, though. So much more.

Abruptly, he pushed back his chair and stood. "Let's put away the leftovers. We can finish the wine after we've done our stargazing."

Kate didn't appear to be put off by his change in tone. "Sure," she said, then removed the napkin from her lap and set it on the tabletop. Without commenting further, she gathered up the salad bowl and tongs, while Jack picked up the wooden peel with the uneaten portion of the pizza sitting on it. They both went inside, and he took care of packaging everything up and putting it in the fridge, since he knew where the storage containers and the plastic wrap were kept.

"I'm going to grab my jacket," she told him. "It feels like it's starting to get chilly."

"Good idea."

It was hard not to watch her go, to allow himself to drink in her long legs in the close-fitting jeans, the curve of her ass, nicely rounded despite her overall slenderness. But he forced himself to focus on what he was doing, to make sure she didn't discover him gawking. He'd hoped that sitting down and having something to eat and drink would relax him, but he felt even more keyed up. The way he was reacting to Kate now—he hadn't responded to a woman like that in a long time, if ever.

Behave yourself, he though. *You're going to look at the stars, and then you're going to go to bed early and hope you have a better grip on yourself tomorrow.*

Problem was, he didn't know if he'd feel any different about her the next day....

15

THEY TOOK A DETOUR TO THE GARAGE, WHERE Jack brought out the telescope from a storage area in the back of the space. "I wouldn't trust this baby with any of the people who've rented out the house," he explained as he took off the vinyl cover that protected it from dust. "But it won't take long for me to set up."

Kate nodded, then followed him out of the garage and back up to the main level of the property. The telescope was a big one, with what appeared to be a mount for a camera and a whole bunch of complicated dials and switches. It looked like it must have been very expensive. No wonder Jack didn't leave it out for the Airbnb-ers to play with. Homeowner's insurance would have taken care of any damage to the property itself, but she doubted it would cover something like that telescope.

He led her to the rear of the house, where the

landscape seemed to stretch toward eternity in every direction. The moon still hadn't made an appearance, but that hardly seemed to matter because of the fiery splendor of the sky overhead, the starlight so bright, she could still see the faint outline of her shadow behind her.

After setting down the telescope, Jack said, "Look up. You see it?"

Kate tilted her head upward. A huge misty arch seemed to cover half the enormous vault of the heavens, glowing in the darkness. "That's the Milky Way?"

"Yes. You need to be someplace like this, with hardly any light pollution, to be able to really see it. Tucson is lucky—they're a designated Dark Sky city, so even in the city limits, you can still see a lot."

She'd heard the term before, knew that it meant a town or city where the local ordinances ensured that businesses and homeowners followed strict guidelines so the lights on their buildings were directed downward rather than pointing up at the sky. Never in a million years would Phoenix follow those rules, so she hadn't needed to adhere to them in her city planning work, but it was still nice to see the practice being followed here in the Tucson area. All right, Jack's house was actually fifty miles outside Tucson, but she'd visited Colin in Jerome and was still able to see the lights of Phoenix from almost a hundred miles away, so distance didn't always help.

"It's beautiful," she said. And it was. Smudges of

light that could be stars, or galaxies, or nebulae. Hundreds of millions of them crowding into an area she could cover with the palm of her hand. And yet… watching them didn't make her feel any better about her current situation. Wasn't looking up at the stars supposed to provide you with a sense of proportion, to make it seem as if your own petty problems weren't that big a deal? Problem was, she didn't think the problems she was facing—or that the Arizona witches had to deal with—were petty at all. She didn't exactly sigh, but she did let out a breath before she went on, "I guess this is where I'm supposed to say that they all make me feel small or something."

Jack chuckled, then bent over the telescope and made a few minute adjustments, as though he had a specific target in mind as he focused it. "Don't feel bad. I never really bought into that idea, either. It's not like looking at the stars is magically going to make your own problems go away."

"Oh, good. I was worried that I had a raging ego issue or something, since I didn't really see the attraction in being insignificant."

He straightened then and looked over at her. Even in the darkness she could feel the impact of that gaze, the way his eyes seemed to focus on her and nothing else.

"I don't think you're insignificant."

A tremor went through her. It had to be the night breeze, growing colder now that the sun was gone and the dry air released the heat it had held during the daytime. Somehow she managed to give a small laugh, albeit not a very convincing one. "Well, that's good to know. So what are we looking at tonight?"

"Saturn," he replied, in quite a different tone of voice. "It's very clear, so you should be able to make out its rings without too much trouble. Come take a look."

With an odd reluctance, she moved toward him. It wasn't that she didn't want to be near Jack, more that she was a little afraid she wouldn't be able to conceal her reactions to him if they were in close proximity. But to hang back would be even more obvious, so she walked over to the telescope. "Do I need to do anything in particular?"

"No," he replied. "Just be prepared for the image to be a little shaky. Atmospheric interference. It's something people usually aren't prepared for when they look through an actual telescope for the first time. Look in here," he added, tapping the eyepiece, which jutted out from the main body of the instrument.

Bending down, she did as he asked, bringing her face close to the eyepiece. Although Jack stood off to one side, he was still very close—less than a foot away—and she was acutely aware of him, the faintest scent of cologne on the cool night air, the slight crunch of the hard-packed sand under his feet. She almost fancied she could feel the warmth coming from his body, although she knew that had to be her imagination. He certainly wasn't standing close enough for her to sense something like that.

She wrenched her mind away and made herself concentrate on the image inside the eyepiece. Yes, there it was—a small planet, faintly peach in color, its disk partially eclipsed by the rings that encircled it. She thought she could even see the shadow of those rings on the planet's surface. So small, and yet she knew it was hundreds of times the size of Earth. As Jack had said, the image did seem to jump around slightly, and she had to work to keep it in focus. It wasn't like looking at a still photograph at all. And yet…it seemed so much more real.

"It's beautiful." Yes, she'd just said the same thing a moment earlier, but she didn't know if she possessed the words to express what she thought of what she was seeing, a world so many millions of miles away from where she stood.

"Yes."

When she looked up from the telescope, she realized Jack wasn't gazing up at the heavens, however. No, he was staring right at her. For the longest moment they stood that way, both of them frozen, as though they knew that whatever either of them did next would change both their futures forever.

Jack took the first step. He came toward her, closer, then closer again, and then his arms had gone around her, and his mouth was lowered to hers. And oh, God, the touch of his lips sent a shockwave through her, a burst of heat so intense she forgot about the cold desert wind as it pierced her denim jacket, forgot about everything except that he was holding her and kissing her, and it was better than anything she'd ever experienced before.

That miracle of a kiss lasted for a very long time. At last, though, he drew away—not far, just enough so he could reach down and push a strand of wind-blown hair away from her face. His dark eyes searched hers, looking, she thought, for some reassurance that it was okay, that he hadn't just done something desperately stupid.

No, he hadn't, but....

"I shouldn't have done that, should I?" he asked at last, voice quiet, worried.

"I—" Kate had to stop there, because she honestly wasn't sure what she should say. The kiss had been amazing, and she knew she wanted another one, but.... "I don't know," she said at last. "I mean, I wanted you to. To be honest, for the past two days I've been thinking about what a kiss from you would be like. But with everything that's going on, with what happened to Jeff...." The words trailed off, and all she could do was shake her head. "Are we crazy?"

"I know I am," Jack replied. "Crazy about you. Believe me, I know how inappropriate this is. I thought I could stay professional, not let you get to me. But it looks like I was wrong."

"Well," she said, trying to smile, "if you really thought I was that irresistible, maybe it wasn't the best idea in the world to bring me down here to your desert hideaway."

He let out a grim chuckle at her comment. "You're probably right. It just seemed the safest place…that is, safe from the warlock. Clearly, you weren't safe from me."

"I don't want to be safe from you," Kate returned, a little surprised at her own boldness. Wasn't this where she was supposed to retreat into platitudes about how the timing was bad, and maybe they could revisit this after all the other craziness blew over? But she realized she couldn't do that. She didn't want to. Never in her life had she ever met anyone like Jack Sandoval, and if the timing was spectacularly bad, so be it. Either people would understand, or they wouldn't. If they didn't…well, she'd deal with those repercussions when the time came. She looked up into Jack's dark eyes, saw the trepidation and dawning hope there. "I want to be with you."

And she went to him and wrapped her arms around his waist, felt his lips touch the top of her head, then move once again to her mouth. Oh, yes, this was exactly what she wanted. His arms were so strong, the beating of his heart so steady. She was safe here. She knew he would keep her safe.

When they moved apart this time, he reached down to cup her cheek. "You amaze me."

Had anyone ever said that to her before? She didn't think so. "Well, I think you're pretty amazing, too."

He laughed. "Thank you. And I'm also getting cold—how about we move this party inside?"

"We didn't get much stargazing in."

"Do you mind?"

"No."

"That's what I thought." He picked up the telescope, and they headed back into the courtyard, where he deposited the instrument on the covered patio. Then he opened the door. "After you."

The warmth inside the house did feel good. The half-drunk bottle of wine still sat on the counter, flanked by their glasses. Jack picked them all up and pointed her toward the Arizona room on the east side of the house. "The show isn't totally over. Follow me."

They went into the enclosed patio, and he set the glasses on the table there. After filling each one halfway, he put down the bottle of Sangiovese and extended one of the glasses to her. She took it, glad that he was allowing them this little bit of breathing space. Where would the evening end? She didn't know for sure, but it felt good to sit here, to watch the jagged mountains to the east become backlit by the rising moon. It was now past full, not entirely round, but still large and bright nonetheless.

Kate sipped her wine, eyes adjusting to the semi-darkness. Across the table from her, Jack stirred.

"Mind if I ask you a question?"

"Um, sure." *Please don't let it be anything too incriminating....*

"Why Jeff? I mean, I don't want to speak ill of the dead, but...."

Oh, damn. Well, the question would have come up sooner or later. She had another sip of Sangiovese to fortify herself, then said, "You're not the first person to ask me that question, if it makes you feel any better."

"I'm not sure it does, but thanks for letting me know."

"Well...." She had to stop there, not because she didn't know the answer, but because she wanted to think of the best way to reply, one that wouldn't sound trite, or silly, or self-pitying. And then she realized if she sat there and waited for the perfect words, they'd never come. With a lift of her shoulders, she said, "When I was in high school, I was kind of awkward. Braces until my junior year, gawky. I wasn't exactly the type to attract male attention, if you know what I mean. It wasn't until I got to college that I came into my own, so to speak. And Jeff was the first guy to pay that kind of attention to me. I mean, I dated a little, but it wasn't like anyone was really pursuing me."

Jack's head tilted to one side. Was he thinking over her words, or merely attempting to picture her as the awkward girl she'd once been? "Late bloomer" was what Colin had called her. And he'd been right. Yes, she wasn't going to assume false modesty and try to say that she hadn't grown into her prettiness, but every once in a while she still found herself startled to look into the mirror and see the woman she'd become, rather than the skinny girl with the mouth full of braces and the hair that never did what she wanted it to.

After taking another sip of wine, she went on, "Jeff was different then, too. He played football. Was good at it, too, although he knew he wasn't good enough to catch the eye of any pro recruiters. Anyway, he was sort of a golden boy, and I suppose I was flattered beyond belief that he would show any interest at all in me. But...." She hesitated. Okay, she'd kissed Jack, and so their relationship was now on a very different level than it had been even a half hour ago, but was it right for her to be completely honest now? How much did she really want to share?

"But...?" he prompted. The light from the rising moon had begun to fill the room, and she could see his features more clearly now, the strong outlines of his nose and chin, the shimmer of moonlight along his dark hair.

God, he was good-looking.

She swallowed. "But I guess for Jeff, getting me was sort of like winning a game. He worked very hard at our relationship when we were dating, was kind of the perfect boyfriend—flowers on my birthday, a romantic date on our six-month anniversary. That sort of thing. As soon as he knew he had me...pretty much as soon as we were married...that all disappeared. I was a wife. He'd already won the prize. So I guess he figured he didn't have to work at it anymore. And there I was, this stupid deluded girl, twenty-three years old, starting to realize I'd made this huge mistake. I was just too stubborn to admit it to anyone, let alone myself."

"I'm sorry."

All she could do was shrug again. She didn't quite trust herself to look at Jack, and so she kept her gaze fixed on the rising moon, on the pale wash of its light across the desert stretching beyond the windows. "Don't be. It's a pretty common tale, after all. I'm just glad I figured out that I needed to leave sooner rather than later. We didn't have kids, and I only lost a few years of my life." Oh, that sounded terrible. She wished she hadn't made that particular comment. Those years weren't really "lost," after all. She'd gotten her master's in urban planning during that time. Anyway, how could she possibly compare four years of nagging unhappiness to what had happened to Jeff? He'd lost his entire life....

"Did you want kids?"

This time Kate did shift in her chair so she could face Jack. He looked politely inquiring, but nothing more than that. What did he think about having children? He'd made it to his mid-thirties without getting married or starting a family. Did that mean he didn't want them? And what a thing to be worried about, when they'd only shared a couple of kisses and nothing more.

"Someday. I guess I didn't think about it that much, because I was so busy with school. Jeff didn't seem all that interested, although Nancy had started her nagging campaign for grandchildren early on. She'd never thought much of my work on my master's degree, didn't see why I had to work so hard instead of focusing on my marriage. There was no way in the world I could have told her that the marriage probably lasted as long as it did because I had school to distract me. If I hadn't been so preoccupied, I probably would have noticed Jeff's faults as a husband a lot sooner."

Had she said too much? Maybe brutal honesty wasn't the best angle to take here, although Kate knew she couldn't take any of it back now. Besides, she couldn't help but think that it was better for Jack to know everything and make his own decisions.

He was quiet, and didn't respond right away. The silence seemed to press on her, so Kate said, "What about you? I kind of got the impression from Jenny that most witches and warlocks get married pretty early, that she was an exception. But you didn't, either?"

"No." Jack moved in his chair, as though he was made slightly uncomfortable by her question. "It's what was expected, but I didn't want to get married just because that's what my family wanted. Anyway, with four older brothers, I didn't have to worry about making my parents happy and giving them grandchildren. My brothers started in on that while I was still in high school. After a while, everyone sort of let it alone. It was kind of a joke in the clan—Jack, the confirmed bachelor."

What could she say to that? In her heart, she hoped it would be different with the two of them, but maybe that was the same hope every other woman he'd ever dated had harbored. Not that she could call what they were doing now "dating." Even so, she wasn't going to pretend there hadn't been other women before her, probably quite a few.

"This is different, though," he continued, his voice calm, but with an intensity which belied that calm. "I'm not going to lie, Kate. I've been with quite a few women over the years, some witches, some not. I never found what I was looking for. At least, not until now."

Her heart began to pound, although she told herself she couldn't get too hopeful. Maybe he'd felt this same way when he began all those other relationships, only to realize that yet again, something wasn't working.

But he got up from his chair and came over to her, reached down and took her hands in his so she would have to stand up, too. His fingers were warm and strong, and she never wanted him to let go.

"I could say a lot of things right now. That you're different. That I was struck by you from the first moment I saw you. That I've been trying my damnedest to ignore how I feel, because I knew I couldn't have timed all this more badly if I tried. All those things would be true." He stopped there, his grip tightening on hers. Not painfully so, but as if he needed to make sure she wouldn't try to pull away. "But that doesn't matter if you don't feel the same way."

"I do feel the same way," she said, her voice little more than a whisper. "I've been fighting it this whole time, too. My brain and my heart have been having quite the conversation."

"I'll bet." He smiled then, and pulled her close. "I want you, Kate. But we can take this as slowly or as fast as you like. Because I know that you've had a lot of shocks lately, and I don't want you to make any big decisions if you don't feel like you're ready yet."

Oh, she was ready. She could feel it in the way her body responded to his slightest touch, the rush of need for him, the ache in the very center of her being. Would he think less of her, though, for being with him so soon after the two of them had met, especially when that meeting had occurred under such horrific circumstances?

"I—" Kate paused and moistened her lips. "I can

only think how this is all going to look to someone on the outside looking in."

Jack didn't move, but she could tell from the way his mouth tightened that he hadn't wanted to hear her say that. However, he remained silent, clearly waiting for her to go on.

She summoned her courage, the same grit that had allowed her to finally walk out on her marriage even though at the time she didn't have many prospects—no job, no place to stay, although she knew in a pinch that she could have moved in with her parents, unwelcome as that prospect had been. "But we're not on the outside looking in. We know how we both feel. And you know that I hadn't loved Jeff for a very long time, that a piece of paper might have said we were still married, but we sure as hell weren't husband and wife. So I guess what I'm saying is that I don't want to wait. I'm here with you now. I don't want that to change."

No chance to say anything more than that, because in that same moment, Jack pulled her to him, covered her mouth with his, deep kisses so she could taste the wine on his tongue and something else, a flavor that was uniquely his. This time she didn't hold back, but pressed herself up against him, feeling the hard muscles of his chest against her breasts, and something else that was damn hard, pushing against her leg.

His hands moved up and buried themselves in her

hair, and she kept kissing him, dizzy from his touch and maybe, just a little, from lack of oxygen. That didn't matter, though. Nothing mattered except the taste and feel and scent of him.

Then he let go of her, but only for a brief moment, just to slip his arms under her, lift her up. They left the Arizona room, and he carried her through the dimly lit house, going down the hall so he could enter the master suite and set her down on the bed. Almost as soon as he had done that, he lay next to her, kissing her again, even as his hands moved over her body, pulling her blouse from her jeans, undoing her belt buckle. The blouse went up and over her head and landed somewhere on the floor, but she wasn't paying much attention. How could she, when his hands were now gliding over her bare flesh, moving up to unhook the front clasp of her bra, his fingers moving across her breasts?

She gasped, and knew she needed to see him, too. Fingers fumbled with the buttons of his shirt, and then it was gone as well, revealing his muscular torso, his smooth brown skin, with only a light dusting of dark hair on his chest.

Jack didn't give her much time to admire him, however, because his mouth closed on one of her nipples, and she gasped and shut her eyes, then arched up against him. With his free hand, he pulled her jeans downward, taking her underwear with them. A faint *clunk* as they hit the floor, belt buckle and all, but she couldn't pay any attention to that, not when his hand was moving upward along her thigh, not when his fingers slipped into her, stroking.

Oh, God. It had been a long time. Too long. Yes, she had a battery-operated girl's best friend, but it wasn't the same. How could it be? A vibrator didn't know exactly where to touch her, the way Jack was doing now. All of her worry and frustration was gone, replaced by need, replaced by the realization that he was about to make her come.

Which she did, her body clamping down on his fingers, making sure she didn't miss a single shudder-inducing moment. And she cried out, knowing it was okay because there wasn't anyone else around to hear.

Except the coyotes, she thought with some amusement as she gradually returned to herself. *I'll bet you just gave them a run for their money with all the noise you made.*

Well, she'd just have to make sure she had Jack join in, too.

Once she'd caught her breath, she took hold of his belt buckle and unfastened it, then undid the buttons on his jeans. Underneath, she could see the way he strained against his dark underwear. Only one thing to do about that.

Her fingers curled around the waistband of his pants, his boxer briefs. Down they both went, joining the pile on the floor. And holy hell, he was big. She'd guessed he probably would be, simply judging by the size of the erection she'd felt pressed against her as they kissed, but still…damn.

Refusing to let herself be intimidated, she wrapped her fingers around his shaft, stroking. He groaned, and more or less collapsed against the sheets, letting her do as she willed. And she knew exactly what she wanted to do.

She bent down and pulled him into her mouth, savoring the faint saltiness of his skin, feeling the hardness of his flesh. One of his hands moved to touch her hair, but lightly—he wasn't forcing her, that was for sure. He was letting her be in control.

Which was exactly what she wanted. She drew him deep into her mouth, then moved back up again, and down again. More and more, while his breathing quickened and his fingers dug into the comforter, holding on to it tightly as she pleasured him.

Should she stop? No…she wanted to make him come. After all, she was sure they could think of something to do while he was bouncing back, so to speak. So even when he let out a faint sound of protest, as though warning her she was about to hit the point of no return, she didn't hold back, kept moving her tongue over him until at last his entire body stiffened and he spilled into her mouth.

Kate swallowed it all, enjoying his flavor, and, even more than that, the way she'd been able to get him to orgasm. After wiping her chin, she moved up next to him and snuggled against his chest.

For a moment, he didn't say anything, the only sound in the room his harsh breathing. And then, "Jesus Christ."

"Was that okay?"

"'Was that okay'?" he echoed, and chuckled. "That was so far beyond okay, I don't think there's a word for it."

"Good."

His hand stroked her hair. "I think I'll need to return the favor."

"Excuse me?"

Jack didn't reply, only pulled her up so he could kiss her, lips strong against hers. Then his hands moved down her body, and he was lifting her, pulling her away from him so he could lower her onto his mouth.

Oh, my God. That was the last coherent thought to cross through her mind, because after that all she could do was reach out and hang on to the iron headboard while he pleasured her with his tongue, slowly, with languorous, perfect precision, as though he thought her the most delectable treat in the world. The orgasm he'd already given her had been intense enough, but she could tell, from the way every nerve ending flared with heat and need, that he'd only been getting her warmed up.

When the climax hit, she hung on to the headboard and screamed again, a raw sound, the release of too many months without this kind of touch. No, it had been far longer than that; Jeff had never been one to reciprocate when it came to oral sex, and by the time things were falling apart, she was only too glad to avoid that kind of intimacy.

This…this was entirely different. Never in her life had she come like this.

And Jack didn't give her any time to recover, because while the echoes of the orgasm still shivered through her, he lifted her from his mouth and lowered her onto his cock, now obviously recovered from his own climax. It didn't even matter that he was so much bigger than what she was used to, because she was so wet that she easily slid onto him, let him fill her.

"Oh, God," she moaned, and his hands closed on her breasts, caressing her, fingers playing with nipples that had never felt this sensitive before.

She rode him, and once again felt her body warm with heat and need, so alive, so ready for him. This orgasm was quieter than the last, and preceded his by a few seconds, when he bucked up into her, a deep groan accompanying his climax, as she felt him come inside her. No worries there, though—she wasn't a McAllister witch, able to recite a charm to ward off unwanted pregnancy, but the pill did just as nicely when it came to that sort of thing.

And then she collapsed next to him, heart pounding, and he pulled her close, kissing her again, kissing her with a wild abandon that seemed very unlike his usual controlled self. She wrapped her legs around him, not because she expected him to penetrate her again so soon, but just because she wanted as much of her touching him as possible.

His arms tightened around her. As he lifted his mouth from hers, he said, "Now I understand."

"Understand what?"

"Witches and warlocks...we're just supposed to know when we're with the right person. I'd never felt that before. Maya used to tease me when I would tell her I was waiting for the perfect woman. She said the perfect woman was always out there—the real trick was recognizing her when I saw her." Jack touched Kate's cheek, then moved his hand downward so he could caress her mouth. "I recognize you, Kate. This was what Maya meant. I didn't want to acknowledge it at first, because I knew that to anyone looking in, this whole thing would be crazy. But you're the one. It just took a little while for my head to catch up with my heart."

What could she say to that? This was what she'd hoped for with Jeff and failed so miserably to achieve. Knowing that you were with the right person, that something in your soul called out to something in theirs. Even so, she hesitated. This was all so new. She didn't know if she dared tell him what she already knew in the depths of her soul.

But apparently he didn't have the same misgivings, because he said, "I love you, Kate. I think I loved you almost as soon as I saw you."

He'd said it first. He was braver than she, that was for sure. "I love you, Jack. Crazy as all this is…I love you. I want to be with you." She hesitated for a moment, then added, "Even though I have absolutely no idea what we're supposed to do next."

A smile, his teeth flashing white in the semidarkness. "For now? Sleep. In the morning we can start to figure everything out."

Sleep. That sounded like a good idea. To fall asleep in Jack's arms, here in his desert sanctuary. Right then, she refused to believe that anything bad would happen. How could it, when she'd never felt so safe and happy before in her life?

16

Morning sunlight slanted across the bed. Jack opened his eyes and blinked, thinking that surely everything from the night before had been some sort of fever dream born of his need for Kate, his hope that they might somehow be together.

No dream, though, because there she was next to him, her hair a scatter of sun-warmed brown against the pillow. One hand was curled up against her cheek, a curiously childlike position. But she was no child. No, she was definitely all woman.

As he shifted his position, she stirred, eyes opening slowly. They widened as they appeared to take him in, and a crooked little smile settled itself on her mouth. "Good morning," she said.

"Good morning," he replied. And it was. He couldn't think of a better morning than this, waking up to her, knowing that she loved him. "Sleep well?"

"Like a log." She pushed herself up a sitting position, although she made sure to keep the sheet pressed up against her naked breasts. A tinge of pink colored her cheekbones.

As much as Jack would have liked to see those beautiful breasts again, he wasn't going to chide her for her reticence. They'd made love in the dark, with only the light of the moon slipping in past the blinds to illuminate their joining. Now it was bright day, and he wasn't surprised that she might feel a little shy.

"How about some coffee?" He already knew that she needed coffee in the morning as badly as he did, so he figured that was a safe question.

This time her smile was one of gratitude. "Love some."

"Coming right up."

His clothes were strewn all over the floor, so there really wasn't any way to prevent her from seeing his naked backside as he got out of bed. Trying to act nonchalant, he slid from under the covers, then went over to the dresser and got out a clean pair of underwear and some shorts and a T-shirt. He dressed quickly, all too aware of her eyes on him. Funny, because this certainly wasn't the first time he'd woken up with a woman in his bed—although not the bed here in this house—and yet this was the first time he'd really felt self-conscious. Maybe it was because none of those other women had mattered to him the way Kate did.

"I'll be there in a minute," she said as he pulled the T-shirt over his head. "All my clothes are across the hall."

"No worries."

As he headed toward the kitchen, he could hear her get out of bed and pad across the hallway to the room that was supposed to be hers, although he doubted she was really going to spend much time there. They'd gotten fresh coffee at Trader Joe's, so he went about heating up the water and putting the filter and Italian roast in the coffeemaker. No Keurig here; he'd decided it was probably better to have a low-tech coffee solution in a place that would be rented out to strangers.

He looked around, thinking that he wasn't sure if he really wanted to use the house as a vacation rental any longer. Now it felt like a sacred place, the spot where he'd made love to Kate for the first time. Where he'd realized that he did love her, that his heart wasn't the barren ground he'd begun to believe it must be.

She came into the kitchen, her sleep-mussed hair pulled back into an elastic band, her body now covered in a tank top and some knee-length yoga pants. Well, sort of covered—the clothes fit her snugly, and he could see the contours of her breasts easily enough through the pale green top.

Just the sight made him begin to harden, and he pulled in a breath, willing the erection to go away until a more opportune time. The sex last night had been spectacular, but now it was morning, and reality had a way of intruding at that particular time of day.

He busied himself with getting down some mugs as he said, "Coffee should be ready in a few minutes."

"Sounds great." She went over to the window and peered out, but there really wasn't that much to see, just a bright morning sun shining down on the fresh green of the manzanita trees, a light breeze blowing through the wild grasses and flowers. It looked to be a perfect day.

A perfect day for what, though? That was the real question. He didn't think their foe would approach the house in bright sunlight; so far, except for the trashing of his apartment, the warlock in question clearly preferred to work in darkness. Anyway, if someone who harbored dark intent was lurking anywhere in the vicinity, he would have felt it through the wards he had placed on the perimeter of the property.

"Everything's fine," he said as he poured coffee into each of the mugs he'd set on the counter. "We're alone here."

She gave a guilty start, then turned away from the window and back toward him. "Of course. I mean, I should have remembered that. You told me that the wards would let you know if anyone tried to come close."

"Exactly. So have your coffee, and we can figure out what we need to do today."

Without replying, she came over to him and picked up one of the mugs of coffee, and blew on the surface of the liquid. "What do we need to do? You made it sound as if we just had to sit tight while Luz talks to Connor and Angela, that it was up to them to figure out what to do next."

He went to the fridge and got out the small carton of milk they'd purchased, pouring in only enough to turn his coffee a milk chocolate color. "Well, yes, I am sort of waiting to hear what they have to say, but that doesn't mean we can't do some work of our own while we're down here. I have a cousin in Tucson, Consuelo. She's the clan's expert on this kind of magic. I already talked to her once about your—about Jeff's case, but with everything that's going on in California, I thought it would be a good idea to speak with her again."

Kate didn't look exactly thrilled by that suggestion. "Is it safe?"

It would have been nice to be able to tell her that her worries didn't have any true basis, but Jack knew that wasn't the case. He'd reassured her over and over that they would be safe in their desert refuge, and now he was telling her that he wanted to leave the house down here in Tubac and go back up to Tucson.

"I don't see why it wouldn't be. For one thing, it seems pretty obvious that our warlock doesn't know where we are, so we don't need to worry about being followed. Also, Consuelo has her house warded even more securely than this one. Even if something did try to attack us there, I don't think it would get very far."

His words didn't appear to reassure Kate, though. She didn't answer immediately, only blew on her coffee a few more times before taking a very cautious sip. When she spoke, however, she didn't offer any protests. "Well, if you think it will be all right...."

"I know it will be. I'll send her an email."

This time, one of Kate's eyebrows arched slightly. "Email?"

"Consuelo kind of lives out in the middle of nowhere. She doesn't have a phone, and there's no cell service where she lives. She has satellite internet, just like I do here."

"Ah." This time, Kate shot him an arch look. "So when were you going to give me the wifi password?"

He couldn't help chuckling. "We were a little busy last night. But it's Tubac256. Guess I'd better change it, though—that's the password my agent set up for the last batch of guests. You can use it now, though, if you want to check your email or something."

"No, I'll wait until the password's been updated. I talked to my mother yesterday—and left messages for Colin and Sam—so I'm probably okay for a while." She took a larger swallow of coffee this time, then added, "Am I making breakfast?"

He gave a rueful shrug. "Well, yeah, unless you're okay with runny scrambled eggs."

Kate grimaced and sent him a rueful but still affectionate look. "Never mind. I'll take care of it."

After setting down her mug, she went to the refrigerator and got out more of the supplies they'd picked up the afternoon before—a carton of eggs, bacon, a package of English muffins. Even though she couldn't know where everything was located, she got all the necessary items assembled in a remarkably short period of time.

As she beat the eggs in a yellow ceramic bowl, she asked, "So you really think your cousin Consuelo will be able to help out with all this?"

Good question. But the older witch had spent years researching magic's darker aspects, tracking down its more esoteric manifestations. She might have more insight on how to handle a null, for example. The little Jack had heard on the subject had made it sound as though those witches and warlocks who could destroy all magic around them were nearly invincible, but he refused to believe that. No one was invincible. Everyone had their weak point.

"More than anyone else I can think of," he said, and drank some more of his coffee. "In general, we don't like to explore the darker aspects of our powers. They can be very strong, but they can also make us reckless. And that's one thing we really can't afford to be, not when we have to live amongst those of you who don't have any magical ability, not when we're so outnumbered. So Consuelo is something of a rarity. I think she's tried a few times to take some of my younger cousins under her wing, to teach them what she knows, but they haven't been very receptive."

"She doesn't have children?"

"No." Which was another rarity. He knew that she'd been married a long time ago, but her husband had died young, before they could start a family. No one really talked about what had happened to Consuelo's husband, and Jack hadn't spent much time wondering about the circumstances of his death. In a clan as large as his, it was hard enough to keep track of one's immediate relatives, let alone the fourth cousins twice removed, or whatever Consuelo was to him.

Kate appeared to think that over for a moment, then said, "Well, it does sound as if she's the person to talk to. And it'll give us something to do."

"What, were you worried about being cooped up in the house all day with me?"

A slow smile, one that spread over her features like the spring sun coming up over the desert. "No, I'm pretty sure we could figure out something to do to amuse ourselves. But being overly distracted probably isn't a good idea, not with what we're up against."

Jack couldn't argue with that statement. He watched as she poured the beaten eggs into a skillet where butter had been heating up and melting, and thought once again of what it had felt like to taste her, to plunge deep into her. Yes, going to bed would definitely while away the hours, but…they'd taken a risk last night, wards or no. Spending all day in that kind of activity could put them in danger. They'd be far too distracted.

"You're right," he said. "I guess we can't really pretend like we're on vacation down here. Do you know how to shoot?"

The question caught her off guard, he could tell; she startled slightly and turned away from her work on the stove top so she could give him a worried look. "You mean, shoot a gun?"

"Yes."

"Sort of. That is, I went to the range with Jeff a couple of times. I really didn't like it—the noise, the realization that I was holding something deadly in my hands. But yes, I know how to shoot. Why?"

"Because you just never know."

"A gun against a warlock?"

She appeared so skeptical that Jack couldn't help chuckling. "We're not supernatural beings, Kate. We're just people who happen to have some special abilities. We bleed, same as everyone else."

"What about the demons?"

He felt himself sober abruptly. "Well, yeah, demons generally don't care if you plug them full of semiautomatic rounds. But that's what my defensive spells are for. And I'm still not sure if we'd even be facing demons. Consuelo said it appeared that they'd been summoned and then dismissed once their work was done, whatever it was. You don't really keep them around on a leash. That's way too dangerous, even for the person summoning them."

For a moment, she didn't say anything, only turned back to the stove and pushed the eggs around in the skillet. "This is all academic, right?"

Should he lie to her, reassure her that he was just trying to be thorough, tell her they'd hidden themselves well enough that they really didn't need to worry?

No, he would never lie to her. She deserved better than that. "I don't know," he said frankly. "I'm just trying to make sure we have as many bases covered as possible."

Again she didn't reply right away. In silence, she opened the package of English muffins and extracted several, then split them apart and stuck them in the toaster oven. "You're kind of freaking me out, Jack."

"I want you to be freaked out."

That remark made her turn around back toward him, hazel eyes questioning. "Excuse me?"

"Being a little scared is okay. It helps you to keep your edge. Too scared, and yeah, then you lose your focus. But we both need to keep it together, because I honestly can't tell you what might be coming next."

She nodded. Even though she was fairly tall, right then she looked small and frightened, like a kid who'd just realized the monsters under the bed might be real. Her expression made him go to her and wrap his arms around her waist. She immediately leaned into him, her arms reaching around him as well so she could hug him tightly.

"Don't worry," he said. "Everything is going to be okay."

Whether he was telling her the truth remained to be seen.

Such a beautiful spring day, and yet Kate couldn't allow herself to enjoy it. Not really. She sat in the passenger seat of the Jeep and watched the landscape pass by outside, every mile bringing them a little closer to Tucson, and to this cousin Consuelo. What would she be like? Kate imagined that someone who'd spent most of their life researching dark magic must be somehow dark as well, bent and twisted. No, she was just manufacturing an image based on movies she'd seen and books she'd read. Jack would never take her to meet someone who wasn't on the up and up. If the clan didn't have someone who specialized in this stuff, how would they know how to fight it?

To be honest, her current nervousness only had a little to do with leaving the sanctuary of the house in Tubac, and a lot more to do with the fact that Consuelo would be the first person to meet Kate after...well, after she and Jack had slept together. Under normal circumstances, that wouldn't be such a big deal—this wasn't the 1800s, after all—but when you had witches thrown into the equation, all the norms sort of went out the window. Would Consuelo be able to tell just from looking at her that she and Jack had been intimate?

No, that was ridiculous. Kate didn't profess to be an expert on the witch community, but nothing Jenny had said during the time she'd been married to Colin seemed to indicate that sniffing out whether people were sleeping together was a common witch talent, like seeing the future or casting illusions. Anyway, Kate knew that, of all the things which should be preying on her mind, worrying about whether anyone in the de la Paz clan might think she was a loose woman should be pretty far down the list.

As they drove, she checked her phone. A message from Colin, saying he was glad she'd let him know what was going on, and that Jenny was doing fine and they both wanted to hear from her soon. He ended the message with, "A de la Paz warlock? I always hoped that someday you'd come over to the dark side."

The comment made her smile. "Dark side," indeed. She did have to admit that being involved with a warlock would make some things easier—she definitely wouldn't have to worry about hiding anything about Jenny's family from Jack.

There was also a text from Sam letting her know that her friend had gotten Kate's message and that she hoped everything would be okay, and to please call her when she had a chance, that Sam would be available after six that night. Kate hoped she'd be able to make that call, but at the moment she really didn't know what was going to happen next.

On the other hand, Jack spent half their drive deep in conversation with Luz, who was waiting for Angela and Connor to arrive at her house for their meeting. Since Jack had the hands-free setup going through the Jeep's sound system, Kate was able to hear every word.

"…no reply at any of the numbers I called. Not that I have so many contacts in the Santiago clan, but Caitlin had given me Olivia Hernandez's number —Matías Escobar's sister—and she didn't answer, and I also had the contact information for Simón's younger brother Cristían, and he didn't pick up, either. So then I called the number I had for Simón and Beatriz Santiago. Just to see what would happen."

Kate could feel her own eyes widen, and Jack apparently was just as shocked, because he said, voice rough with worry, "Why would you do a thing like that?"

"Because I wanted to see how this—this interloper would react. And to show that I am the *prima* of the de la Paz clan, and not someone to be easily intimidated."

"So you spoke with him?"

"Not at first. It was actually Marisol who answered the phone."

"She's living at the Santiagos' house now?"

"I got that impression. Actually, it was difficult to get much of anything out of her. I can't claim to know her at all…this was the first time I'd ever spoken to her…but she sounded almost drugged. Dreamy and not making very much sense. I tried to ask her what had happened to Simón and Beatriz, and Marisol just said that they'd gone away, and she was the *prima* now, but she couldn't really talk because she had so much to do."

Jack's fingers tightened on the steering wheel. "Did you ask her what it was that she had to do?"

A pause, and Luz replied, "As I said, I tried. She just gave a strange little laugh and told me that she was going to do over one of the spare bedrooms. Because of the baby."

"The baby? *Whose* baby?" he demanded, and Kate felt a horrible creepy-crawly sensation move down her back. After all, it was pretty obvious from what Caitlin had described in her vision what had happened to the Santiagos' *prima*-in-waiting after the screen went dark, so to speak.

"I don't know. Afterward, I talked to Caitlin and asked her if she'd seen any indication in her vision that Marisol was pregnant. Caitlin said that no, she hadn't, but of course if Marisol was only a month or so along, she wouldn't be showing anything anyway.

But I don't think that's what she was referring to. I think she believes that this man, this null, has already gotten her with child."

The coffee and eggs Kate had consumed only an hour or so earlier flip-flopped in her stomach. She honestly didn't know what was worse—that Marisol should be so sure already that she was pregnant, or that she seemed so happy to be planning for her rapist's child.

From the grim set of Jack's mouth, it seemed obvious enough to Kate that his thoughts ran along more or less the same lines. When he spoke, his voice was tight but controlled. "What did she say after that?"

"She said she had to go, but that Joaquin wanted to talk to me."

"Joaquin. That's the null's name?"

"Apparently. There was a pause, and I could hear her speaking to someone in a murmur, although I couldn't really make out what they were saying to one another. And then a man came on the line. He said, 'Hello, Luz. What is it that you want?' I told him that, as the *prima* of the de la Paz clan, I was gravely concerned by his actions. He told me that what happened in Santiago territory was none of my concern and that I should mind my own business. Then he added, 'It is better this way. I have what I want. But if you press me, Luz, I will carry the fight to you, and I do not think you will much like what happens next.' After that, he hung up."

"Charming character," Jack commented, although Kate could tell he was being sarcastic to cover up how deeply Luz's narrative had disturbed him. "What did he sound like to you?"

"His accent was quite thick. I don't think he is a native speaker of both English and Spanish, the way so many in our clan are. It seemed clear to me that he must have learned English later on. His voice was somewhat deep and rough, but I couldn't really tell much from it. Anyway, Caitlin has already described him, so we know that he is probably in his forties. The accent only backs up her description of him being Hispanic."

Luz sounded very calm…almost too calm. What sort of effort had it taken for her to make that call in the first place, and then stay on the line as that monster, that murderer, spoke to her? Kate didn't know if she could have managed it.

"Well, it's another piece of the puzzle. That news about Marisol, though…." Jack let the words trail off, but Kate could see the way his nostrils flared in disgust. "Anyway, we'll just have to keep trying to put things together. I'll let you go now, since we're about to get off the freeway. But call me and let me know what Angela and Connor had to say."

"I will." Luz paused before adding, "Be careful."

"I always am."

He pushed the button on the dashboard to disconnect the call. Because they were just pulling off the highway then, he didn't say anything for a moment. It wasn't until he had the Jeep pointed toward the foothills east of Tucson that he said, "Jesus."

"That was...pretty bad," Kate ventured. "What do you think the null is doing to Marisol? Drugging her? Putting some kind of a spell on her?"

"Probably the latter, although it's hard to say for sure." Jack's brows drew together behind his dark glasses. It seemed like he was paying extra attention to the road in front of him because he didn't want to look over at her, as if by doing so he'd reveal too much of the horror he must be feeling. At least, Kate assumed he must be horrified. She knew she was. "Just because he's a null doesn't mean he doesn't also possess some secondary talents. It happens sometimes, though people who possess two strong talents at the same time are rare. Controlling other people—sort of like what Matías Escobar did to Roslyn McAllister and Danica Wilcox—could be another gift. And if that's true, it means the null...this Joaquin person...is even more of a threat than I'd previously thought."

Wonderful. This just kept getting better and better. Kate tried to figure out what would be worse— to be taken by such a person and understand every-thing of what was happening to you, or to have your mind clouded by magic so you thought that what he was doing was something you actually wanted. Since both prospects sounded equally horrible, about all she could do was shudder.

"I know," Jack said. He lifted his right hand from the steering wheel and laid it on top of hers for a moment, gave it a reassuring squeeze. "I can't sugar-coat this. About the only promising thing in Luz's conversation with the null was that it sounded as though he wanted to be left alone, that he wouldn't bring the fight to us unless we pushed it."

Kate was glad of the pressure of Jack's hand against hers, the warmth of his skin. Too soon, though, he took it away, gripped the steering wheel with both hands. She could see why—they'd just turned off the main street they were following away from the freeway and off onto a dirt road, its surface turned into a washboard of ruts after too many years of summertime monsoon rains and no apparent main-tenance to smooth it out again.

"Will you do that?" she asked. "That is, would Luz and Connor and Angela let something like this go?"

"I'm not sure," Jack replied. They'd slowed down to a modest twenty miles an hour or so, but dust still plumed away from their tires at an alarming rate. Good thing Consuelo expected them, because there was definitely no way of sneaking up on someone out here. "Usually we all try to keep things on the down-low, no matter the cost, because a war between witch clans is the fastest way to let civilians know that something's been hiding behind the scenes all along. On the other hand, can we really stand by and let this Joaquin person—and whoever else might be working for him—get away with this? To kill a *prima* and her consort, to murder the *prima*-in-waiting's own consort? Those crimes are completely beyond the pale."

And those probably weren't the only deaths on this Joaquin's conscience. Kate still couldn't quite figure out the connection, but it was becoming more probable to her that the warlock who'd murdered Jeff also had to be working for the null. Also, what had happened to Lucinda Santiago in all this? Caitlin's communications with her had been cut off, and so no one seemed to have any idea as to her fate. Maybe the null had murdered her, too, deeming her to be of little use because, although she was the *prima*'s daughter, she wasn't a strong enough witch to have been the *prima*-in-waiting.

So many questions, so few answers. Even without the stakes being so impossibly high, Kate would have found the entire situation beyond frustrating, just because she wasn't used to being kept so much in the dark. In this day and age, instant communication and information were pretty much a given. But not here. The man who had taken over the Santiago clan might as well be on the dark side of the moon for all they really knew about what he was doing now.

The road curved, and then Jack turned down a narrow lane barely big enough to let the Jeep through. Here, the washboarding was so bad that he slowed down to a scant ten miles an hour. Even so, Kate found herself reaching for the "Jesus handle" above her head so she wouldn't get jostled around too much. On either side were scrubby manzanita bushes and the stark shapes of saguaro cactus, and golden desert broom. There was nothing here that should have made her feel so uneasy, but as they pulled up in front of a low, sprawling adobe house, she felt it again, an uneasy churn in the pit of her stomach.

Jack turned off the engine and climbed out of the vehicle, and Kate did the same. Dust swirled away from the Jeep, and the air smelled like sun-warmed dry grass. Cactus flowers bloomed on all sides, their colors a riot against the mellower shades of sand and rock. It was very warm, almost hot. And yet she couldn't help shivering.

"Consuelo's lived here forever," Jack said as he led her to the front door, which was adorned with a cruci-fix. "She doesn't drive—some of the family here in Tucson takes turns coming out here with groceries. I think her sister has been pressuring her to sell this place and move to a condo in town, but she won't hear of it."

Despite her uneasiness, Kate couldn't help smiling. "Well, I have to admit that a witch living in a condo sounds a little funny."

His eyebrow went up. "But apartments are okay?"

"For some reason, yes."

He chuckled. Clearly, whatever was bothering her didn't seem to be affecting him. Maybe that was merely because he happened to be a warlock trained in defensive magic, and he knew for a fact that nothing bad waited for them on the other side of the door. After all, Kate was a civilian, one who didn't know very much about those sorts of things. She probably had a bad case of the heebie-jeebies now because of the conversation she'd just overheard. Some of the things Luz had said were enough to make anyone uneasy.

"Consuelo?" Jack knocked on the dark wood of the front door. "It's Jack and Kate."

No response. Kate tilted a glance up at him, and hoped her expression was merely one of mild curiosity rather than outright worry.

He offered a shrug. "It's a big place, and Consuelo is…well, she's a big woman, and not as light on her feet as she used to be. It takes her more time to get from one place to the other than it does most of us."

What could she do except nod? Kate didn't want to give voice to her disquiet, so she only said, "Ah, that makes sense."

Jack knocked again. "Consuelo?"

Still no answer. Had she gone out? No, Jack had just said she didn't own a car, had family members bring her groceries to her. But she could be in the bathroom, or on the other side of the house, or….

Something that sounded like a curse in Spanish, made under his breath, and Jack laid both palms flat against the age-darkened wood of the door. His eyes shut. Once again his lips moved, but this time Kate thought he might be reciting the words to a spell.

Then his eyes flared open, and he put his hand on the door latch and lifted it, and swung the door inward.

Kate's hands went to her mouth. *Oh, my God….*

The place had probably always been somewhat cluttered. Now, though, it was a welter of books and papers and statues and incense burners and other bric-a-brac she couldn't identify. Everything had been thrown around with enough violence that it looked as if hurricane-force winds had driven their way through the house.

Jack charged into the front room, hands raised, as if ready to cast a spell of protection at the slightest sign of an attack. "*Consuelo!*"

Only silence.

He looked over his shoulder at Kate. "You stick right behind me. Understand?"

"Yes." No way in hell was she going to try playing the hero. She'd let Jack handle this. He was far better equipped to deal with whatever might be waiting for them in this empty house.

Slowly, he began to move forward, through the

wreck of antiques and religious icons. Kate wondered at that a little, even though she knew the de la Paz clan was fairly Catholic. She supposed she hadn't expected to see such obvious signs of faith in the home of a witch, especially one who studied the darker aspects of the supernatural world.

And then, from somewhere down the hallway…a low moan. Jack hurried in the direction of the sound, which seemed to be coming from a room off to the left, a space which had once apparently been a library but now looked like a mountain of discarded books.

It was from under the pile of books that the moan came again. "Hurry," Jack said, going to the source of the sound and beginning to claw books out of the way. Kate followed suit, grabbing volume after volume and tossing them to one side. She began to see the shape of a woman under those books, curled into a fetal position as if to try to protect herself from her attacker, her long gray hair loose from its bun and falling down to obscure her face.

As Jack pushed the last of the books out of the way, she moaned again. He knelt down next to her. "Consuelo? What happened?"

Another moan. Now that the books had been cleared away, Kate was able to see the terrible claw marks on the older woman's face and throat, the mottling of livid bruises that made it almost impossible to tell what color her skin actually was.

Jack scrabbled in his pocket for his cell phone.

"I'm going to call Valentina. She'll fix you up, and then you can tell us what happened."

"No." The syllable came out as a harsh whisper. Consuelo's eyes shut, and she shook her head almost imperceptibly. "What has been done…cannot be undone. It is well. I will be with *mi esposo* Esteban soon."

"Consuelo—"

"No." Her eyes flared open briefly, the whites marred by a series of broken veins. "You listen to me, Jack. This—this is an evil you cannot fight alone. Go tell Luz. Tell her…." The words trailed off, and once again Consuelo's eyes shut.

"Tell her what?" Jack asked, his voice rough with urgency.

But whatever it was that Consuelo wanted him to tell Luz, it had died with her. She did not move after that. All Kate could do was stand off to one side, her entire body paralyzed with worry. What if whatever had done this to Consuelo was coming back?

At last Jack pushed himself to his feet. When he turned toward Kate, his face appeared utterly without expression, bleak, as though he didn't dare let himself betray any reaction to his cousin's death.

Kate whispered, "I'm so sorry…."

He held up a hand. "She made her peace with it. But we have to figure out what happened here. So much for thinking the warlock wouldn't strike in broad daylight. He must have decided it was worth the risk, since Consuelo's house is so isolated. Her nearest neighbors are far enough away that they probably wouldn't have seen or heard anything."

"What was the warlock trying to find?"

A long pause as Jack surveyed the damage around them, the lifeless body of the woman on the floor. "I have no idea. Consuelo collected a lot of rare texts on dark magic, so maybe there was something here he specifically thought he could use. I don't know if we'll ever be able to figure out what went missing—I know Maya had encouraged Consuelo for years to get all this in a database somewhere, told her she'd ask one of the cousins who was computer-savvy to help. But Consuelo always said no, that these were works of power and not something to be trapped in a computer. Maybe she had records written down somewhere, but considering the shape this place is in…." He stopped there, the way his hands hung limp at his sides a better indicator of the helplessness he currently felt than anything he might say.

Kate went to him and put one arm around his waist. "Well, we can worry about that later. Who should we call? I know you said Consuelo didn't have any children, but…."

"Ana, her younger sister—she lives here in Tucson. It's often her kids who bring out Consuelo's supplies. I don't think I have her phone number, though."

"Who does?"

"Luz. The *prima* has the contact information for

everyone in the clan." Once again Jack stopped. He pulled in a breath. "Jesus. I deal with this sort of thing every day, but…."

"It's all right," Kate said. She hugged him closely. "I understand. It's different when it's someone you know."

A bitter smile twisted his lips. "Yes, I guess you'd know that better than anyone else. All right, I'll call Luz. Do you want to wait in the car?"

At once Kate shook her head. "I'll stay with you… and with Consuelo…until her relatives can come." She hesitated, then added, "Whatever did this…it's not coming back, is it?"

"I have no idea. I don't feel anything off. That is…." He went quiet for a minute, clearly trying to figure out the best way to articulate what he was feeling. "I can feel that it was here, sort of how you can smell the stink of chicken carcass in the garbage even after you've taken the trash out. But it's gone. It did whatever it needed to…got whatever it wanted."

The room was stuffy, verging on hot, but Kate couldn't help shivering anyway. "Whatever that was."

"Yes. The problem is, I'm not sure we really want to find out what the warlock took…because that means he'd be using it against us."

17

Consuelo's sister Ana, and Ana's daughter Isabel and son-in-law Manuel, arrived within the half hour. Jack was glad to see Manuel with them, because, while he might have been able to get Consuelo's body into the back of his Jeep with only Kate's help, it would have been difficult. This way, Jack and Manuel were able to manage the unpleasant task while Ana, Isabel, and Kate stood off to one side Both Ana and Isabel wept; Kate was dry-eyed but pale-faced, clearly far more upset than she wanted to let on. Not that she didn't have every right to be upset. She didn't know Consuelo, true, but she'd also been first on the scene when her estranged husband was murdered, and no doubt coming here had only brought back those painful memories. This crime scene hadn't been nearly as brutal, true, but it still was the last thing either of them had expected to see when they entered the house.

It would all be handled very quietly. Jack couldn't recall the name of the de la Paz cousin who owned the funeral home here in Tucson, but that was where Consuelo would go, until her services were held a few days from now. There would be no inquiry; the victim had been in her late seventies, and extremely overweight. No one would question her death, and none of the clan members would speak of it as anything except the sort of everyday tragedy one might expect of an elderly relative who lived alone.

And the monster who had murdered her would get away.

No. Jack refused to believe that. Sooner or later, this murderous warlock and the dangerous entities he controlled would make a misstep. One person couldn't go up against an entire clan and hope to win. The death of Jeff Nichols wasn't anything that affected them directly, and so there had been no need for any of them, except Luz in her role as *prima,* to get involved with that crime. But Consuelo was one of their own.

Jack said a few comforting words to Ana and Isabel, thanked Manuel for his help. They drove off in Manuel's Ford Explorer, leaving Jack and Kate alone once again.

He looked over at the house. It appeared innocent enough, just a shabby adobe structure baking in the midday sun. No one looking at it would be able to tell that someone had just been violently attacked within those thick walls.

"What now?" Kate asked. Her voice sounded tight to him, like she was doing everything in her power to stay calm and controlled, even though he knew that inwardly she must be freaking out. Was she beginning to wish her path had never crossed his, that she had never discovered the darkness lurking behind the world of bohemian witches and warlocks she'd first encountered in Jerome?

As he gazed down into her clear hazel eyes, turned golden in the bright sunlight, he realized he couldn't let himself think such things. Yes, she was troubled, but he didn't see anything of regret in her face. Whatever happened next, she wanted to meet it at his side. And he loved her all the more for that.

"We'll head up to Scottsdale, talk to Luz. With any luck, Connor and Angela will still be there. Luz made it sound as if they planned to stay over for a late lunch, so I'll call as we're driving and tell her to keep them until we can get there. It's only an hour and a half away."

Kate nodded. "All right. Besides…." She stopped there, her wide, friendly mouth pursing slightly.

"Besides what?"

"Well, I was just thinking it would be a good idea to head someplace that wasn't the house. Just in case there's something around here, something that might…follow us."

At once he took her hands and pulled her to him, sensing she needed the reassurance of his touch right then. "I think it's gone, Kate."

"But do you know that for sure?"

He hesitated. To be honest, while he didn't sense anything lurking around the property, how much did that really mean? His skills lay in defensive magic, in fighting something that had already made itself known to him. If a presence was strong enough, he could feel it…sometimes…but his skills in that area certainly weren't infallible.

"No," he said. Her lips tightened, and he could see her swallow. He went on, "I promised myself that I would never lie to you, Kate, and I'm not about to start now. I don't feel anything here right at the moment, but I'm not an expert. You're right that it's probably smart to go elsewhere first. Even if it's waiting here, watching to see what we do next, it's not going to be too happy to discover that we're headed straight for the *prima*'s house…especially when the *prima* in question has her counterparts from up north visiting. So let's get going."

Kate nodded and followed him over to the Jeep. He waited until they were off the narrow lane that led to Consuelo's house and partway to the freeway before he called Luz again. This time, the call went to voice-mail, which told him she was probably in the middle of her convo with Connor and Angela. Jack hated to leave this kind of a message on voicemail. He didn't have much choice, however, so he quickly explained what had happened with Consuelo, and said that he and Kate were on their way up to Scottsdale and they'd very much appreciate it if the *prima* and *primus* from northern Arizona would hang around until they got there.

After that, there wasn't much to do except head north on I-10 and be glad of every mile he put between them and Tucson. As they were passing through Picacho, he looked over at Kate and said, "Sorry."

She shifted in the passenger seat and sent him a quizzical glance. "Sorry for what?"

"I don't know…dragging you into all this."

To his surprise, she smiled slightly. "As I recall, you kind of got dragged into it first, because of Jeff. Things just…happened…after that."

That was one way of putting it. Still, he wished vehemently that none of this was happening, that they'd met some other way. For God's sake, he'd had the most spectacular sex of his life with her the night before. They should've gone out to brunch, visited the art galleries in Tubac, enjoyed the day together, come back to barbecue and an evening of leisurely lovemaking. Instead, he'd brought her—inadvertently, yes, but still—to yet another crime scene, to a place where she'd had to watch someone die in front of her eyes.

"Yes, but—"

She reached over and laid a hand on his leg. Crazy that even the most comforting of touches should send such a thrill through him. He didn't want to be going to Scottsdale. He wanted to head back to the house in Tubac and make love to her again. Insane? Maybe. Or maybe not really, considering that one of the most human reactions to death was the desire to have sex, to prove you were still alive.

But it wasn't happening this afternoon. After they got back to the house? Well, he'd have to see how Kate felt. Right now he didn't see any desire in her expression, except the need to offer him what comfort she could.

"It's okay, Jack," she said quietly. "This is—it's all awful. There's no other word for it. But if I have to go through all this, I'm so very, very glad that I'm able to go through it at your side. Anyway," she continued, her tone somewhat more brisk, "shouldn't I be comforting you? You're the one who just lost a relative."

True enough, although he wasn't what you could call close with Consuelo. She was part of the Tucson branch of the family, and so their paths didn't cross very often, especially in later years, where she hadn't shown much inclination to leave the house, not even for the clan get-togethers they usually held sometime in the spring. "It's…well, I can't say it's all right, because of course it isn't, but I'm also not the sort of person to pretend to mourn someone I didn't know very well. If it had been either of my parents, or one of my brothers…." He stopped himself there, because he really didn't want to think what his reaction might have been if he'd lost someone that close to him.

Kate seemed to take the hint, because she asked, "Can you tell me about your family? I mean, your immediate family, not the de la Paz clan itself."

"What's to tell? My parents live in Phoenix, in the same house where all of us were born."

"You were born at home?" She seemed surprised by that revelation.

"When you've got healers in the family, it's not as big a deal. No hospitals for most of us de la Pazes, unless it's something really serious that a healer can't handle. I'm the youngest of five—usually we witch-folk keep our families a little smaller, just because witch blood tends to breed true, and it's hard to keep a low profile if you're multiplying at a rate to take over the earth." Kate chuckled at that remark, and he allowed himself a small smile. It felt good to be talking about subjects like this, rather than all the doom and gloom of the past few days. "But my mother wanted a girl, so they kept trying…and then when I came along, that's when she gave up and said it must be God's will."

"Well, I'm glad you're not a girl."

He grinned. "Yeah, me, too. My oldest brother is married to Luz's sister, so we're connected a little more closely than most. Luis is a lawyer. The rest of my brothers are kind of all over the place—one's a landscape architect, another a chemist, and Tomás is a librarian, of all things."

"What made you want to be a cop?"

"A couple of things. I like to work at puzzles until I solve them. Also, we try to have a couple of us on the various police forces in the area—it helps in case something happens that's witch-related and needs to be swept under the rug, so to speak."

That comment didn't seem to win Kate's approval. Her brows drew together, and she shot him a troubled look from under her eyelashes. "What, you'll cover things up if it looks bad for the witch community? That doesn't sound right."

"That's not really what we do," he responded, his tone as gentle as he could make it. Kate might understand something of his people's need to keep things quiet, but since she wasn't a witch herself, she couldn't possibly understand it at gut level the way he and everyone else in his family did. "I mean, look at Matías Escobar. Of course I helped to make sure he'd be locked up for the rest of his life, because he's a bad guy. But a very important part of what I did was to ensure that the supernatural elements of the case were downplayed, or shown to be part of his own particular obsessions, nothing to do with reality. That's how we make it work. We don't want the bad guys to win. But we also can't have them expose us for what we are."

This explanation elicited a nod, albeit a somewhat troubled one. "I suppose I understand. I can tell you have far different problems to deal with down here than the McAllisters do in Jerome."

There was an understatement. For the most part, the smaller clan got to exist in their little bubble and not worry nearly as much about hiding their true selves. Hell, even the civilians who lived in the little mountain town were carefully vetted so they could be let in on the secret. But here, rubbing elbows with non-magical people on every side? You could never let go. Not really.

"Yes, we do." He drummed his fingers on the steering wheel. "The real reason I became a cop, though, is that I wanted to make sure the bad guys would be brought to justice. And that's why I'm not going to let this thing go." As she watched him, her expression troubled, he added, "No matter what."

Jack parked his Jeep in front of Luz's elegant hacienda-style home. This time, Kate noted the perfectly groomed desert-style landscaping out front, the cactus studded with blooms in fuchsia and yellow. They went through the courtyard, past a tiled fountain that splashed into the quiet afternoon air, and up to the tall door of dark carved wood. Once again, Kate had to fight back a wave of uneasiness. Yes, she hadn't faced any disapproval from Consuelo, but that was because the unfortunate woman had been attacked and on death's door when Kate and Jack arrived at her house.

Here, though…inside was Luz Trujillo, the *prima* of the entire de la Paz clan, along with Angela and Connor Wilcox. Never mind that, according to Jenny, Angela was a year or so younger than Kate herself, and therefore shouldn't be all that intimidating. She was still a *prima,* and her husband a *primus,* and therefore both forces to be reckoned with.

Jack rang the doorbell, and a moment later Luz opened the door. Just like the last time Kate had seen her, Luz wore a dead-simple but probably very expensive dress, her dark hair pulled back into a low chignon. Although her expression appeared tense, she smiled when she saw Kate and Jack, and said, "You made good time." Her focus shifted to Kate, and she added, "It's good to see you again, Kate."

Was there a subtext to those words? Had Luz somehow managed to detect the shift in Kate's relationship with Jack? She managed an awkward smile and said, "Hello, Luz."

Seeming to sense the awkwardness of the moment, Luz said, "Come on inside. We're all in the living room."

Kate trailed along behind Luz and Jack, trying not to be too obvious about looking from side to side and taking it all in. Yes, she'd been here before, but that time she and Caitlin and Alex had hurried in so quickly that she hadn't been able to note much about her surroundings. Her second impressions only reinforced those first glimpses she'd caught, telling her that this house was very different from the witch-owned homes she'd seen in Jerome. The de la Paz *prima*'s home could have been lifted from the Spanish countryside somewhere, with its red-tiled floors, white plaster walls, and wrought-iron fixtures. Everything here looked as if it had been in the family for years, and well-loved during that time. Not shabby, just not model-home perfect, either.

On the leather couch in the living room sat a dark-haired couple, both of them very attractive, the woman with striking green eyes and long wavy hair, the man tall and movie-star handsome. They stood as soon as Kate and Jack entered the room, although neither of them smiled. "I'm Connor," the man said. "And this is Angela."

Angela held out her hand to Kate, and she took it. "Very nice to meet you," Kate said.

The other woman's mouth quirked. "Well, I'm not sure about 'nice,' considering the circumstances, but I'm glad for the chance to meet you. Jenny speaks very highly of you."

A flush heated Kate's cheeks. She had no idea that her sister-in-law had ever discussed her with the clan's *prima*. "Jenny's awesome."

"So she is." Angela looked over at Jack. "I'm sorry, Jack. Luz told me what just happened to your cousin."

He nodded. His face wore the tight, blank expression Kate had come to recognize as the one he put on when he wanted to make sure he didn't betray his emotions. "I'm positive it's the same person who murdered Jeff Nichols, and who sabotaged Kate's car. My best guess is that he was after something in Consuelo's collection."

"Right, her collection," Connor said. "Luz was telling us something about that. Were you able to figure out what was taken?"

Jack's lips pressed together. Kate guessed that subject was a sore spot with him. "No. The house was trashed. I think that Ana—Consuelo's sister—will have some of her closer relatives out there to put the house back together as best they can. But I don't know if that will help us. Consuelo had her own system for keeping track of everything, and we may never be able to determine what's missing."

That response made Connor frown slightly. He looked like he was about to speak, but Luz forestalled him by saying, "Please, everyone, sit down. We have much to discuss, and hovering like this won't help."

Connor and Angela exchanged a glance, then settled themselves back on the couch. Jack inclined his head toward the end of the sofa nearest a matching leather armchair. Clearly, he thought that Kate should sit there. She followed his silent request and took that position, while he sat down in the armchair next to her, and Luz took the one across the coffee table.

"How long had Consuelo been collecting these items?" Angela asked then.

"Most of her life, I think," Luz replied. "She inherited her great-aunt's collection, then built on it. But I don't think that Adelina—she was Consuelo's great-aunt—kept any better records than Consuelo did."

"Do you really think that was wise?" Connor put in. "I mean, if she had books and artifacts of such power, then it would have been a lot safer to catalogue them all."

In the chair beside Kate, Jack stirred, as if in annoyance. However, Luz didn't give him a chance to speak. "Perhaps. But you must realize, Connor, that the sort of conflict the McAllisters and the Wilcoxes experienced over the last century or so was quite unique to your clans. We de la Pazes have lived here in peace for generations. There was no one to challenge us. We had no reason to expect that anyone would seek to harm us. So while you might think it was irresponsible of Consuelo not to safeguard her collection, in her eyes, she had no real reason to do so, other than a good set of warding spells, just to be safe. Clearly, they were not sufficient, and now we must all suffer the consequences of that lack."

"And this warlock—whoever he is—is very powerful," Jack said. "Consuelo would have tried to protect herself, but it's obvious her own gifts weren't enough to save her. We can't blame her too much."

Angela nodded, her big green eyes worried and sad. "We're not here to blame anyone. We're just trying to figure out the best way to protect our own people…and those connected to them. Kate, Luz said you were targeted as well?"

"The warlock hexed my car," Kate replied. She tried to ignore the little wrench in her midsection that seemed to occur whenever she thought of her poor wrecked Jetta. "I survived, but only because Jack had his clan's healer take care of me right away. So yes, it seems like I'm on the list, for whatever reason. Jack thinks it's because, as a civilian who's connected to a witch clan, I'm an easier target."

"So…revenge against the McAllisters?" Connor said. "And your cousin Consuelo was collateral damage because she had something this warlock wanted?"

"It sounds that way," Luz said. "But with the Wilcoxes and the McAllisters on such good terms these days, one has to look farther afield to discover who would bear such hatred for your clan."

"Well," Angela ventured, speaking slowly, as though she was still trying to work her way through the tangle of evidence, "I'd say the Santiagos have reason to be angry, because of what happened to Tomas and Jorge Aguirre. Not so much Matías, because he was never truly one of theirs, but taken in on sufferance because of his mother's healing skills. But maybe there are some in the clan who think we were too harsh with the cousins, that they shouldn't be counted as guilty because Matías forced them to go along with his schemes."

"Those two weren't innocent," Jack said. His dark eyes were narrowed, angry. "They knew exactly what they were doing, were only too happy to go along with Matías' schemes."

"Yes, Jack," Luz said. "We all know that. But this is a question of what the Santiagos might believe."

"But are the Santiagos in a position to be doing much of anything right now?" Kate put in. "I mean, because of what happened to their *prima* and her consort...." She let the words trail off, not wanting to go into any more detail. Not that she needed to; from the way everyone's expressions grew even grimmer, she could tell they knew exactly what she meant.

"That's the really scary thing," Angela said. She clasped her hands on her knees and leaned forward slightly, delicate features taut with worry. "We have this—this null out there, doing Goddess knows what. I have to guess that he's running things, but is he really in charge of the warlock who's running amok here in southern Arizona, or are these two unrelated issues?"

"I don't believe in coincidence," Jack said flatly. "Not one bit. I don't know why they're working together, but they have to be. There's no other real explanation for all this blowing up at the same time. What we have to do is try to connect the dots."

"Difficult, when we don't have much to work with," Luz responded. She tapped her manicured nails on her knee; looking at her, at her elegant chignon and the simple dress of pale peach she wore, Kate would have said Luz must be one of Scottsdale's ladies who lunch, trying to work out a problem with a charity banquet, and not a series of gruesome murders. "We know this man's name. Joaquin. Caitlin gave us a description, but that same description could match a number of my cousins here in the Phoenix area. We know he possesses very strong powers. It is possible he is the same one who murdered Kate's estranged husband and my cousin Consuelo, but that doesn't seem likely. Especially Consuelo's murder. One would think that this Joaquin would have to stay in California and continue to consolidate his power. He would not take the risk of coming here."

"No, probably not," Angela said, and gave a small sigh. She ran a hand through her wavy dark hair, mussing it. "Which means we have to be on the lookout for someone with no description, who works in darkness or at least in isolation, where he can't be seen."

"And leaves no real trail behind, either," Jack said. "Faint traces, gone quickly. There's no way of tracking him down."

"So we just have to play defense rather than

offense," Connor said. He reached over and took his wife's right hand in his left before continuing. "We've already gotten the word out amongst our clans. The McAllister elders have strengthened the wards protecting Jerome, and the Wilcoxes are shoring up their defenses, too. People have been told not to be alone, especially at night."

"Much the same here," Luz added. "Everyone is on their guard." Her gaze shifted to Jack. "I am not sure your hideaway is the best place for the two of you."

Kate could feel herself stiffen. Through all of this, one thing that had heartened her was the knowledge that they'd be able to go back to the house outside Tubac, find solace in one another's arms. She hoped Luz wasn't going to suggest that she go and stay with her parents, or maybe head up to Clarkdale to hide out with Jenny and Colin. That was the last thing Jenny probably needed, what with the baby due to show up in the very near future. If she'd been able to give any real assistance to the new mother, that was different, but Kate didn't know the first thing about taking care of babies, whereas there were plenty of seasoned pros in Jerome just waiting for the chance to help out.

"It's fine," Jack replied, his tone once again flat, inviting no further arguments. "I've got that place warded within an inch of its life. Nothing's getting to us there. Its safety is that no one knows it's mine."

"You could say the same thing for a hotel room."

His expression didn't change. "Maybe. Maybe not. They're pretty strict about checking I.D.s these days, and I don't have the powers of illusion to make mine look like something they're not."

"But I do," Luz said mildly. "I can see that your mind is made up, however. You have more expertise in these sorts of things than I do, so I won't argue with you."

Thank God. If Kate had been sitting right next to Jack, she might have sagged gratefully against his shoulder. As it was, all she could do was shoot him a quick smile, and hope that he could see how relieved she was.

One corner of his mouth lifted slightly, but that was his only response. He turned his attention to Luz and said, "One thing Consuelo said when I met with her a few days ago stuck with me. She said that Jeff Nichols' murder had taken place during the night of the full moon so the person who cast those spells would get the maximum benefit from them. She then said there was an equal strength in the dark of the moon. Since that's still more than a week off, maybe we have some breathing space to try to regroup, to plan our next steps."

"If the warlock waits that long," Connor said. "If I were in his position, I probably wouldn't."

"Spoken like a true Wilcox," Jack returned with a faint curl of his lip.

Luz sent him a reproving look. "Jack, that is not helpful at all. We all know that Connor is nothing like his brother. So." She stopped there, appearing to gather her thoughts. "While we can all hope that this warlock does wait until the dark of the moon, we can't place all our faith in such a thing happening. What we should do is attempt to figure out what his next target will be."

"Well, me, isn't it?" Kate asked, then flushed a little as everyone turned their attention to her. "I mean, he tried once, but who's to say he won't try again?"

"Because I won't let it happen," Jack said.

While those words sounded brave, and she was glad to hear them, Kate didn't know if she could put all her faith in them, and that uncertainty sent a chill through her. Not because she believed Jack wouldn't fight for her, but because this warlock clearly had no scruples, nothing he thought was below him. If he needed her dead, then he would keep on trying.

"And I'm not completely sure about that," Luz told her. "He might have decided that going after you was too much of a risk. I do not know much about the sort of blood rituals used in your estranged husband's murder, but one would think that a civilian's death would not impart as much power as that of a witch or warlock. Wasn't that the main reason Matías Escobar and his followers kidnapped Roslyn and Danica, tried to kidnap Caitlin?"

No one spoke for a moment. Luz did have a point; based on what Kate had heard about those terrible crimes, the rogue warlocks had specifically wanted witch blood to fuel their spells. Yes, the current theory seemed to be that the warlock who'd committed the most recent murders had killed Jeff to send a message, rather than because his blood held any particular innate power, but wouldn't it make more sense for him to now go after de la Paz witches or warlocks, rather than a civilian who'd already foiled one of his murder attempts?

To be honest, all of this was starting to make Kate's head spin. Up was down and down was up. The only thing she thought she could be certain of was the man who sat a foot away from her, his dark eyes watching her intently, as though he guessed at the turmoil within her.

"Yes, that much was pretty clear," Angela said in response to Luz's question. "And that's why we all have to be on guard. Right now, though, I think our best hope is for Caitlin to have another vision, one that can provide some more information. Has she said anything to you?"

"No," Luz replied. "That is, I spoke with her late this morning, just to be sure she didn't have any new information for me. But her visions do not come on command, as we all know, and she had nothing else to give me. If she had, she would have called right away. She's very conscientious."

The approval in Luz's voice was clear. Kate couldn't help but wonder what it would be like to have a mother-in-law who actually liked and appreciated you, instead of nitpicking every last thing. Then she pushed the uncharitable thought away. Nancy might have been an utter pain in the ass most of the time, but that didn't mean she deserved to lose her only child.

"And I've talked to Marie, the Wilcox seer," Connor said. "She's not getting anything, either."

Well, great. Kate understood that witches and warlocks were just people, human beings who might be in possession of some very special gifts but who certainly weren't all-powerful, or infallible. Still, she really wished their second sight could be a little more help in this particular instance.

"Then I think we must leave things here for now," Luz said. "We can only do what we can."

"As little as that might be," Angela remarked. She let go of Connor's hand and stood, and he rose from his seat on the couch a second or two later.

Luz offered her a tired smile. "We will get through this, even if things don't look very hopeful right now."

"I know, but…." A lift of her shoulders, and Angela turned toward Kate. "It was good to see you, Kate. I'll let Jenny know you're doing well." Accompanying this last comment was the barest flicker of her eyes in Jack's direction. "But I suppose you'll be up in a few weeks, when the baby comes."

"That was the plan," Kate responded, although she felt a frisson of unease, as though she wasn't sure she'd actually be there to greet her new niece or nephew. That was just being morbid, though. As Luz had just said, they'd get through this…somehow.

Angela and Connor made their goodbyes, and Luz saw them to the door. When she came back, she looked even more tired, although she summoned a smile and said, "Why don't you stay for dinner? I know David would like the chance to talk."

"Thanks, Luz," Jack replied. "But I think it's better if we get back before nightfall. Just in case."

She nodded and didn't bother to argue. Obviously, she hadn't expected Jack to take her up on the offer. "That might be a good idea. Then take care… and be careful."

"We will."

Luz gave Kate a smile. "You're in the best hands in the world. Everything will be fine."

As she closed the front door behind them, Kate and Jack headed into the courtyard, then out through the gate. It was only after he'd started up the Jeep and began to pull away from the curb that she let out a chuckle.

"What's so funny?" he inquired. It was clear he didn't find anything particularly amusing about the situation.

"Well," Kate replied. "Luz just said I was in the best hands in the world. And I have to agree with her." She let her gaze slide over to where he had his fingers wrapped around the steering wheel. "But I'd kind of like you to show me again. Just to prove she was right."

The tight set of his mouth relaxed, and he actually smiled. "Well, Kate, I'll have to make sure I do just that thing."

18

JACK DROVE TOO FAST ON THE WAY BACK TO Tubac, but he didn't bother to moderate his speed. If they got pulled over, his Scottsdale P.D. identification would get him off the hook. Anyway, it wasn't as if he'd floored it or anything. Eighty-five was a perfectly reasonable rate of speed when the limit was seventy-five.

A quick glance over at Kate told him she probably wasn't paying much attention to how fast they were going. She had one hand curled around the seatbelt as she stared out the window, although the abstracted look in her eyes seemed to indicate that she wasn't paying much attention to the landscape passing by.

"You all right?" he asked.

She didn't precisely startle, but from the way she appeared to somehow snap back into herself, he could tell she must have been very far away. "I think so. That is…." A lift of her shoulders, and she knotted her hands in her lap. Even from where Jack sat, he could see the way her fingers were shaking, and her voice sounded small as she went on, "I mean, I don't have much choice but to be all right. Flipping out isn't going to help the situation any."

"No, probably not," he said, but he kept his tone gentle. Anyway, he could understand her feeling overloaded. He was close to that himself, although he had more experience dealing with abrupt ups and downs, just because of his work. Also, his mind kept replaying that scene in Consuelo's house. Whatever had attacked her hadn't given a damn that she was an elderly woman. She looked as if she'd gone a few rounds in an MMA tournament.

"And your cousin…." Kate began. She turned toward him, eyes wide and worried. No, not worried. Downright scared. "Who would do that to a defenseless old woman?"

"A monster who didn't give a shit that she was old, or a woman. She had something the warlock wanted, and she was in the way. I'm glad that at least she hung on until we got there, though. That way, she wasn't alone when she passed."

From the way Kate appeared to relax slightly at those words, it appeared that he'd come up with exactly the right thing to say. "I hadn't thought about it that way. I—well, I don't know if it makes me feel any better, but you're right. I just wish we'd gotten there early enough to prevent what happened to her."

He'd been thinking the same thing, although he honestly didn't know if they could have done that much good. Were his defensive spells really strong enough to fend off that kind of an attack? He'd never had much need to use them, and they'd certainly never been put to that sort of test. The last thing he would have wanted was for Kate to be placed in any kind of jeopardy. If he'd confronted the warlock and failed, then she would have been left alone with no defenses at all against someone who'd already tried once to have her killed.

"Maybe," he said. "It would have been dangerous, though. Anyway, we can't go back and change the past."

"I thought you witches and warlocks could. At least, Jenny mentioned something about one of the Wilcox witches being able to do that sort of thing."

"Danica Wilcox did," Jack said. "Under very special circumstances, and in a feat of time travel she hasn't been able to repeat since. No, I'm afraid the one thing we can't do is change what's already happened. All we can do is try to make sure the future isn't in jeopardy."

His reply didn't seem to sit very well; her wide mouth, usually so warm and amiable, tightened as she pressed her lips together. For a long moment, she didn't say anything at all, only redirected her attention to the highway in front of them. "How dangerous?" she asked finally. He raised an eyebrow at her, and she continued, "How dangerous is it going to be to go up against this person? I'm getting mixed signals from you."

"Maybe that's because I don't know for sure," he said calmly. "I can only make educated guesses. When Luz said that our family hadn't been involved in any real conflict with other witch clans for generations, she was only telling the truth. I practice my defensive spells because that's my talent, but it's one that would have been of more use hundreds of years ago. Until now, anyway."

Kate's expression softened slightly. "I guess I hadn't thought about it like that. I suppose it is hard to know for sure when you haven't had any real opportunity to prove yourself."

"Right. And also, I don't know if the warlock was alone when he attacked Consuelo, or whether he summoned a few demon buddies to come and help him out. That makes a huge difference, too. The wards I have set up might repel them. *Might.* The rules work differently for beings like that. It's not like dealing with just another witch or warlock."

"Oh." She went silent again, expression shuttered. What she was thinking, Jack had no idea, but he had a feeling she was probably trying to decide whether or not going back to Tubac really was that great of a plan. Maybe she was starting to think that a nice anonymous hotel room in Phoenix or Scottsdale might have served them better.

"If we're not safe in Tubac," he told her, "it means we're not safe anywhere. Or at least, unless you include staying somewhere with a bunch of other witches and warlocks surrounding you to help out with defense." Jack paused, frowning as he wondered whether it would have been smarter for them to pack up and head north with Connor and Angela. In Jerome, there would have been a lot more magical backup to draw on. The de la Paz clan was bigger, but spread out all over the greater Phoenix area and down into Tucson. They mingled with the population, didn't try to keep themselves separate, which meant they wouldn't be as useful when push came to shove.

Well, it couldn't be helped now. He'd walk the property when they got back to Tubac, check the wards. Feel the wind. If he thought anything seemed even slightly off, then they'd pack up their things and get back on the road, and head up to Jerome as fast as they could.

"It's all right," Kate said after a lengthy pause. "I trust you."

What could he say to that? About all he could do was hope that her trust wasn't entirely misplaced.

~

As they came down to the dirt lane to the house, Kate was relieved to see that everything looked exactly as they'd left it. What she'd expected to find, she really didn't know, but it still felt good to catch that first glimpse of the place, surrounded by its mesquite trees and flowering cactus. And after they pulled into the garage, again she was glad to sense absolutely nothing as she got out of the car. Okay, she wasn't a psychic or a witch, but in general her intuition was pretty good. She'd had a bad feeling the second she exited the Jeep back at Consuelo's house. She definitely didn't get that feeling here.

Whether or not Jack felt it, Kate couldn't be sure, but he did seem somewhat more relaxed as he led her up to the main level of the house, then paused in the hallway to look around. "I think it's okay," he said.

"Me, too," she replied.

"How about a drink?"

That sounded like an awesome idea. All right, by that point it was nearly four in the afternoon, and she hadn't eaten anything since breakfast, but she wasn't hungry. Or rather, somewhere on an intellectual level she realized she should probably eat something, but the thought wasn't at all appealing. "Yes, definitely," she said.

"And some of the cheese and crackers we got at TJ's," he added. She must have looked dubious, because Jack went on, "I know it feels strange to be thinking about eating in the midst of all this, but we can't go completely without. You'll feel better. Trust me."

Kate couldn't argue with that. Having a nibble of cheese and a few crackers wasn't the same thing as trying to force a steak or a burger down her throat. "Okay."

They went into the kitchen and got everything together, then took it out to the patio. The air was warm, almost hot. It felt good, and there was something about the scent of dry grass drifting on the breeze that made Kate relax slightly. This was a good place. How could anything bad happen here?

Jack poured white wine for the two of them and handed a glass to Kate. She took it gratefully, then sipped it at. Tart and cold, and just what the doctor ordered.

"Better?"

"Yes," she said. "Much better."

For a few minutes, they sat in companionable silence, drinking their wine, helping themselves to some of the tapas-style cheese. Something tight and scared and anxious deep within her began to relax, to quietly unknot itself. Across the table, Jack sent her a slightly questioning glance, and she nodded.

"I'm okay," she said. "I think it's going to be okay."

"It will," he agreed. "Sometimes when you're in

the middle of it, you can't see beyond the darkness into the light. But it's always out there. It doesn't forget you, even if you might lose sight of it."

"'The arc of the moral universe is long, but it bends towards justice,'" Kate quoted.

Jack gave an approving nod. "I like that."

"I can't take credit," she told him. "It's something Martin Luther King once said."

"It doesn't matter who said it when it's true."

"I suppose so. But I think that's what we have to cling to—that no matter what's going on around us, no matter how awful things might seem—in the end the universe does tend to right those wrongs, even if it doesn't follow the timeline we might want."

For a minute, Jack was silent. Then he said, "I want to make love to you again, Kate."

A shiver went through her. Was she ready for that, after everything that had happened today? Despite what she had just said about feeling better, could she open herself to him like that?

Of course she could. What was more, she knew she should. She couldn't shut him out. She needed to reaffirm the attraction that had drawn them together. More than attraction. Love. Desire. Everything she hadn't been expecting, but which the universe had sent to her at exactly the wrong time. Or maybe the right time. Was there a wrong time to fall in love, as long as that love didn't hurt anyone else?

She extended a hand to him, and he took it, then pulled her to him so he could kiss her, over and over, his lips strong and demanding. He needed this, she could tell, maybe even more than she did.

Jack led her to the sliding glass door and pushed it aside. A blast of cool air touched her face, almost shocking after the warmth of the breezes that flowed across the patio. But then she wasn't thinking of much of anything, because he scooped her up in his arms and carried her down the hall to the bedroom, where he grasped her shirt and pulled it over her head, then reached back to undo the clasp of her bra. His hands closed on her breasts, caressing, and he bent and took a nipple into his mouth, suckling on her, even as he fumbled with the button of her jeans.

Oh, yes, this was what she needed, his strong fingers stroking her, awakening little ripples of pleasure from deep within. They fell onto the bed, and she reached for his belt buckle and undid it, then pulled down his jeans and underwear. Wrapped her hand around him as they kissed, bodies pressed tightly against one another, all need, all want, searching for a few moments of blissful oblivion. And then he was sliding into her as she gasped and wrapped her legs around him, driving him deep, their bodies rocking together, finding their rhythm, those ripples of pleasure turning into a flood as he filled her, the world disappearing. Or rather, the world became him and no one else, just Jack, his dark eyes so deep she thought she would drown in them, that she could drown herself in him, lose herself forever. But that was all right, because he would always find her.

They came together, crying out in the same timeless moment where she became him and he became her. It had never been like this with anyone else, because Jack was the match to her soul. She clung to him, shuddering, and then…slipped away into the quiet of sleep, sheltered within his arms, safe.

Forever.

Somewhere, a phone was ringing. Jack cracked an eyelid, saw that the room had grown dusky and dim. A quick glance at the clock on the bedside table told him it was seven fifty-two. He and Kate had both collapsed after that bout of frenzied lovemaking, both of them clearly needing the release of sleep after the day's events.

He realized the phone wasn't his, had to be Kate's, since it had that annoying Apple-standard ringtone going. Where was it? Off in the house somewhere; he vaguely recalled that she'd dropped her purse on the kitchen counter as they came inside.

"What?" she mumbled, and turned over in bed next to him.

"Phone," he said. "Yours."

She sat up in bed and pushed back her tousled hair. "Oh. Guess I'd better check it. I don't really feel like it, though."

Jack kissed her, savored the taste of her mouth as he held her close. She chuckled, a throaty sound that made him want to pin her back down against the sheets.

The phone stopped ringing. "Oh, great," she said after she pulled away slightly. "Now I've missed it."

"Go take a look, see who it was," he said as he reached down to pick up his discarded clothes. "I'll rescue the food we left out on the patio."

A nod, and she pushed herself out of bed and began to collect her own clothing and put it back on. A minute after that, she was headed down the hallway toward the kitchen.

He followed almost immediately afterward, less than thrilled with the way he'd let himself just jump right into bed with Kate. Yes, it had been amazing, but he'd meant to check the wards before night fell, and now he'd have to decide whether it was worthwhile to take a flashlight out there and wander around in the darkness, or whether they could let it go for another night. After all, it was nowhere near the dark of the moon. They had time. Maybe.

Kate's phone remained silent. Hopefully, whoever had called had left a voicemail. Jack went out onto the patio and gathered up the remnants of their snack, including the half-drunk bottle of wine. Maybe they should make something a little more substantial, finish the rest of it. Absolutely no tingles from his spider sense, which meant the wards hadn't picked anything up. As he'd thought, they would be fine here. And he wanted them to be fine here for a very long time. Maybe it was crazy, but right then all he could think of was how wonderful it would be to stay here, to somehow make their lives together in this place of open vistas and skies so blue, it almost hurt to look at them.

"Jack!"

Her cry was so frightened, so sharp with urgency, that he nearly dropped the bottle he held. He hurried into the kitchen, saw her standing there with her iPhone in one hand and a look of terror on her face.

"What is it?" he demanded, setting down his burden of bottle and plate on the kitchen counter.

In response, she held the phone out to him. "Listen."

Since the screen was unlocked, all he had to do was hit the little "play" arrow on the phone's voice-mail. From the speaker came a strange voice, thin and oddly sexless. "You thought you could hide? Your parents will suffer the same fate as your husband if you don't come to their house. Now."

The message ended there.

"We have to go," Kate said, her eyes wide and frantic.

"Kate, that's exactly what this person wants you to do. You can't take that kind of risk—"

"You heard the message! He—she—whatever that was, they said they were going to kill my parents! We have to go now!"

He knew he couldn't reason with her. This could be an empty threat, a trap set specifically to draw Kate away from the house in the Tubac, or the warlock could actually be with her parents, holding them hostage until their daughter appeared. Even if that were the case, Jack knew the warlock wouldn't let them go. He'd kill all of them, and use their blood to power his nefarious schemes.

"Kate—"

"No," she said. "This is not...not negotiable. We're going now. Jeff is dead, and your cousin Consuelo, and he's going to kill my parents if I don't do as he says. You want to think of a plan? Fine. Think of it as we're driving."

Gone was the woman who'd moaned in his arms only a few hours earlier. This Kate was wild-eyed but determined. Jack had a feeling that if he didn't agree, she'd try to steal his car keys from him and go on her own. Which of course would be suicide.

"All right," he said, holding up his hands. "All right. Call back and say you're on your way. Then we'll go."

She pulled in a ragged breath. "Okay."

As he watched, she pulled up the number on her contacts list and made the call. He could tell she must have gotten the answering machine, because she made no greeting, only said, "I'm leaving now," and then ended the call.

"Put your shoes on," he said quietly, and she glanced down at her feet, startled, as if she hadn't quite realized that she wasn't ready to walk right out the door.

"All right," she said, and headed back toward the bedroom.

Since he was completely dressed, he didn't have to worry about such things. Instead, he went and fetched his gun and shoulder holster from where he'd stowed them in the top shelf of the coat closet, and strapped them on. He still had his doubts as to whether the gun would do much good, but he felt better having it with him.

A moment later, Kate emerged from the bedroom. Her gaze flickered toward the shoulder holster, but she didn't say anything, only gave a grim nod and then headed down the stairs that led to the garage.

Jack followed. He remained silent, because he could tell that she was in no mood for conversation and would probably view any attempts at dialogue as yet another way to dissuade her from this mission. That was where she was wrong; he knew when someone's mind was made up, and arguing with Kate would have only angered her more.

They both got in the Jeep, and he backed out of the garage. Good thing the solar lights along the driveway had come on and were doing their best to drive back the darkness, because it was black as pitch out here, the moon still hidden behind the eastern hills. Once they were out on the lane that led to the property, he turned on his high-beams and increased his speed somewhat—but not, he guessed, fast enough for Kate.

Even breaking the speed limit all the way to Tempe, they wouldn't make it in less than two hours. A lot could happen in that amount of time. Kate's face in the reflected glow of the dashboard was grim, lips pressed together. Clearly, she'd done the same mental math, so he wouldn't bother to point it out to her.

Should he call Luz? Or would putting the alert out to all the de la Pazes in the area only make the warlock decide they'd broken the terms of their agreement, thus making the Campbells' lives forfeit? Jack knew they were dealing with someone who possessed unknown powers and resources. The last thing he wanted to do was put any of his clan members' lives at risk.

Damn it.

His hands clamped down on the steering wheel, and he depressed the accelerator a little further. Now they were skating along at a hair under ninety. He knew that, in general, the state cops wouldn't pull you over for that kind of speeding. Tickets over ninety were a lot more expensive.

"Kate, reach into the back seat and get out the portable flasher light, then affix it to the roof. That should allow us to go a lot faster without worrying about getting busted."

Pale-faced, she nodded, then undid her seatbelt so she could twist around and retrieve the light from the rear seat. A moment later, she was unrolling the passenger-side window, and then placing the light on the roof. As soon as he could see the flashing red illumination reflected on the hood of the Jeep, he floored it, pushing the speedometer past one hundred, up to one hundred and five. He didn't dare go faster than that; this vehicle was built for sturdiness and off-roading, not high-speed chases.

Still, at this rate, they'd knock a good half hour off their travel time, maybe more. Carefully, he pried his phone loose from his pocket.

"Who're you calling?" Kate asked. She was hanging on to the "Jesus handle" above her, but looked a little more composed now that they'd increased their speed.

"Luz. I need to let her know what's going on."

"So she can send people to help? You can't, Jack— the warlock told me to come alone. It's bad enough that I have you with me."

Although he knew what she meant, the words

stung a little. Still, he kept his voice calm as he replied, "I'm not asking her to come help. I know that would be taking too much of a risk. I'm just letting her know what's going on. She knows not to spook this person."

With obvious reluctance, Kate said, "All right. Just —just make it really clear that she needs to stay away."

"I will."

He made the call. Luz didn't answer immediately, which didn't surprise him all that much—it was now past eight o'clock, the time when she and her husband David had probably settled down in front of the television to relax and take their mind off all the day's turmoil.

But then she picked up. "What is it, Jack?"

Some days he didn't know whether to curse or praise caller I.D. "I just wanted to let you know that Kate and I are on the way to Tempe. The warlock is at her parents' house, threatening them."

"I'll be right over."

"No, you can't do that. I have no doubt that the warlock would sense you coming and react negatively. He's expecting just Kate."

"And yet you're with her."

"Because I sure as hell wasn't going to let her go alone. But I'm just another warlock. You're the *prima* of the de la Paz family. Big difference."

A long pause. Luz said, "I don't like it, Jack."

"You don't have to like it. Just understand. It's going to be fine. This is our chance to stop this person before he does any more harm."

"And you're ready to do that?"

"More than ready. I'm done, Luz. This bastard is going down."

Luz's sigh came clearly through the speakers. "Be careful."

"I always am."

He ended the call then before she could say anything else. In the seat next to him, Kate stirred.

"I'm surprised she didn't argue with you more."

"I'm not. She knows she'd lose."

Despite everything, Kate chuckled slightly. "Are you always this sure of yourself?"

"Not always," he replied, and risked a quick glance sideways at her before he returned his attention to the road. At the speeds they were going, he didn't dare anything more than that. She was still pale, but now she looked more determined than frightened. "For example, I'm definitely not sure of myself when it comes to you."

She tilted her head so she could glance over at him. "Me? I would have thought it was pretty obvious how I felt about you."

"True, but we haven't had much of a chance to talk about it."

"We will," she said, then added, her voice firm, "after all this is over. We can talk about what we want to do next. I know we'll make it work somehow, because I've seen how Colin and Jenny make it work. But we've got to make sure my parents are safe first."

"Of course." He really couldn't ask anything more of her than that. They'd just have to find a way to survive the next few hours.

And then…well, they'd have to see.

19

Her parents' house in Tempe looked innocent enough as they pulled up and parked at the curb. Kate saw that the porch light was on, along with several lights on the ground floor. Nothing remarkable about any of that, which she guessed was the whole point.

She also didn't notice any suspicious vehicles anywhere nearby, but what self-respecting evil warlock would leave so obvious a clue? Maybe he'd parked on the next street over. Hell, maybe he'd taken an Uber, or teleported. Who knew? At this point, how he'd gotten there didn't really matter. How he left was the real issue at hand. If there was any justice in the world, he'd be taken out in a body bag.

On the way here, she and Jack had discussed their plan of attack. They'd decided that Kate would approach the front door alone, while he went around to the rear of the house so he could reach the back door in the utility room and let himself in that way, using his inborn magic to open the door if it happened to be locked. Warlocks and witches could sense one another's presence, but only when they got within a few feet of each other, which meant Jack should have the element of surprise on his side.

"Try to keep him talking," Jack told her as they used the bulk of the Jeep to shield themselves from any watchful eyes inside the house. She'd climbed across the driver's seat so she could let herself out on that side; Jack had turned off the emergency light as soon as they got off the freeway in Tempe. "I'll be there as quickly as I can, but there might be a small lag."

"What if he blasts me right away?" Kate asked, wishing her voice didn't quaver so much.

"That's not the purpose of all this," Jack replied. He rubbed a thumb over her palm, clearly trying to reassure her. "If he wants to use your blood, your energy, there's a ritual involved. Hitting you with a fireball while you're standing on the doorstep won't do him any good."

She cracked a wry smile, trying to take some refuge in humor. "Oh, that makes me feel so much better."

"You'll be fine. Trust me. Just go now."

Her heart began to pound, but she managed to

sound calm enough as she said, "I will. See you in a minute."

As she came out from the shelter of the Jeep and began to walk up the path to the front door, she thought she saw a blur of darkness moving somewhere off to her right. Jack, shielded by some spell to conceal his presence? She didn't dare look in that direction, though, just in case the warlock was watching from inside the house. No, she could only make her feet continue to carry her up to the door. As her hand moved to ring the bell, the door swung inward, although she didn't see anyone there.

Great. Not only was this warlock an evil son of a bitch, he was also apparently into cheap theatrics. Since she knew she had to go on, couldn't turn back now even though her heart was hammering in her chest and her back was slick with cold sweat, she stepped inside. The door slammed shut behind her, and she jumped, then sucked in a breath and called out, "Mom? Dad?"

No answer. Well, the lights were on in the living room, so she'd go there. Heart hammering in her chest, she turned right so she could head past the dining room and on toward her destination.

Only to stop on the threshold, hand going to her throat. Sitting there, bound to two side chairs, were her parents. Her mother's eyes met hers, pleading, despairing, tears staining her cheeks. The source of her despair became clear enough as Kate focused on her father, saw the way he sagged there, lifeless, blood pouring down his pale yellow polo shirt from the slit in his throat.

A cry of despair choking in her throat, Kate surged forward—only to feel a hand like steel clamp down on her bicep, preventing her from moving any farther. She looked over her shoulder to see who had detained her, and her mouth dropped open.

This had to be the warlock. Those dark eyes, baleful, somehow glaring with an evil reddish light, could belong to no one else. But…the warlock was no warlock at all, but a witch. Tall, almost as tall as Jack, but slender, and beautiful in a harsh way, like the basalt cliffs on the Rio Grande gorge above Taos, New Mexico.

"Hello, Kate," said the witch. Her voice was thin and sharp, but unlike the way it had sounded on the phone, definitely female. "I'm glad you were able to follow instructions."

"Who—?" Kate broke off there. Did it really matter who this evil woman was? What mattered was stalling her until Jack could get in here. The words sounding far too shaky, she asked, "Why are you doing this?"

"Revenge, of course. Revenge on my father's behalf, and revenge for my brother and what you all did to him."

From the chair across the room, Kate's mother watched this exchange with terrified eyes. Voice taut with fear and pain, she cried out, "We never did anything to anyone!"

"Oh, forgive me," the witch said. "Not you directly, but the family of the witch your son married. Guilt by association."

"Witch?" Lynda's frightened hazel eyes fixed on her daughter. "Is she saying that Jenny is a witch?"

"Mom, I—"

"You can explain everything to her later, Kate. Or perhaps not. I need the energy from both of you to complete the ritual, to return to my brother the power that was stolen from him."

At those words, a horrible realization began to dawn within her. There were three men whose powers had been taken by Angela and Connor Wilcox, and yet Kate doubted this woman was here to avenge either of the Aguirre brothers. "You're—you're Matías Escobar's *sister?*"

"Half-sister, actually. His bitch of a mother stole him away from my Papa, came running here to America, hoping to hide from him and shelter amongst those weaklings, those Santiagos. But soon Matías will come into his own again, and will be able to take up his duties as his father's heir, helping to run the Santiago clan."

Oh, God. It all made sense now. The man Caitlin had seen in that vision was Matías Escobar's father, come here to seek his revenge, first on the Santiagos who had cast out his son, and then on the McAllisters for taking his powers away.

And now as she focused on her surroundings—careful to avoid looking at her father's pale, staring face, because she knew otherwise she'd break down in hysterics—Kate saw how a series of symbols had begun to be painted on the walls of the living room, symbols that dripped red with blood. Not as many as she'd seen in Jeff's apartment, because, as the Escobar witch had just confessed, she was only partly done with the ritual. She'd need to kill Lynda, and then Kate, to summon the power she required.

"Kate, down!"

The words carried across the space, heavy with command. Jack barreled into the room, hands extended in front of him. He obviously intended to cast a spell and didn't want her caught in the crossfire.

Wrenching her arm from the Escobar witch's grasp, Kate dropped to her knees. A burst of crackling energy jetted out from Jack's fingers, catching the witch off guard. She stumbled backward, but instead of falling, she propped herself up against the wall and began to laugh. From behind her, Kate heard her mother let out a screech of fear and surprise.

"Oh, you'll have to do better than that," said the witch, apparently ignoring her audience.

"I intend to."

Not knowing what else she should do, Kate began to crawl across the floor, heading to the chair where her mother was tied up. If she could only get her free, then Lynda could run out the back door, go to fetch help.

If there was anyone around who could help.

Another burst of energy whizzed overhead, but it seemed to stop while halfway across the room, halted in its tracks by a billowing plume of black, foul-smelling smoke that appeared to have come from nowhere. Which, Kate supposed, it had. That was how magic worked.

"You can't defeat me," the Escobar witch said, her tone almost bored. "I've spent many years studying these arts. I have my father's strength. You are soft, like the rest of your clan. You do not know what it is to suffer for your art."

"True," Jack replied, sounding amused. An act, Kate knew, but one she hoped the witch might fall for. "Around these parts, we prefer to take joy in the use of magic. If you're suffering for it, then I think you're doing it wrong."

This verbal salvo must have angered the Escobar witch, because she snapped out something in Spanish. Immediately afterward, a bolt of reddish lightning zinged through the air, striking Jack in the shoulder. He cursed and fell to his knees.

Kate wanted to scream his name, but she didn't—she knew that would only distract him, and he had to keep all his focus on the witch, on keeping his defenses up. Luckily, the Escobar witch didn't appear to be paying any attention to Kate as she crawled her way across the floor, possibly for the same reason. For now, the woman had to maintain her own defenses. She probably thought she would have plenty of time to deal with Kate and her mother later.

"Had enough?" the witch asked. "I do not need you for this spell, de la Paz warlock. You can walk away from all this. That is what my father told your misguided *prima,* after all. Let us rule things in California, and we will leave you alone. Forget this woman, this 'civilian,' as you call them, and just walk away."

"I don't think so," Jack replied. His voice was tight with pain, but it didn't waver. "You see, I'm a cop. My job is to protect innocent people like these women here from criminals like you."

The Escobar witch drew herself up, red-painted lips curling. "A criminal? I am no criminal. My cause is a righteous one."

"Tell it to the judge, lady."

He made an odd motion with his hands, holding one steady while he pushed outward with the other, and immediately Kate's ears popped, as though Jack had somehow displaced half the air in the room. The burst hit the Escobar witch squarely in the midsection, and once again she stumbled, this time catching her foot on one of the steps that led into the sunken living room.

That wasn't enough to deter her, though, because

she countered with another of those lightning strikes, two of them hitting Jack simultaneously. At once he collapsed face first on the carpet, smoke rising from his shirt. A few yards away, Lynda gasped. She didn't really know who Jack was, and had to be out of her mind with fear, but clearly she understood that the man who'd just been struck down was the only person who could help them.

No. No, Kate thought. *This can't be happening. He has to get up.*

But he didn't move. By that time, Kate was only a few feet away from him. She glanced back over her shoulder and saw the Escobar witch getting to her feet, unsteady, but with a malevolent smile touching her full lips and a triumphant light in her coal-black eyes. Limping, she began to make her way across the room to the spot where Kate crouched.

Clutched in the woman's right hand, hidden before now by the long black robes she wore, was a curved, evil-looking knife.

Shit.

Kate backed away, scrabbling now on her hands and knees. So close to Jack. He had to get up. But he wasn't moving.

But there, mostly hidden by his body, was his gun in its shoulder holster.

"It doesn't hurt," the Escobar witch said, her voice almost friendly. "What I did to your husband...that hurt, I'll admit. But I had to bring my assistants to this plane. Now that they are here, it takes less to appease them."

"Oh, really?" Kate replied, not caring how inane she sounded. Her fingers reached for the holster, fumbled with the snaps that held the gun in place. "Still sounds like they're kind of high-maintenance. Maybe you should look for different friends."

"I assure you—these 'friends' are very useful."

There…the 9mm was free, sliding cold and heavy into Kate's desperate grasp. "Then make sure you say hi to them for me."

A click of the safety, and she lifted the gun, aimed directly at the witch. Head shot? Kate didn't know if she'd be able to pull that off. Better to shoot her right in her cold black heart.

The sound of the gun going off was louder than anything Kate could have imagined. Of course—the only other time she'd shot a gun, she'd been wearing ear protection. The noise echoed in her ears, ringing like some infernal bell.

And then—there was the witch, slumping to the blood-spattered carpet, her black clothing wet with the stuff. Her dark eyes were wide, startled.

Knees shaking, Kate got to her feet and approached the wounded woman, gun held at the ready. The witch's eyes met hers, narrowed with pain. Incongruously, she smiled.

"I will not live to see my father's dominion," she

whispered. "But my blood on its own is enough to complete the spell."

With one swift motion, she raised the curved blade she held, whispered a few words in a language Kate didn't recognize, and then drew the edge across her own throat. Blood, red-black in the dimly lit room, gushed from the wound, further soaking the carpet.

A harsh keening sound. The sensation of cold, leathery wings beating at the air. The ground trembled underfoot, and from somewhere in the house came the tinkle of broken glass.

Then, just as suddenly, as it had come, the supernatural disturbance ended. Whatever the Escobar witch's death had summoned, it was gone now.

Kate let out a hiccupy sob and ran back over toward Jack. After making sure to engage the gun's safety once again, she set it down on the coffee table. "Jack? *Jack!*"

Blearily, his eyes opened. They focused on her first, and then moved toward the lifeless figure of the woman lying on the floor. An expression of incredulity moved over his features, and she couldn't help laughing. Laughter tinged with hysteria, perhaps, but still.

"See?" she said. "I told you I knew how to shoot."

EPILOGUE

Jack set down his phone and looked across the patio table at Kate. Despite the losses she'd suffered over the last few weeks, she now appeared almost serene, as though she was ready to put the past behind her and look forward to the future.

To a future with him.

"That was Luz," he said.

"Oh?" After all the necessary cover-up of her father's true cause of death, after the dust had settled and the dead had been buried, Kate made the decision that she couldn't live in Scottsdale anymore. Too many terrible memories, too much to remind her of what she'd lost. Her parents' house had been put on the market, and Lynda had moved up to Clarkdale to be near her new grandson. The shock and sorrow would always be with her, but at least she could try to focus on the newest member of the family, a welcome distraction from the horror of her husband's murder.

And since Jack refused to remain in Scottsdale without Kate, he'd resigned his commission with the police department. What he was going to do with himself, he wasn't sure…but if what Luz had just told him was true, he had a feeling all of them were going to be very busy for the foreseeable future.

Watching Kate carefully, he said, "We had to be discreet about making inquiries, because this is going to turn out to be an embarrassment for everyone involved, but it seems that the Escobar woman's spell did what she intended it to. About a week after the night she died, apparently Matías Escobar walked right out of the prison in Florence and disappeared."

"He *what?*" Kate set down her coffee cup. Even though she'd been working outside in the yard the past few days and had begun to pick up something of a tan, she now looked deadly pale. "How is that even possible? Wasn't he in a maximum-security prison?"

"His sister's death provided the energy needed to restore his gift. Remember, his power was controlling people with his voice, getting them to follow his commands. He probably wanted to take some time to experiment with it, to make sure that it truly was working the way it used to before Connor and Angela took it away, but once he'd determined that he was back in the game…." Jack paused there and picked up his own coffee. It had gone lukewarm during his conversation with Luz, but right then he just wanted the caffeine. The shock of the news the *prima* had just shared made him feel far too tired. "Matías would have used his power to charm a few guards to let him out and walk him out of there. Once he was free, he could have found someone in the town near the prison to literally give him the shirt off their backs, most likely a car, too. No doubt he's already joined up with dear old dad in California."

"But…." Kate drew in a breath, the worry clear in her face. "But what are we going to do now?"

"I'm not sure," Jack replied. He reached across the table to take her hand in his. Her fingers felt cold, fragile. In that moment, he vowed that she would never suffer harm or loss again, no matter what happened.

"Just know that I'll always be here for you. I'll always protect you. And if the Escobars bring the fight to us…we'll be ready."

The Witches of Cleopatra Hill series will continue with *Deep Magic*, due out in October 2017.

THE ARIZONA WITCH CLANS

The McAllisters (Jerome, Arizona, and the Verde Valley)

Angela McAllister (Wilcox) – *prima*, or head witch, of the McAllister clan

Rachel McAllister – Angela's aunt

Bryce McAllister – one of the McAllister clan's elders

Allegra Moss – one of the McAllister clan's elders

Margot Emory (Wilcox) – formerly one of the McAllister clan's elders, now married to Lucas Wilcox

Sylvia Emory – Margot's mother

Ruby Lynch – former *prima* of the McAllister clan

Henry Lynch – son of Ruby McAllister and Patrick Lynch

Tobias Miller – fiancé of Rachel McAllister

Sonya McAllister – Angela's mother, deceased

Boyd Willis – a McAllister warlock

Micah Landon -- an absentminded artist

Floyd Barnett – lives above the store next to Rachel's

Rosemary McAllister – lives on the other side of Rachel's store above the tea shop

Susan Callery -- an artist with a studio in the same building as Tobias' flat

Efraim Willendale -- runs the post office

Wyatt McAllister -- owns a B&B on Paradise Street

Dora McAllister – Great-Aunt Ruby's caretaker

Jocelyn Riggs -- the clan's strongest medium

Kirby McAllister – a cousin of Angela's and one of her "caretakers"

Tricia McAllister -- the new clan elder after Margot Emory steps down

Richard McAllister – Tricia's husband

Caitlin McAllister (Trujillo) – daughter of Tricia and Richard; a seer

Michael McAllister – Caitlin's older brother, a chef

Roslyn McAllister -- Caitlin's first cousin; youngest sister of Jenny and Adam

Marcus McAllister -- Tricia McAllister's older brother, father of Jenny, Adam, and Roslyn

Lysette McAllister – Marcus' wife and mother of Jenny, Adam, and Roslyn; a civilian (non-witch)

Jenny McAllister – eldest daughter of Marcus and Lysette McAllister

Adam McAllister – only son of Marcus and Lysette McAllister

Roslyn McAllister – youngest daughter of Marcus and Lysette McAllister

Evan McAllister—a distant cousin of Angela's; the clan's "fixer"

The Wilcox Clan (Flagstaff, Arizona, and the northern third of the state)

Connor Wilcox – *primus* (head warlock) of the Wilcox clan

Damon Wilcox – former *primus* of the Wilcoxes, now deceased

Lucas Wilcox – a cousin of Connor's, now married to Margot Emory

Mason Wilcox (McAllister) – Connor's cousin and a friend of Angela's; now married to Adam McAllister

Danica Wilcox – Mason's younger sister

Joseph Wilcox – Mason and Danica's father

Olivia Wilcox – Mason and Danica's mother

Andre Begonie – Angela McAllister's father

Marie Wilcox (Begonie) – a cousin of Connor's, the Wilcox clan's seer

Eleanor Garnett – the clan's healer

Darrell Wilcox – a Wilcox warlock gifted with heating the area around him

In the 1880s:

Jeremiah Wilcox – the Wilcox clan's *primus*

Nizhoni – Jeremiah's second wife, a woman of the Navajo

Jacob Wilcox – Jeremiah and Nizhoni's son

Samuel Wilcox – Jeremiah's brother

Edmund Wilcox – Jeremiah's brother

Nathan Wilcox – Jeremiah's brother

Emma Garnett – Jeremiah's only sister; children are Louis, Susan, Marcus, and Jeffrey

Aaron Garnett – Emma's husband

Grace Wilcox – Samuel's wife; five children are Benjamin, Addie, Esther, Clay, and Dorothy

Lida Wilcox – Edmund's wife; their three children are Kathleen, Annabelle, and Wyatt

Jennie Wilcox – Nathan's wife; their four children are Oliver, Calvin, Levi, and Victor

The de la Paz clan (Phoenix, Arizona; Tucson, Arizona; and the southern third of the state)

Maya de la Paz -- *prima* of the de la Paz clan up through *Protector*

Alex Trujillo -- Maya's grandson

Diego Trujillo -- Alex's older brother

Alicia Trujillo – Alex and Diego's little sister

Letty Trujillo – Diego's wife

Luz Trujillo – Alex and Diego's mother and Maya's

daughter; *prima* of the de la Paz clan after the end of *Protector*

David Trujillo – Luz's husband and father of Alex, Diego, and Alicia

Valentina de la Paz – the de la Paz clan's healer in the Tucson area

Alba de la Paz -- the healer in the Phoenix area

Zoe Sandoval – the de la Paz clan's *prima*-in-waiting

Zander Sandoval – Zoe's little brother

Luis Sandoval – father of Zoe and Zander

Andrea Sandoval – mother of Zoe and Zander, Alex Trujillo's aunt (Luz and Andrea are sisters)

Luis de la Paz – Alex's cousin; works at the family's store

Jack Sandoval -- Luis Sandoval's youngest brother; a detective with the Scottsdale P.D.

Miguel de la Paz -- a private detective

Oscar de la Paz -- with the Tucson P.D.

Defender

Bad Blood (August 2017)

Deep Magic (October 2017)

Books 1-3 and Books 4-6 of this series are also available in two separate omnibus editions at special boxed set prices.

THE DJINN WARS

(Paranormal Romance)

Chosen

Taken

Fallen

Broken

Forsaken

Forbidden

Awoken (July 2017)

The first three books of this series are also available in an omnibus edition at a special low price!

THE SEDONA FILES

(Paranormal Romance)

Bad Vibrations

Desert Hearts

Angel Fire

Star Crossed

Falling Angels

Enemy Mine

The first three books of this series are also available in an omnibus edition at a special low price!

TALES OF THE LATTER KINGDOMS

(Fantasy Romance)

All Fall Down

Dragon Rose

Binding Spell

Ashes of Roses

One Thousand Nights

Threads of Gold

The Wolf of Harrow Hall

Moon Dance

The Song of the Thrush (November 2017)

Books 1-3 and Books 4-6 of this series are also available in two separate omnibus editions at special boxed set prices.

THE GAIAN CONSORTIUM SERIES

(Science Fiction Romance)

Blood Will Tell

Breath of Life

The Gaia Gambit

The Mandala Maneuver

The Titan Trap

The Zhore Deception

Refugees (September 2017)

ABOUT THE AUTHOR

Christine Pope has been writing stories ever since she commandeered her family's Smith-Corona typewriter back in the sixth grade. Her work includes paranormal romance, fantasy romance, and science fiction/space opera romance. She fell under the Land of Enchantment's spell while researching her Djinn Wars series and now makes her home in Santa Fe, New Mexico.

To be notified of new releases by Christine Pope, please go to www.christinepope.com and sign up for her newsletter.